FIRST ON THE ROPE

THE CLASSIC OF FRENCH LITERATURE

FIRST ON THE ROPE

ROGER FRISON-ROCHE

TRANSLATED BY JANET ADAM SMITH

Vertebrate Publishing, Sheffield
www.v-publishing.co.uk

THE CLASSIC OF FRENCH LITERATURE

FIRST ON THE ROPE

Roger Frison-Roche

Translated by Janet Adam Smith
Thanks to the children of Janet Adam Smith – Andrew, Henrietta, Adam and John Roberts – for their permission to use this translation.

First published in France in 1942 under the title *Premier de Cordée* by Arthaud.
First published in the English language in 1949 by Methuen & Co. Ltd, London.
This paperback edition first published in the United Kingdom in 2019 by Vertebrate Publishing. Reprinted in 2019 and 2020.

Vertebrate Publishing
Omega Court, 352 Cemetery Road, Sheffield, S11 8FT, United Kingdom.
www.v-publishing.co.uk

A CIP catalogue record for this book is available from the British Library.

ISBN 978-1-911342-45-8 (Paperback)
ISBN 978-1-911342-44-1 (Ebook)

10 9 8 7 6 5 4 3

Production by Vertebrate Publishing.
www.v-publishing.co.uk

Translator's introduction

In dealing with the measurements and climbing terms in this novel, I have aimed at using the forms that would be most natural to English-speaking mountaineers climbing in France. So I have kept the heights of mountains in metres rather than feet; also the length and diameter of ropes, and distances except when it is a question of walking so many yards or moving a few inches.

For readers who are not mountaineers the following brief glossary may be useful:

Aiguille: sharp peak, usually rock.
Alp: mountain pasture.
Belay: hitching the rope over a projection; the projection itself.
Bergschrund: the great crevasse which separates the glacier from the rocks on upper snowfields.
Cornice: projecting mass of snow on a ridge, generally formed by the prevailing wind.
Couloir: steep gully.
Crampons: iron or steel frame with spikes, fitted on to the boot for use on steep snow or ice.
Föhn: south wind.
Névé: snowfield above the snow line.
Piton: spike of iron or steel which can be driven into rock or ice.
Rappel: descent of steep slope or rock face by means of a double rope round a belay.
Sérac: pinnacle of ice, found mainly in icefalls.
Verglas: thin coating of ice on rocks.

Rope attaches the members of a party together; *line,* which is thinner, is used for rappels.

PART 1
THE BIRTH OF A VOCATION

Chapter I

The two men had left Courmayeur that morning at the hour when the dew rises in blue wisps from the stone-tiled roofs. They walked quickly up the road to Entrèves and passed the little mountain village still asleep in its green hollow. The track to the Col du Géant goes up from there, tacking up the hillside between low stone walls, its erratic course dictated by the layout of the fields.

At this early hour, the cattle were coming out of the barns, horns up, muzzles steaming, and all their bells a-tinkle. A few peasants were already at work in the tiny fields that dot the stony slopes: they paused for a moment as the two strangers passed, glanced up and, doubled over their tools, took a good look at the travellers who greeted them with a civil 'Good morning.' 'Morning,' answered the peasants. Soon the checkerboard of tiled fields gave way to larches. The valley looked wider now, and the murmur of the Dora down below could be heard more clearly. At the first zigzag, where the path begins to attack the slope in earnest, the two climbers halted. The younger was first to stop – a strapping young fellow who up till then had walked jauntily enough, jumping up on the stone walls, mowing down the nettles in his path with a sweep of his ice-axe, stopping suddenly to look back at the village perched in the angle of the two mountain walls, the peaceful valley, and the distant landscape shimmering blue under a sapphire sky. A few yards behind came the older man, who had walked up at a slow rhythmical pace, bending his knee slightly at each step as if trying to feel the earth under his thick nailed soles.

'That's enough larking, Pierre, my boy,' he grunted as he joined the other. 'Let's put our sacks down and have a breather.'

They slipped their huge guides' rucksacks off their shoulders: they were made of solid Valais leather, marked by sun and air, scratched and worn by the rub of rock. Then, sitting on the bank by the side of the path, legs apart and elbows on knees, they rested for a moment and got back their breath. The silence was broken by the young man:

'How long from here to the Col, Uncle?'

'Six hours. Two from here to the Mont Fréty inn,' the old man counted them off on his fingers, 'from Mont Fréty to the foot of the rocks, an hour and a half; from there to the hut on the Col, you have to reckon three hours, with heavy sacks – and it's going to be hot, so I'd best go in front and set the pace. You'd walk your legs off at the rate you're going – and I'm sixty years old. Mercy on us, sixty years old, and they want to make me retire! As if my strength didn't count for something! Look at these hands, young fella-me-lad: do you think they can't get a proper grip? Mark me, these hands of Red Joseph's have never let go, never, I tell you, not even on the Pic Sans Nom that day when half a ton of rock came down and I took the whole weight of the rope in my fists.'

'There aren't any hands to touch yours in all the valley, Uncle; with them, you're as firm as a rock – I've seen that very well for myself these last few days. But what can you do about it, these are the regulations and we've got to put up with them. Anyway, you won't need to leave the mountains, the president of the Club Alpine Français offered to make you warden of the Couvercle hut.'

'Don't say another word about it, my boy. It's a dreary way of ending my days, waking people up in the small hours and getting tea ready for parties setting off on a climb.'

'Sorry, Uncle, I hadn't meant to hurt you.'

'Take your pack, and get a move on.'

Joseph Ravanat, generally known as Red Joseph, was one of the heroes of the French Alps; he had been called the guide of kings and the king of guides. This was the end of his last big expedition. According to the rules of the Chamonix Corps of Guides he had to go on the retired list at sixty, and take no further engagements. Even though he could still keep the title of guide, he had no longer the right to keep his name on the books of the Guides' Office and take his turn on the roster. This is the inexorable law of the mountains, which demand for their service men in the prime of life and health. And Ravanat, still at the top of his form, cursed and grumbled, as cross as any old salt forcibly barred from the sea, and wished that the end of his climbing career had come in hot blood with a fall, on one of those many first ascents that starred his record.

The two men started up again in silence. Ravanat walked in front, back bowed, leaning on his ice-axe, his left hand hitched into the strap of his rucksack to take some of the weight off his shoulders. Pierre Servettaz followed, adapting his stride to the older man's, in the knowledge that at this rate they would reach the hut without undue effort and before nightfall. A newcomer to the Alps noticing the general deliberateness of their progress would have been surprised at the lightness with which the two mountaineers put their feet down on the loose stones of the path. Not a pebble moved, and their bootnails bit evenly into the ground.

The old man climbed without a word, his eyes fixed on the path ahead, careful not to break the rhythm of his stride. His face – burned by the sun, battered by storms and worn by years of hardy and strenuous life – was wrinkled and dried up: years ago he had stopped having anything to sweat off. He was an odd sight, this old guide with his brick-red complexion and twinkling lively eyes, deep-set under bushy red eyebrows that were always twitching, as if they'd been stuck on; and the wonderful pirate's moustache that he was always absentmindedly stroking, did nothing to lessen his general air of Saracen ancestry. His long, bony frame was rough-hewn, his hands were like flails, knotty, freckled and covered with hair – red-brown like the rest – and the fingertips were all worn and cracked by the rocks. Hands, as he liked to point out, that never let go their grip.

Chapter II

So this was the end of Ravanat's last expedition. During the last few days he had traversed Mont Blanc, from Chamonix to the Italian side, as guide to two young women from whom he had parted at Courmayeur. His nephew, Pierre Servettaz, a strong young man of twenty-two, had at his own request accompanied them as porter.

Pierre, who was learning the hotel business, had a passion for the mountains; whenever he could, he was off to climb in the Mont Blanc massif with his friends. Well set up, climbing with the confidence that comes from belonging to a family of hereditary mountaineers, he was always a welcome member on a rope. His father, Jean Servettaz, a man of forty-five, was considered the outstanding guide of the present generation; but – though he would on occasion deny it – he had up till then spared no pains to educate his son for another life.

'It's enough to risk one member of the family,' he often pointed out. 'Pierre will run a hotel – it's a job that brings in more cash with less danger.'

In anticipation of that day he had already, during the leisure hours of the off-season, added a storey to the 200-year-old chalet that he owned at Moussoux, just above Chamonix, hard by the woods of Prin and just out of the way of the avalanches of the Roumna Blanche.

Pierre had followed the line indicated by his father. In order to know his trade inside out, he had been in turn accountant in Paris, cashier in Lugano, assistant chef in London, hall porter in Berlin and receptionist in Innsbruck, going from one course of instruction to another, conscientiously taking it all in, and already fluent in three foreign languages. His trip across Europe had matured him early and had also increased his nostalgia for his own countryside. He was an obedient son – in Savoy paternal authority is no laughing matter – and was successfully equipping himself to run the small hotel that it would be his business to enlarge and make prosper. He was always having old Payette's experience held up to him – a guide like his father who had made his two sons the most considerable hotelkeepers in Chamonix. But in his own heart, he looked forward to his future life with no enthusiasm whatever; he envied the local lads, who from one year's end to the other led the free and hazardous life of guides. He had a vague feeling that here was a calling with something noble about it, something indefinable, that even the mountain folk themselves could not rightly understand, but that made different men of them, initiates of a mysterious world whose secrets no outsider could share.

For the time being, his love of the mountains was mainly physical: it satisfied a craving for action and recreation. He was drawn to the peaks by ties of blood and birth; his father was a guide; his grandfather and his great-grandfather had guided many generations of travellers; and the archives of the Priory of Chamonix, from the earliest times, bore witness to Servettaz after Servettaz who had walked on the mountaintops, been smugglers, chamois hunters, crystal gatherers. He alone, the first of his line, was going – admittedly against the grain – to break away from the path destined for his breed. Hitherto, Pierre had not tried to analyse the source of the happiness that he felt when he passed beyond the grassy alps to the solitude of the high peaks. Was it because he found in his struggle with the mountains the perfect antidote to those long monotonous spells in city hotels? Was it the pleasure of coming back once a year to his own friends, the good simple folk of his own countryside, of sharing meals with them on great slabs of granite heated by the sun? Was it the unutterable happiness that comes on a mountaintop when, mind and body still at full stretch, the climber tastes the full joy of hard-earned victory?

He would not have known what to answer and he felt he could not analyse his own feelings. 'I couldn't live in the plains,' he would say. 'I've got to be among the hills – but I don't exactly know why.' Nothing short of a catastrophe could have revealed the full depth of his inclinations and shown him what his future life ought to be. This catastrophe, which threatened to destroy all the plans that a prudent father had made for Pierre, had happened the day before.

Chapter III

Two days earlier, starting from the hut on the Aiguille du Goûter an hour before daylight, Joseph Ravanat and his party had reached the top of Mont Blanc without any difficulty. It was 1 September 1925, a remarkably fine year in the Mont Blanc region. But a storm had suddenly burst over their heads as they were coming down the Italian side by the long and difficult route of the Rochers de Mont Blanc – a storm of the utmost violence, though it lasted barely an hour. Several times lightning struck the rocks near the perch where they were sheltering after having left their ice-axes at a respectful distance so as not to attract the discharge. Snow and hail had alternated with never a moment's respite, covering the mountains with a new coat of white; then in a few moments a wind from the north had partly blown away the mist and once more revealed the sun and large patches of blue sky.

Ravanat – quite unmoved, for he had seen many a storm as bad as this – had given the word to resume the descent. As porter, Servettaz went first, followed by the girls, and the old guide came down last, safeguarding the whole party, rope taut, and himself ready to check the least slip.

This was certainly no place for slipping; the party had started down a couloir of ice overlaid with new snow that plunged at an angle of sixty degrees towards the Miage glacier some 2,000 metres below. Danger sharpened Pierre's faculties; deliberately, he cut steps for the girls with great blows of pick and blade. Ravanat, standing erect in his steps, watched him without a word and his face showed his satisfaction. If his brother-in-law had so wished it, Pierre Servettaz could have been a first-class climber. 'A pity,' said the old man to himself, 'a pity to make a plainsman of him.' The improvement in the weather did not last long. A curtain of mist from the Dôme du Goûter crept down the south face of Mont Blanc; it swallowed up the party with its icy and impenetrable breath, and a fine snow-like rime began to fall. In the mist Ravanat could barely distinguish the outline of Servettaz who, forty-five metres lower down, showed himself more and more hesitant over the line to follow. Soon the guide realised that he would have to go down first, as he was the only one who could find the way among these little rocky outcrops that appeared here and there on the ice slope, cut off by deep channels down which hissed runnels of snow.

'Wait a minute, Pierre,' he said, 'you're bearing too far over to the left, let me go first, all these hummocks look the same.' Servettaz obeyed, but not without some misgiving; going down last was as good as taking on the position and responsibility of the guide. As long as he was going down first, well held by the rope that linked him, through the two clients, to the solid pillar that was Ravanat, he felt himself absolutely secure. Several times the girls, who were exhausted and numb with cold, had stumbled in their steps; each time, with a masterful pull on the rope, Ravanat had checked a slip and re-established their balance.

'Stand up, ladies,' he commanded. 'Stand up straight in your steps.'

The fate of the party now depended on the hands – strong enough, but inexperienced – of the porter. Deliberately, he drove his ice-axe up to the head in the snow and belayed the rope round the shaft while Ravanat, who had overtaken the party and checked up on the general line of advance, was already cutting steps with one hand, three strokes of the axe to each step, to the full length of the rope. With all his faculties heightened by this struggle with the elements, Servettaz kept his eye on the two clients. He did not worry about his uncle, for he had never put a foot wrong on snow, but every instant he had to brace himself against a possible slip by the girls, whose tiredness had slowed down their reactions. And he could not help wondering if an unexpected pull might not drag him from the steps where he stood in precarious balance – heels dug in, nails biting into the ice – and send him hurtling down towards the old man, who was hacking away without a pause. If that happened it would all be over; and Servettaz pictured the fourfold tumble, and the bodies hurtling from one side of the couloir to the other.

For the first time in his life Servettaz held in his hands the lives of human beings for whom he was responsible. Bit by bit the anxiety in his heart gave way to a new feeling of strength, self-confidence and pride. His pulses no longer throbbed so quickly, and when his turn came to climb down last, a critical moment when there was no question of his being held, he resolutely dug his heels into the slope and, face outwards, using his axe to maintain his balance, he came down to join the others.

For six hours that, under such a strain, seemed to pass like so many minutes, Servettaz safeguarded the party; a last rope's length brought him down to the level glacier where Ravanat and his clients had already flopped down on the snow. The old guide was tired; six hours of step-cutting, with one hand, and on a downward slope, was too much of an effort for a man of his age. Ravanat thought of his coming retirement. Down in the valley he put any such thought out of his mind; but up here in this waste of snow and ice, he found himself viewing with misgiving the three hours before they could reach the hut on the far side of the glacier. When he considered they had rested long enough, he got up and announced quite simply, as if he had already nominated his successor, 'Go ahead, Pierre, I need to take it easy'; so the young man took on the leadership of the party. And with a confidence he had never expected to feel he guided it through the chaotic jumble of crevasses and séracs, on a glacier that was quite new to him, and yet somehow seemed strangely familiar.

So Pierre experienced the climber's deepest satisfaction, of leading a rope. He no longer followed blindly, trustingly, without thought or question; he had become the leader, the man who commands and fights, who shoulders the responsibility, who has other lives dependent on him. He felt himself cut out for the part and gloried at the prospect of the struggles that lay ahead.

His placid future as a privileged hotelkeeper had just been swept away like a straw by the storm whose last tattered clouds were now retreating eastward, leaving the mountains white and mysterious. A violet haze hung over the glacier basin, and the walls of the gaping crevasses showed purple in the dusk.

Chapter IV

The sun was high in the heavens when Ravanat and Servettaz, after more than two hours' going from Courmayeur, emerged from the larches on the high pastures of Mont Fréty. Their pace had not varied during the climb: always that long, supple stride, with the bending at the knee, the stride that looks slow to the hurrying novice – as if the struggle with the mountains allowed any hurry! – but is so beautifully adjusted that it lets the climber go on for hours without feeling tired. The two men put their sacks down on the rustic table beside the little inn, leaned their axes against the roughcast walls, and went straight through the door into the guides' room.

'Morning, everyone,' said Ravanat. And Servettaz echoed him, 'Morning, everyone.'

They sat down at the common table, content to rest. The proprietress knew their habits and without waiting for an order set down before them two steaming bowls of soup, a great hunk of Gruyère, fresh from the mountains of Catogne, and half a round of bread. Placidly, the two sliced the bread and cheese into the soup; Ravanat ground the pepper mill over it, covering the surface with a grey film that took some time to absorb. Pierre, though his manners were naturally more refined, set himself to copy his uncle's simple actions; he also ground the pepper and slowly stirred his spoon round the thick earthenware dish. They sniffed the steaming mixture; the cheese made long strings that clung to Ravanat's moustache, but the old man went on eating, with his Opinel knife open in his right hand, elbow on the table, and beret pushed back off his forehead. Abruptly he cut off the troublesome sliver of cheese, but in the old-fashioned setting of this mountain inn there was no vulgarity in the action; it recalled those high-cheeked nomads of the Asian steppes who grip a piece of meat in their jaws and then slice it off level with their lips.

In a corner of the room, sitting on a three-legged stool beside the open fire of crackling larchwood, the old retired guide who ran the hut waited for them to finish their meal. Pierre was the first: he cleared his plate and with his spoon chased a last piece of cheese that had stuck to the dish. At last Ravanat too came to his final mouthful; he wiped his moustache with the backs of his gnarled fingers, then, pulling his beret on to his head, brought himself to utter a word or two.

'Well, Josêt, how goes it?'

'Mustn't grumble, mustn't grumble,' answered the old man in that sing-song French of the Val d'Aosta that neither time, nor man, nor the elements will destroy. 'Yesterday the snow was down as far as this, but today it's clear up to the Porte; there's probably plenty lying up on the rocks of the Col. Bah, a bit of snow isn't going to worry you, Red.'

'If you want anything taken up yonder, let's have it. The lad and I have plenty of room in our sacks.'

'First time the young chap's been this way?'

'Yes, he's my nephew, Jean Moussoux's boy; going to be a hotel-keeper later on.'

'There's always a chance, Uncle, I might be a guide instead,' put in Pierre, who had been listening deferentially to the two old men.

'If it depended on me, I'd certainly advise you to go on as a guide; you've got a turn for it. I saw that, way up under the Aiguilles Grises. To come down steps in ice, the way you did, you have to be' – and here Red Joseph fumbled for the right word – 'you have to be born to it; anyway, it's a matter between you and your father.'

The innkeeper gave them a great round of new bread, which had come up that morning with the mule, and a letter for his cousin up at the Col. Joseph put the letter into the inner pocket of his jacket, Pierre made the round of bread fast under the flap of his rucksack, and, after saying goodbye, the two set off again across the pastures.

From Mont Fréty to the Col du Géant there are two stages. The first takes you up the excellent mule track that zigzags between the two precipices gouged out by the glaciers each side of the arête leading up to the Col du Géant. To begin with, you go across the most beautiful pastures, dotted with boulders, carpeted with dwarf rhododendrons and short grass, and gay with the blue bells of gentians and the yellow tufts of arnica; then, bit by bit, the flowers give way to moss and lichen. Stones encroach on the grass, and the path, that began by climbing in broad sweeps, now zigzags restlessly from side to side as if looking for a way out, unable to escape from the ridge that gets narrower and narrower till it merges into the rocky face. This is the way to the boulder-strewn arête up which a sketchy track leads to the Col. Climbers call this point the Porte: it is indeed a majestic portal opening on to the world of high mountains.

At the top of the pastures, just under the rocks, stands a little shanty for the porters who serve the Col. The mules stop there, 2,800 metres up, and from this point provisions are carried on the porters' backs to the tiny hut 3,341 metres high, just under the Col.

Ravanat and Servettaz rested a good quarter of an hour before tackling the arête. They recovered their breath and looked at the view – familiar to the old man, quite new to the younger – of the Graian Alps. It was a perfect day and, to the south, range on range stretched to the horizon. Near at hand were the alps of the Val d'Aosta: the Grivola – *ardua Grivola Bella* – the Gran Paradiso, the white basin of the Ruitor; the giants of the frontier chain between France and Italy, the Sassière, the Ciamarella – the country of the *bouquetin*, the ibex – and further to the south-west, the Vanoise group. Eastwards extended the Swiss mountains line upon line; in the foreground the Vélan, dwarfed by the enormous mass of the Grand Combin; then, in the distance, the Zermatt peaks, with the Matterhorn, and the great nose of the Zmutt ridge, black above the clouds; and the snows of Monte Rosa, soaring high above the earth, and merging their dazzling whiteness into the pearly haze.

Clouds rose from the valley, clustering above the hollows, mingling, forming fleecy billows that soon swallowed up all the valleys from the Col Ferret to the Col de la Seigne. Over to the west showed a still more unearthly scene. In front, like an outpost, towered the granite spire of the Aiguille de la Brenva, banked by that curious taper of rock that the Courmayeur guides call *le Père Eternel;* behind it, the basin of the Brenva glacier, and the glacier itself, stony and dirty, crawling down between its moraines, spilling over the last great icefall, spreading like a leprosy on the Val Veni, to come to rest finally in the larch woods of Notre Dame de Guérison. Here and there the torrent from the Combal lake came into view, finally forcing its roaring way out of an ice cave, about the level of the meadows of Entrèves. Still further back, reared up the tremendous Pétéret arête, over 3,500 metres high – the ominous-looking pyramid of the Aiguille Noire, seamed with dark couloirs, the delicate airy spires of the Dames Anglaises, and finally the majestic upthrust of the Aiguille Blanche, a dome of ice crowned with threatening cornices, and linked by a slender silver thread to the main mass of Mont Blanc. This southern face of the mountain, Himalayan in its scale and grandeur, towered high in the air; from this point of view it seemed to hurl a scornful challenge to the two climbers.

From time to time, over by the Red Sentinel, a sérac fell. It sounded like a thunderclap in the thin high air, and long after the noise had died away, a cloud of iridescent dust could still be traced, forerunner of the avalanches that would sweep down on these high and icy plateaux.

Chapter V

The two climbers hardly bothered to look at the view. All they were thinking of at this moment was a rest and a break. From here to the Col, it was a matter of three hours. They set off again in the noonday heat, Ravanat always in front, and in a few minutes reached territory barred to plainsfolk. They passed into the world of rock and ice with the easy confidence of veteran mountaineers.

They reached the limit of the new snow, which was melting quickly, just under the great boulder that makes such a landmark for climbers. From there the way winds airily and easily up a shattered arête, and the drop on each side increases at every step. The wet snow clogged up the soles of their boots; every time they lifted a foot its outline was stamped out on the stones, and their tracks were printed in black on the whiteness and cold of the mountainside. Occasionally, with a quick tap of the axe, they cleared their heels of snow and sent the lumps flying.

The wide gully on their left was swept by snow that swished down towards the valley, gouging out little runnels that joined up to make one big furrow from which volleyed, like bullets from a machine gun, a constant flow of stones, ice, and snow loosened by the thaw.

They were only an hour from the Col when they met a party going down; a Courmayeur guide and porter with their client. Leaving the client to go on in the porter's charge, the guide stopped for a word or two.

'Going home, Ravanat?'

'Aye, we're homeward bound, as you see. But we've still got to do a bit of drinking up yonder,' joked Red Joseph.

'They haven't the heart for drinking up there,' answered the Italian, 'one of your men has come off on the Dru.'

'One of us, Mother of God!' (And old Ravanat crossed himself.) 'Do you know who it is?'

'Can't tell, it was two guideless Englishmen who gave us the news. They'd heard it down at Montenvers. They say a rescue party's already started.'

'What a trade ours is! They must have been caught in that storm the day before yesterday, and high up on the rocks you can't get away with that sort of thing. Have you any details?'

'Not a one. But anyway Brocherel is on the lookout; he'll let us know. We'll be sending a deputation over for the funeral; we'll pass the word on to the guides of Breuil and Valtournanche. At the end of the season, when the worst risks are over and you're beginning to look forward to a bit of rest – it isn't really fair to be killed then. You'd better get on and so had I – it's getting late, and it won't be long before this snow freezes.'

Ravanat and Servettaz started up again, but the bad news was like a weight on their feet. The old man in particular could hardly conceal his anxiety: he had too many friends, too many relatives out on expeditions at the moment, and there are not so many guides who will undertake the Petit Dru.

'It certainly seems to be one of our men, Pierre, but which one?'

And he tried to remember the expeditions posted up in the Guides' Office before he left Chamonix: Armand à la Bolla Nera was fixed up with two Americans, and at this moment he should be somewhere in the Dolomites. Alfred à la Colaude was having a look at the East Face of the Grépon, so it couldn't be him; Zian des Tines had planned to start two days after Ravanat for the same traverse of Mont Blanc, so he was out of it too; Joseph à Jozon? – might be him. He was a chap who would never let on where he was going for fear he might be robbed of a first ascent.

Ravanat turned over all the possible names in his mind, and Pierre too, though not so well informed, tried to solve the melancholy problem. As he climbed, one awful thought dogged the old man and embedded itself more deeply in his mind at every step. What about his brother-in-law? Where had he been off to? A week ago, he had still been in the Oberland, but that engagement must have come to an end. It doesn't take long to get back to Chamonix from the Hollandia hut up on the Lötschenlücke – down the long valley that leads to the mouth of the Lötschberg tunnel, and then by train round by Brigue and Martigny. Jean Servettaz could easily have got back to Chamonix in time to start again for the Charpoua hut and the Dru. He was never the man to turn down a possible expedition, and people were always telling him off for working himself too hard.

Ravanat turned all this over in his mind, without breaking the rhythm of his stride; but when the turns of the path brought him face to face with his nephew, he could hardly conceal his anxiety and fear. 'Suppose it were Jean,' he kept thinking.

Pierre climbed up without a word, but with a weight on his heart. He had a presentiment of some fearful tragedy, and forced himself to suppress the thought that became more vivid at every step. Suppose it were his father! Even just to think that his father might have fallen seemed sacrilegious to him; a Servettaz never falls. But he remembered the storm that had overtaken Ravanat and himself on the south side of Mont Blanc; he had enough experience of the mountains to know that, on rock and above 3,000 metres, you can take no chances with a storm. And, like Ravanat, he weighed up the possibilities. His father had only been due back at Chamonix the night after they had started; would he have had time to set out again at once for the Dru? A vain question, that he turned over and over in his head. He determined to ask his uncle's opinion.

'Uncle,' he called in a voice heavy with anxiety, 'if it were … '

'Shut up, can't you, shut up. I know what you're thinking. It's only too true that anything can happen in our trade, but that your father should fall on the Dru, that's not possible. He's done that climb more than thirty times … another man might fall there, but never him.'

'But, Uncle, there was that storm, you remember. Let me go ahead. I can't wait to make certain, I'll climb faster than you. Brocherel must have had further news.'

'You stay where you are. *If* something had happened to your father' (and for the second time Ravanat crossed himself), ' – *if* – which God forbid – then more than ever it would be our business to keep fresh. Listen, you must save your energy, and so must I. They'll need us over there. Keep going at this pace. We've passed the place where the Englishman was killed in '97, in half an hour we'll be up. Try and be patient. See here, my boy,' (and here a softer note crept into Ravanat's rough voice) 'there *is* something we can do. Whoever it may be, the man who's at this moment somewhere on the face of the Dru is one of us. Let's pray for him, to our Lady of the Dru, and of the Géant and of the Grépon.'

The old guide took off his beret and knelt down in the snow at the edge of the cliff: Pierre followed suit. Facing the sunset that lit up the horizon for hundreds of miles, they repeated some Paters and Aves. The abyss at their feet yawned deeper than ever, and the valleys were already blue under their veil of mist; an icy wind blew up from the gullies and whistled through the gaps in the arête.

By the time they rose to their feet, the snow was beginning to crunch under their boots, and their footmarks, that had hitherto shown black, were now printed on the hard snow. They both shivered.

'Come on, we'll catch cold,' said Red Joseph.

As they came up to the hut a huge sérac crashed away to their right, under the snowy saddle of the Col du Géant; it made a tremendous din, and it was some time before the echoes faded away in the still air. Little by little the noise died away as night came on, and the only sounds that broke the stillness were the tinkle of their axes on the rocks, and later, the dull thud of boots being kicked against the wall of the hut as the climbers tried to get rid of their clogging lumps of snow.

Chapter VI

In the living room of the hut three parties of climbers were steadily eating and drinking by the light of a smoky lamp; their wet ropes, coiled up in a corner of the room and stiff with frost, showed that they had just arrived from a long Glacier expedition. Ravanat crossed the room, followed by Pierre; in the dim light they made for the kitchen. As they passed, the diners recognised Red Joseph, famous from La Bérarde to Cortina, and gave him a friendly greeting.

The kitchen was a big square room, low-roofed and built entirely of wood: a narrow window with double glass and one adjustable pane let in some air without admitting too much cold. The Aiguille Noire de Pétéret and the Dames Anglaises were framed in it, as if a painter had arranged the composition, and at this late hour, though it had been long dark in the valleys, the tops were still faintly illuminated from behind by a pearly light that clung to the crests and lit up the curving cornices. Although everything was carefully shut, a chilly draught blew through the kitchen and round the living room, and the windowpanes were decorated with a pattern of frost.

Brocherel, the warden, was busy at the stove. At the common table, several guides and porters were eating and, as usual, talking about their climbs. Cretton of Champex was there, the younger Zermatten from Saas-Fee, the great Carrel from Valtournanche, and three Chamonix men, Joseph à Jozon who had traversed the Rochefort arêtes that morning, his porter Camille Lourtier, a promising young fellow, and Zian from Tines, who had already won a reputation as a rock climber. After making a successful ascent of the Mer de Glace face of the Grépon he had come down the same way, bivouacking with his English client at the Tour Rouge.

Thence, without pause, they had come on up to the Col du Géant. Red Joseph must know the news already, they said to themselves; we know the cheerful rowdy way he usually comes into a hut. Today Joseph wasn't joking: he looked anxious and withdrawn, and didn't say anything.

Brocherel spoke first.

'Heard the news?' he asked simply.

'For God's sake, who is it?' demanded Ravanat roughly. Behind him, Pierre was waiting in agony; in spite of the cold, great beads of sweat stood out on his sunburned face. The guide gave him a compassionate look before answering.

'Jean – yes, your brother-in-law – his father,' said Brocherel, pointing to Pierre, who went white as a ghost. 'Struck by lightning on the Petit Dru, you know, above that perpendicular bit of wall just under the summit ... Cretton here brought us the news ... ' (Brocherel fumbled awkwardly for his words, and blinked his tear-filled eyes.) 'This rotten stove's still smoking ... It happened the day before yesterday in the storm. The porter, that young son of Clarisse des Bois, brought down the client; they had a night out at Straton's bivouac, and early yesterday morning they got down to the Montenvers. By this time the rescue party must have reached the Charpoua hut – only I'm not so sure they'll make it, for there's new snow and verglas everywhere above 3,400 metres. It only just thawed here at midday.'

The guides bowed their heads, overwhelmed by the dreadful news. Pierre drew back into the darkest corner of the kitchen, put his sack on the ground, and realising at last the full extent of his loss, he let himself go in tears which he did not even try to wipe away.

Ravanat came up to him and his great hand, that could grip the rock so firmly, shook as he laid it on Pierre's shoulder. He did not speak; words are superfluous at a moment like this. All those present were good friends, and Servettaz knew he could depend on them, but the friendly weight of Ravanat's rough hand on his shoulder gave him more comfort than anything. At last he raised his head – and his eyes were as red as if he had been walking on a glacier without his dark glasses – and said with rare pride:

'Father didn't fall, Uncle, did you hear? He was struck by lightning.'

'You could take your oath about that,' said Zermatten slowly, in his grating German-Swiss accent. 'Servettaz was never a fellow to let go his hold.'

This tribute from the great Zermatten went straight to the young man's heart. His father had died in harness as a guide, and the porter had brought the client down. Servettaz could have hugged Clarisse's Georges for that – for having brought down Jean Servettaz's client safe and sound.

There was a long silence as each man pursued his own troubled thoughts. Then, nature reasserting herself, the guides turned again to their food. For them the hardest part was over: Joseph and Pierre had been told. This was what they had dreaded on seeing the newcomers enter the hut.

Brocherel signalled the two to take their places at the table.

'Sit you down; the bad news won't have made you any less tired after your climb.'

'That's right,' said Pierre resolutely, 'you must eat something, Uncle, for I propose that we should start off again in an hour. The others must be up at the Charpoua hut by now, and I don't want anyone to say that I didn't go with Father on his last journey. Come on, I'll set you an example.' Pierre forced himself to swallow three or four spoonfuls of soup, no more: then wearily pushed the plate away.

'It's no good, I can't hold it down.'

'Be patient, Pierre, my boy. I'd like nothing better than to set out again with you tonight, but we'd be fools not to rest and even sleep a bit. Eight hours' climb, and this shock on top of it – we wouldn't go far. Mercy on us, remember what's ahead!'

'Look you, Joseph,' put in Zian, 'I don't need to tell *you* what to do. You're my senior, you've had more experience than anyone else here, and it's one of your men who's gone. But you have nothing to gain by starting tonight. Not a thing. The séracs are as bad as ever they've been at the end of a season. Three of the snow bridges are in a shocking condition and may go at any moment. Even in broad daylight we had to twist and turn to find the way through: in the dark, you'd end up by sleeping out.'

'Zian's right,' agreed Jozon. 'The séracs are so open that you just can't see the tracks; even the steps cut today have melted, and you'd have to make new ones. That's not a job for anyone to do in the dark, even you.'

The Swiss guides pitched their advice even more strongly. They were all set upon dissuading the two from crossing the Géant glacier by night.

'Listen,' added Jozon, 'you mustn't hold it against us if we don't go down with you in the morning. We can't leave our clients in the lurch: an engagement is binding; but if you like, I'll let you have Camille, and I'll get another porter at Courmayeur; there won't be too many to bring down the body – especially if, as I think, it's right up under the summit of the Dru.'

'I must go off tonight,' Pierre insisted, 'I can't sit here knowing that my poor father's lying unburied somewhere up there in the gullies, under the snow, with the jackdaws wheeling round him.'

'Don't worry about the jackdaws, the body will be frozen stiff and they won't touch it. Listen to the others, Pierre. You must take it from me, after all I'm your uncle, indeed, I'm almost your father now. They're right; if we started now, we'd be going round in circles among the séracs till morning. We'll set out an hour before daylight, and that way we'll hit the best time for getting through. We'll save time – and save our strength.'

Pierre made no reply. His misery was too much for him. He got up and went out on to the doorstep of the hut. He must have fresh air, he felt, to cool his brow. The rocky slabs, covered with frozen snow, glowed in the darkness. A few stars twinkled in the sky above. A strong wind was blowing up from the sleeping valleys where a few lights showed: down there, at the bottom of a great black pit, he could just see the lamps of Pré-St-Didier; a little above them, the straight row of the main street of Courmayeur. The cold was intense. Pierre put up the collar of his windjacket. On the edge of the precipice, with his legs dangling over in the darkness, he sat and brooded with his head between his hands, listening to the solemn voice of the torrent, the only living note in all that stony waste.

After a little while Ravanat came out to look for him. Exhausted as he was, Pierre suffered himself to be led in without a word and stretched himself on the shelf of the dormitory. The loud breathing of guides already asleep alone broke the silence of the hut. He could just make out the line of bodies, each prone in its grey blanket.

Red Joseph sat down on the edge of the shelf and carefully wound up his alarm watch. 'I've set it for four,' he said. Pierre made no answer, for he had dropped off at once into a deep sleep. The old man was the only soul left awake in the hut. He carefully folded his jacket to make a pillow, but after blowing out the candle lay tossing and turning on the shelf. Sleep would not come. He envied his nephew the youth that enabled him to forget present sorrow, at least in sleep. In the still, cold night he looked unseeing at the fearsome outline of the Aiguille Noire de Pétéret, framed in the little window against the paler background of the sky. A tiny star twinkled over the summit, like a mysterious flame lit by some pious hand to keep watch over the dead man. For the first time, Ravanat pictured to himself the scene which he could imagine only too well. Jean Servettaz's body, stuck somewhere on the face of the Dru, under the stars.

Tragedy was abroad on the high mountains. Aloof and lofty, they kept watch over the valleys as well, indifferent to the thoughts of the men who perched on their flanks and huddled together in stone huts.

They had kept this watch for thousands of years; and the only sounds to disturb it now were the rumble of a far-off avalanche or the sharper rattle of stones dislodged by the too rapid return of the frost.

Chapter VII

At four in the morning, three ghostly figures stole out of the hut with lighted lanterns. To save their fingers from frostbite on the icy saddle of the Col, they had put on the rope in the hut, and now walked up quickly and silently, careful not to slip on the icy path. Camille Lourtier went up first, confidently picking out the line of the narrow track. Ravanat came last, keeping a sharp eye on Pierre, who had awakened limp and miserable, and was now walking along mechanically, occasionally stumbling against the loose stones of the ridge and striking sparks with his bootnails from the rocks.

The icy wind which met them on the Col put out Lourtier's lantern. He lit it again and, as his ears were freezing, took the opportunity of a halt to pull his helmet down over his neck. The three men broke into a long stride down the great waste of ice and snow on the French side, cutting straight across the base of the Géant. They came down in long, slithering steps, by the flickering light of the lantern. Beside the Vierge, where the slope steepens, they did a standing glissade. Leaning on the heads of their axes, they got up enough pace to take them with a jump right over the last crevasse before the plateau.

Dawn was breaking. The palest of lights began to tinge the summits. Facing them across the huge glacier basin the pyramid summit of the Aiguille Verte stood up against the sky, supported on the west by a queer-shaped buttress, a sort of hump-backed monster with two horns, evil and absurd. At this distance it seemed to be nothing more than a projection on a ridge of the majestic mountain. Turning their backs on Mont Blanc du Tacul and on the Aiguilles du Diable, now just beginning to catch the light, they took a line towards the Chamonix Aiguilles whose serrated outline, sharpened by distance, was flanked on the west by the marble icefall of the glacier of Envers du Plan. Without a glance at the lofty Dent du Géant, soaring into the sky above them, they continued their long descent. They had eyes only for the Verte. Pierre in particular could not refrain from looking at the evil monster keeping watch at its side. This protuberance was, he knew well, the fatal Aiguille du Dru; and among the many patches of snow on the summit, he strained to distinguish the little platform where his father lay. But distance gave a false impression of innocence to the mountain, seen from here.

They quickly reached the main icefall. The séracs of the Géant glacier were just as the guides had described them at the Torino hut: a shattered and crazy jumble, defended by a series of wide parallel crevasses that forced the party to make several detours. In their hurry they jumped most of the crevasses, bounding over the narrow cracks, sometimes more than eighty metres deep.

Lourtier was leading. It was his last year as a porter, and the way he cut steps, and took an unhesitating line through the labyrinth of the icefall, showed that next season he would be an entirely reliable guide. Joseph came down last, keeping an eye on the movements of the other two and paying out as needed the coils of rope he held in his hand.

In two hours they were through and, balancing their way along a final thin tongue of ice, they reached the rocks under the Requin. The new hut was still in process of construction. Workmen from Piedmont were building the walls, hewing the granite blocks out of the boulders on the moraine. The guides stopped for a moment. Pierre learned for certain that a rescue party had gone up to the Charpoua hut the evening before. As far as they could tell they would be able to join it at the hut that night. They did not take long to come down the moraine and on to the lower plateau of the glacier. From this point, the glacier is dry. The whole of last winter's snow had melted during the summer, and it flowed down grey and dirty like a huge river between its granite walls, forming rapids in the narrows, and descending inexorably towards the valley, pushed down by the snow above.

By nine o'clock the guides were at the foot of the torrent that flows from the Charpoua. They had just lost 1,000 metres of height; now they had to go up 700, over scree and grass slopes, to reach the hut. A trained eye could just make it out, perched on a great rocky knob, a lighter patch against the grey of the mountains.

Chapter VIII

When he set off for the Dru that morning the elder Servettaz had had a foreboding of what might happen. Stepping out of the Charpoua hut at 3 a.m. he had seen summer lightning streaking the heavens in the west, and intermittently silhouetting the darker jagged outline of the mountains against a greenish sky. It was mild, and the footprints on the snow in front of the hut had barely frozen. The guide shook his head, and looked worried.

'We'll have to look sharp if we're going to make the summit. Feeling in good form, Georges?'

'Not so bad, Jean, not so bad,' answered the porter who was busy lighting the lantern and neatly coiling up the rope. 'You've given me a run for my money this season! Never a minute's rest, never time to sleep, from one hut to the next ... Five metres will do between each of us on the moraine, won't it, that should be long enough, and the rope won't get wet then ... You've shown me a bit of the world – the Oberland, Valais, Oisans ... D'you think one candle's enough? It'll last as far as the Shoulder, and we won't be wasting any time with this fellow.'

'This fellow' was their client: Henry Warfield, Jr., a tall, lanky young American nearly six foot six, lithe as whipcord, who never uttered a word and strode over the Alps watch in hand, jotting down in his notebook the peaks climbed and the record times made. Something of a windfall, indeed, to his guide, for he was openhanded and paid double the tariff for each expedition. Moreover, his passion for record times made him the easiest of clients – the party was always back at the hut for lunch and the porter only had to take the barest necessities in his sack. His climbing partner, Douglas Willys Slane, Sr., had passed the guide and porter on to him on the station platform at Brig, after they had done some climbs in the Oberland. Slane had caught the Orient Express for Bucharest, to hunt bear in Transylvania. Warfield and his two companions had gone back to Chamonix, and thence straight up to the Charpoua hut.

Warfield had decided on the traverse of the Dru after one look at the tariff of expeditions at the Guides' Office. It was the most expensive climb, and he deduced that it must necessarily be the most difficult. At that time, in 1925, the Dru was still considered the trickiest of the standard climbs. Today, the newer school of rock climbers are apt to smile at the mention of it; but all the same they're wrong, because every now and then the Dru takes its revenge and devours a climber, as indisputable proof that it is still the same great mountain which Charlet-Straton attempted time and again with his climbing irons before finding the right way up.

The three climbers set off up the moraine, which disappeared into a rocky amphitheatre whose features were barely discernible against the lighter background of the sky. To their right there were shiny patches on the Charpoua glacier, and the sea-green lips of the crevasses gaped evilly in the darkness.

Georges had been right: no time would be wasted with a client like this. They had barely reached the level of the rocky outcrop, at the spot where the track descends to the upper basin of the glacier in order to reach the rocks of the Petit Dru, when he was already urging them on, 'Faster, faster.'

'Just keep on steadily,' said Jean, 'we've the whole day before us; later on we'll see.'

Without question the American could cover the ground at an excellent pace. They lost no time over this first stretch on the rocks in the darkness. Jean knew the chimneys on the Dru by heart: he climbed without a pause, lantern in hand, or between his teeth when a steep part forced him to use both hands. To save time he had put Georges second on the rope. The guide went ahead, silently and confidently, without worrying about the two others; he forced his way up, occasionally helping the second man with a quick pull on the rope. Georges would barely reach a stance before Jean was off again up the next pitch. The porter admiringly followed the skill and agility that made light work of every difficulty. It all looked so easy as you watched him: it was strange to find yourself making heavy weather of the same pitches!

The American showed himself to be a first-class rock climber, and came up easily, safeguarded by the porter; it was indeed an entirely harmonious party, with each man in his place, and knowing exactly what the others expected of him. The rope was always neatly coiled, ready to pay out without a check, or stretched taut, to hold the man without pulling him. Engrossed in the climb, the three lost count of time. Daylight began to show as they reached the Shoulder, where the real tussle with the mountain began. Jean rubbed his hands and surveyed the great face they were about to tackle.

At this point the wall seems, by a trick of perspective, to double back, bend, taper off, and then, supported on the great foundations that reach well down to the icy valleys, to spring up in one leap to the sky. Its topmost pinnacles seem to pierce right through, as if penetrating to the mysteries that lie beyond; the climber feels small and insignificant, crushed by the inhuman scale of the mountain. When the route takes him close to the terrifying precipice of the Nant Blanc, he feels, however well-balanced his mind, the appalling sensation of a bottomless abyss; it is far worse than mere dizziness – he feels that if he were to fall, his body would hurtle through the air and never touch ground till it reached the gaping bergschrund that separates the rock wall from the shattered glacier. Fantastic pinnacles twist in desperate supplication on the knife-edge ridge; at dawn and sunset they glow and sparkle, pink in the morning and purple in the evening: hence their name, Flammes de Pierre.

The climbers had no eyes for the view; they climbed up indifferent to the splendour of the surroundings and the horrors of the abyss. At each stance, Servettaz cast a quick glance to the east: the sun was still hidden by the Aiguille Verte, quite close to them, but there was an ominous redness in the sky, outlining the Verte's dome of ice, and long purple streamers at a height of between four and 5,000 metres. The sky was streaked from east to west by lines of light fleecy clouds, driven by a wind that was so far not perceptible on the mountain itself; these disappeared so suddenly that it hardly seemed possible they had ever been there.

'It's a dirty outlook,' grumbled Servettaz. 'The *ravoures* of the morning are putting water in the mill. That's an old saying with us, Mr Warfield, when the *ravoures* – those long streaks of red – appear at dawn, then it means rain in the afternoon. We mustn't hang around here.'

Crack followed chimney, chimney followed crack in apparently endless succession. The party, now engaged on the hardest part of the climb, reached the Piton, the merest crack, which leads up for twenty metres between two granite slabs. A great rusty peg fixed there by some pioneer of the heroic age affords a little help; above it is the Vire des Cristaux, a white streak agleam with quartz in the red granite wall.

Georges was too busy looking after his gentleman, paying out the rope to the guide, and climbing up himself, to bother about anything else, and never noticed these heralds of the coming storm.

As for Warfield, he was happy climbing in silence, relishing with primitive joy the aerial gymnastics that drew from him an occasional '*Exciting – very exciting*.' He had complete trust in his guide.

There are some things that it is better for a client not to know. Servettaz seized the chance of being alone on a stance with Georges to warn him:

'Have you seen the red streamers? You should have noticed them, the weather's breaking up: first of all the streamers, and now it's the Donkey on Mont Blanc. Look over there!'

A cloud, blown by the west wind, had just settled on the majestic summit; it grew bigger and bigger, covering the Bosses and Mont Maudit, and rolling over the Dôme du Goûter. The guide was all too familiar with this cloud that settled on the monarch of mountains. It is known locally as the Donkey on account of its fantastic shape: it means bad weather, and pretty soon at that.

'Let's go on!' declared Servettaz. 'As long as the Verte hasn't put on its bonnet, we're safe; but keep an eye on it, and look out if it *does*.'

They continued to climb without pause or rest, but Georges kept one eye continually on the far-off cloud that every minute swallowed up some new peak: for the first time he began to feel anxious. The climbers neared the summit, the angle of the slope eased off. They were above the sheer walls, and now tiers of wide terraces, separated by short vertical pitches, constituted the summit's last defences.

As they reached the foot of one of these walls, the Aiguille Verte was covered over – had put on its bonnet, as the saying goes. A heavy cloud hid the top and spread down the face; creeping silently down the side of the mountain it soon muffled the top of the Pointe Croux and the Pointe Petigax, two isolated points on the west ridge above the Col des Drus. It flowed on inexorably, hiding the precipitous couloirs that plunge towards the glacier. On the Italian frontier, the Grandes Jorasses were quickly blotted out, and soon all the 4,000-metre peaks disappeared in the cloud ceiling that seemed to hang at that height, hesitating to move farther down.

Servettaz surveyed the silent struggle of the clouds, the wind, the sky and the mountains. He did not hesitate a moment.

'About face,' he said. 'We've just got time to get down. In two hours the storm will be on us. We must go while the going's good.'

'But aren't we nearly at the top, Jean?' asked Warfield in surprise.

'Barely an hour, sir; and all the difficulties are behind us; but an hour, and another hour, make two hours, and in two hours we'll have to be well below the overhang, believe me.'

Warfield was far from convinced.

'I want to go on,' he insisted coldly. 'I'm paying to reach the top.'

'We all know you pay, Mr Warfield,' answered Servettaz shortly, 'but my job is to bring you back safe. Believe me, I've enough experience to tell you we *must* turn back; the difficulties have been overcome, the climb's as good as done, honour is satisfied – so why insist?'

Warfield's temper was rising.

'I've climbed far harder mountains, guide' (already, in his anger, he had left off calling the other Jean, thus making him feel that he was paying to be obeyed, and that Servettaz was there to do his bidding). 'I've done harder climbs, and I've been caught by storms; and I've always got to the top. If the Chamonix guides are going to be less – '

'You've said enough, Monsieur,' cut in the guide. 'You want to go on, so on we'll go. But the responsibility's not mine. No one's ever accused *me* of cowardice before.'

'I didn't mean that,' Warfield conceded, feeling he had gone too far, 'but there's no danger yet, let's go on a bit.'

'All right, let's go on, and I swear we'll get to the top,' bawled Servettaz above the noise of the wind. 'Get a move on, Georges! Don't let's waste a minute. Look out for squalls. Got your mittens? May as well put them in your pocket.'

Chapter IX

They were now moving at top speed up the broken rocks leading to the summit when suddenly the mist came down. At the same time, from the direction of the Dent du Géant came a peal of thunder.

'Quicker, Georges, quicker! And if the sky falls down on us, well that's just too bad.'

Warfield climbed on unperturbed, with only one idea in his head: to reach the top.

They realised they had reached it by the great gust of wind that forced them to crouch down among the summit rocks. Then it died down, and in the ensuing hush they discerned through the mist the wavering outline of a human figure leaning towards them; the weird silhouette in its flowing robes glowed gently, delicate bluish flames caressed it on every side, vanishing and reappearing, and the grey head was haloed with fire.

'Lightning on the Virgin!' muttered Georges.

This unearthly vision, looming enormous through the veil of mist, dwindled as they approached. Nearby, it resumed its normal size. It was after all only a modest statue of the Virgin, made of light metal and clamped on to a granite pinnacle some 3,700-odd metres above the plains, which was now transfixed and disfigured by the lightning. Little blue lights flickered continuously up and down the draperies and the whole statue, charged with electricity, crackled incessantly. Plainly, the electric disturbance about them was exceptionally intense. The storm played on all the highest peaks and the flashes of lightning followed each other so rapidly that there was no break in the succession of thunderclaps.

The Dru threatened to become the epicentre of the disturbance. The will-o'-the-wisps crackled on the skirts of the Virgin, as if an invisible transmitter was exchanging messages with space. Strange noises filled the air; the climbers were deafened by a buzzing in their ears, while an unseen hand seemed to be plucking at their hair.

'Georges, the bees! Do you hear it, it's the bees buzzing – get down quickly – the thunder's right on top of us.'

Jean Servettaz recognised all the signs that precede a thunderbolt. The others obeyed, realising how close the danger must be, and the three men flung themselves down the steep rocks up which they had just come, shinnying down the great slabs in a frenzy. When they had put some distance between themselves and the summit, Jean pushed his two companions under the shelter of an overhang. Just in time. For with a sound like the clash of titans, a thunderbolt struck the summit they had just left. The mountain seemed to rock on its foundations, and to the climbers it felt as if the Dru had reeled under the impact of some gigantic battering-ram. The thunder rumbled on for a long time, its cannon-roar echoing from side to side of the gullies. Then followed a silence that seemed even stranger than the uproar. Jean's face, seen through the murky atmosphere, looked to Warfield quite extraordinarily grave; his features were drawn and he gave his client a look eloquent with reproach. Warfield tried to make excuses. Jean gave him no time.

'We've escaped that one,' he said. 'Now we must get away! It's not healthy here! Georges, you go first. You will fix the rappel. You, Mr Warfield, must try to go down as well as you came up. There's just a chance we may see the valley again. Only a chance – this is just the beginning.'

A second clap of thunder set the unseen artillery roaring again.

'That one struck the Sans Nom,' declared Georges, taking the rappel line out of his sack.

'If only it would snow,' said the guide. 'I'd rather that than thunder.'

Mist wrapped the narrow platform between earth and sky on which the three men stood. They felt themselves prisoners of the mountains, and the American waited in absolute silence, not wishing by an ill-timed word to bring down on his head the reproaches he so richly deserved. Georges placed the rope for the first rappel. The remains of an old loop of bleached, worn rope were rotting round a block of granite, and he replaced it by a loop of new rope, through which he threaded his fifty-metre line. Standing on the edge of the drop, and straining to see something of the rock below, he cast the line as far out as possible, so that the two ends should not get entangled. It whistled through the air like a lasso, uncoiling as it went, then fell down against the rock face exactly where the young fellow had intended. By this tenuous line the three men slid down.

They climbed down desperately in the milky half-darkness, endlessly repeating the same manoeuvre of coiling up the line, fixing the rappel, throwing the line, and pulling it after them. They cast about for the right way, only recognising the route by the merest details – a stance, a rusty piton in a crack, or an old rope end already stiff with frost.

It was calm again and their casual remarks, amplified by the mist, seemed to come out of a loudspeaker. Two or three more lengths of the line would bring them to the hardest part of the climb. Already the stances were smaller, and several times they had to make extremely hazardous traverses across the face of the rock.

Just as they reached the top of a wall eight or ten metres high, the air hummed very quietly, as if a liquid were being poured. The humming grew louder, and once more they heard that bee-like buzzing. This fatal sound, heard for the second time, made the two guides turn pale under their tan, for this humming and buzzing were once again unmistakable evidence of an abnormal amount of static electricity. The mist, the mountain, they themselves, were so charged with electricity that a thunderbolt was inevitable.

'Quick, man, quick!' yelled Servettaz. 'Georges, chuck down the rappel! Slide down it! And you, Mr Warfield, don't lose a second, just grip the rope with your hands and jump over, hurry, man, hurry ... Ah, here it is, my hair's standing up. Get on, can't you, get on.'

Warfield tumbled rather than slid on to the lower platform where the porter caught him. Above their heads the rope disappeared into the mist. They were waiting for the guide to join them when a frightful flash completely blinded them. An unknown force plucked them off their feet and dropped them again heavily on the granite slab where they lay full length, inert and battered dummies. Neither heard the appalling explosion that accompanied the electric discharge, nor the sullen rumblings of the echo in the gullies.

When they came to, dazed and haggard, the snow was falling steadily, covering the rocks and glazing over the cracks. The flakes were melting on their blackened faces, and the chill soon restored their power of thought. Georges at once looked for his friend. The rappel line was still hanging down the wall, so he stood up and grabbed it, then shook it and yelled:

'Jean! Jean! Answer me! Are you hurt?'

Nothing answered but the wind.

A jackdaw circling round croaked shrilly, and this sound seemed to give life to the desolation.

'The client's all right,' yelled Georges again, as if this bit of luck could make Servettaz answer them. 'I'll have to go up,' he thought, 'he must have been knocked out.' He untied himself from the climbing rope, not without difficulty, for by now it was wet; then, after tugging sharply at the rappel line, he decided it was holding all right. So up he went, up the smooth face, his legs at right angles to it, the soles of his feet pressed against the rock, to the accompaniment of groans and grunts that seemed to issue from the very depths of his being. When his head reached the level of the upper platform, Georges received a shock that nearly made him lose his hold. A horrified cry died on his lips, and he halted, clutching his rope, with no strength left for the last heave up. The wet rope slipped slowly through his numb fingers. At last he forced himself to move and, finding a hold for the tip of his boot, he managed to heave himself face downwards on to the narrow ledge where Jean Servettaz, of the Chamonix Corps of Guides, had just finished his career.

The guide had been struck by lightning at the very instant when he was preparing to straddle the rappel line. He had been struck while standing upright, with his right hand grasping a hold, his left flat against his body, feeling for the rope, and his head bent slightly forward. His whole attitude betokened movement and life. He looked as if he were still on the way up, watching the progress of his party. The fingers of his right hand still gripped the rock. The lightning, entering by the wrist which it had marked with a small dark stain, had come out by the left foot, for the boot was half-scorched. The body was intact, arrested in that attitude so familiar to climbers; only the eyes had taken on a glassy look, and their uncanny stare terrified Georges. He came up to the corpse, and spoke piteously to it.

'Jean, old man, Jean – it can't be possible. After all these climbs we've done together, you can't leave me like this. It's not true, is it? Oh, speak to me, can't you?'

And the porter shook the strange, frosted effigy, unable to believe such a thing could happen. The wind tore at the ends of the red handkerchief that Servettaz had knotted round his neck. This helped to give the dead man a horribly lifelike appearance, just like the waxworks at the Musée Grévin that visitors have to touch before they will believe they are not real. A faint shout from below brought the porter back to reality: it was the American calling. Disdaining to answer, Georges tried to lay the body down on the platform. After a gruesome struggle, he had to give it up. The corpse was apparently stuck fast to the rock. He had not the nerve to force open those clenched fingers and gave up this ill-matched struggle between a dead man and a living. Cutting off several metres of rope, he tied the body firmly to the mountain, so that the wind could not topple it over the abyss. Then, taking off his helmet, he spent a few moments in silent contemplation of his partner on the rope.

Poor old Jean! What a number of peaks they had conquered in the five years they had been climbing together! They knew each other so well, they complemented each other admirably. Jean used to say of his porter, 'He knows what I'm up to so exactly that he's always there to hold my foot when it might slip, or to safeguard the client when I can't do it. I'll never have anyone else with me!'

He was nearer than he knew to the truth. Already he had begun to wonder how he would manage next season, since Georges would by then be a guide. Certainly he would do nothing, out of selfishness, to stop the porter from graduating to the leadership of a party: he was capable of taking anyone up anything, and Jean was proud of his pupil. Georges repaid, in friendship and devotion, the priceless gift Jean had made him in teaching him his trade so well. Thinking of the day when their partnership would cease, the porter had often suggested that Servettaz should then take on his own son. The guide would have none of it: 'Pierre? Don't you go putting such an idea in his head! I'm going to replace you by a chap young enough for me to lick into shape according to my own ideas.' Now all need of a successor to Georges was past. The rope that had linked the partners so closely had been cut, and death, in striking down Jean, had made Georges a leader. He must take over his command in the hour of danger, in the heat of action, just as a private soldier, seeing his officer fall, at once assumes the necessary responsibilities and duties.

The porter shuddered. It was not death he was afraid of! Death was an old acquaintance. You don't spend your life on the mountains from the age of sixteen, as he had done, without rubbing shoulders almost daily with that old swindler: up till now he'd had the best of it, as had Jean Servettaz. But like all guides, like all airmen, like sailors who don't believe they can ever be shipwrecked, in short like all other men who risk their lives daily, the possibility of a fatal accident never entered his head. Yet here, and in a matter of seconds, death had struck down the most experienced of them all, the very one who should have been safe from its blows and stratagems.

'Oh God,' he groaned, 'what can even the best of us do?'

A fainter cry from his client interrupted his reverie. He shook the snow off his clothes and got ready to go down: slowly and deliberately he checked up the rappel; the lightning had spared it, it was all right. Passing the line round his thigh and arm to act as a brake, he slowly started down the face. He had some trouble with the wet rope which would not run easily. With some bitterness he reflected that they still had 600 metres of this face to go down, in bad weather; the fun was by no means over. Death had won the first round, and now they simply had to win the second, and the match.

Now that the snow had come, Georges knew they ran no more risk of lightning; the only deadly enemy was the snow itself. Already the ledges were carpeted with a soft white layer, and the ice glistened ominously in the chimneys.

Chapter X

Georges rejoined the American, who had watched his airy descent on the line without uttering a word. Warfield's teeth were chattering, he lay flat in a corner of the narrow slab, not yet recovered from the shock. The two men looked at each other for some moments. Georges sighed heavily: 'It's been a fine day's work, Mr Warfield. You've had your Dru.'

Warfield hung his head, then, as if waking from a dream, put the question:

'Is Jean dead?'

'Struck by lightning – and we're not so much better off ourselves.'

'Oh –'

'D'you feel any better? We got a powerful battering, I can tell you. Once I remember up at the Vallot hut being knocked out of my bunk by an electrical discharge; but there's no parapet up here, and we came near to going right over.'

The porter leaned over the edge and shook his head gravely.

'What about waiting here, Georges?' suggested Warfield, who was obviously completely played out. 'The snow's bound to stop sometime, and then they'd send out a search-party.'

'The snow's bound to stop! Man, are you crazy? I hope to God that it doesn't stop now; as long as it's new, and falling, there's still a chance of getting down; but if it clears we'll be stuck up here on the face, the frost will make the ropes as hard as iron, and we'll be perishing well frozen ourselves. There's no use moaning and groaning now, we must begin to do something, one death's enough for today – and it's my job to bring you down safely. Stand up now, we'll need everything we've got. You wanted a storm, didn't you? Well now you've had it, and you've got to put up with the consequences, and get down. Up with you! Pick up your rope –

careful with it, the rappel line's very wet.'

Georges gave the orders, and Warfield, confronted with such determination, had to obey.

The snow was now swirling round the rocks, and mingled with the deep note of the wind was a high piercing wail, like a ceaseless rustling of paper; the whole mountain seemed to be moaning! This weird noise was made by the slabs of snow sliding steadily down the white-coated face: soon the gullies would become the natural channels for avalanches. Everywhere the rocks were alive with runnels of snow. It piled up on the ledges, masked the outlines of the rocks, and obliterated every feature under a deadening cover of white.

The porter was soon faced with some nasty problems. From the feel of the rocks he made out that they were getting near the band of quartz; below it, as he knew only too well, they would come to the big overhang of the chimney with a piton.

They traversed to the right on a narrow ledge now so deep in snow that Georges had to clear the holds with his hands before they could move. His woollen mitts were caked with ice, but he worked feverishly, with only one idea in his head: 'I've got to bring this man down safe! Jean trusted me with him, I've got to bring him down: will I get there?' And the young porter pictured the inevitable bivouac and the fearful night that lay ahead. He had no notion of the time, for their watches had stopped. He guessed it might be two hours after midday; at seven, it would be dark.

He spent a long time searching the rocks for the tiny platform where he knew there should be a rope-ring. The mountain was all the same now: an immense wall of snow and ice that disappeared into the mist. The least mistake might prove fatal. He dug into the snow with his hands, ferreting in the ice-filled cracks for the little rope-end so vital to their descent. Beside him shivered Warfield, burbling some ditty with a refrain that repeated itself, like a cracked record, and came oddly from his dribbling lips –

'If you like a ukulele lady … '

And the snow kept on falling. Already it had blotted out their footprints on the narrow ledge.

At last Georges unearthed the rope-ring, shook it, and chafed it in his hands to unstiffen it. Through it he threaded the rappel line, already stiff with frost, and let it fall over into the soft and shifting emptiness below. He told his client exactly what he had to do.

'Come on, Mr Warfield, put your heart in it! Take the line, there's nothing to worry about. Fifteen metres down you'll start swinging free, but you'll make contact again at the foot of the chimney. Now listen! You'll have to let yourself swing like a pendulum towards your right to strike the exact spot to land on – otherwise you'd just go on down the full length of the line into space. Just do as I say, I'm holding you!'

Georges himself passed the line round Warfield, who allowed himself to be handled like a child; he was still dazed and indifferent, and he gently hummed that maddening refrain –

'Ukelele lady like-a you!'

'For mercy's sake, stop that noise, Monsieur, you're driving me mad.'

'If you like a ukulele lady,' droned the American.

At last Warfield let his weight go heavily on the rope, and started to descend. Georges, braced against the rock wall, kept his eye on the climbing rope that linked him to Warfield. All went well at first and the American went down slowly and steadily, then disappeared out of sight, hidden by the bulge of the overhang. A few minutes passed, the rope ran out evenly, and then a terrific pull came on the porter, as the next two metres of the climbing rope ran out in a jerk.

'Careful now, can't you,' he yelled, 'go down gently, and don't get the two ropes entangled.'

He might have saved his breath, for the wind had risen again and was howling like a lost soul across the mountain face. Georges, always braced for a sudden pull, estimated from the length of rope that had run out how far down Warfield had gone: another fifteen metres he reckoned, another ten … All of a sudden the rope whizzed through his fingers and a fearful pull nearly dragged him off his stance; his hands tightened on the rope and he tried to apply a brake, thinking that Warfield must have let go the rappel line, and be dangling like a broken puppet at the end of its string.

At last he managed to check the fall.

'Warfield, Warfield, get hold of the line. Quickly, you fool, I can't hold you like this for ever.'

A far-off, muffled voice floated up to him from the depths.

'I've got the line.'

And the American's weight no longer came on Georges.

A minute or two later the voice came again.

'I've got there, I'm all right.'

Georges could now relax his grip; but his poor numb hands, in their frozen covering, were fearfully burned. There was a red stain on the palms of his mittens, and a dark trail over several metres of the rope.

It was no moment for thinking of himself. Down there Warfield, whose senses were all benumbed, might do something lunatic. In his turn Georges started down by the line. He could hardly refrain from crying out with the pain as, slung out over space, he grasped the frozen ropes. He dangled round and round like a spider at the end of its thread, then with a tremendous jump sideways, he landed beside his client.

'You can't go doing that sort of thing, Mr Warfield,' he scolded him. 'There must be no more letting go halfway down, because after this' – and he displayed his hands – 'I shan't be able to hold you.'

Warfield peered at the burned and bleeding hands with unseeing eyes, and then, still with the same dazed and wandering look, burst into loud and mirthless laughter. 'Ukulele lady like-a you,' he sang, and without giving the porter another look, began to chuck snowballs over the edge.

The only sane member of the party now had another antagonist to add to the snow and the thunder.

'Well, that's the end!' Georges was talking to himself for reassurance. 'He's going off his head – hope to God *I* keep sane. Alone with a loony on the Dru – what a nice trade a guide's is! Come on, my boy, get moving. Loony or not, you'll bring him down safely, got that? You'll bring him down!'

His next job was to pull down the line. It came easily enough to start with; as he pulled one end the other ran up smoothly, but there came a point where it stuck. He voiced his exasperation.

'Won't budge; well, we're done for.'

It was indeed a tense moment; this line was essential for the rest of the descent. Of course, if Warfield had been normal they could have unroped, and used the climbing rope for the rappels, but the American was getting weaker and less responsible every minute, and to let him go down without being firmly held from above would mean certain death for him. This line that refused to come was absolutely vital to them; the whole safety of their descent depended on it.

Georges made a last effort.

He hung with all his weight on the line, but it wouldn't budge an inch. He tried to stir up Warfield who was huddled in the snow and stared at him without understanding.

'Come on, Mr Warfield, give us a hand,' he begged, 'we've just got to get that line down ... But you don't seem to grasp a single thing!'

Warfield not only didn't grasp a thing, he seemed to be possessed by a demon, for he cackled horribly. Georges made yet another effort, he swung on the thin hempen line, like a cathedral bell-ringer; he alone seemed to be responsible for the deep boomings of the storm.

There were calm spells between the fierce gusts and sudden moments of quiet, when all the elements joined in a conspiracy of silence. During one of these, only the swishing of the snow as it poured down the rocks drowned the voice of the American who took up his South Sea song like a *leit-motiv*.

'Ukulele lady like-a you ... '

And implacably the snow fell on the bizarre party.

'Give us a hand with the rope,' begged Georges, who was tiring; he had cramp in his fingers and his arms felt like lead. Warfield went on singing.

'Oh yes!' he suddenly answered, his face lighting up with a new idea. 'Let's ring the bells ... Ringing the bells! Ding dong, ding dong!' He burst into laughter, finding it an exquisitely funny idea. And he added his weight to Georges's.

For several minutes the two men – the one with drawn face and bleeding hands, the other laughing fit to burst – pulled together, hanging on the rope that jigged and danced above the precipice.

But it still didn't budge an inch. Finally Georges gave over.

He pushed back the useless Warfield, who crumpled up in the snow, still humming in time to the broken rhythm of his breathing. This refrain about the tropical beauties of Hawaii and the scented island nights kept him happy, lost in his dream, while the saliva from his ice-encrusted lips solidified into crystals.

To the porter there appeared to be only one way out: to climb once more up that twenty-metre crack, chock-full of snow and ice, unhitch the line, and come down again. That was the only chance, but would he have the strength to do it?

This short climb was pure hell. The rough granite was wet and frozen, and covered with a sort of oily glaze, a kind of verglas on which bootnails slipped without getting any sort of grip. Georges, already at the end of his tether, heaved himself up painfully inch by inch, gasping and breathless, clutching the line in desperation. The snow which poured down the chimney came in at the neck and cuffs of his jacket, chilling his body, and blinding him. He reached the spot where the crack became so narrow that there was no room for more than a knee and elbow. He thought he would never make it; he spotted, on a level with his hand, in a bulge of the face, the big iron piton on which he would be able at last to rest for a minute, but his boots were coated with ice and kept on slipping, and he had to depend on his arms alone. He floundered around for what seemed hours, and thought he would never reach the security of the piton. How did he get there? Later, he swore he couldn't say. At the moment when, at the very end of his strength, he was on the point of giving up and letting go, his left foot, drumming desperately against the smooth unbroken wall, found some sort of tiny foothold. A bootnail had gripped something – it certainly did not give much hold, but it was just enough to enable him to grab the piton, and heave himself on to it.

He breathed again. His position was extremely precarious. The snow poured continuously down the slabs; he had not enough movement in his bleeding and frozen fingers to be sure of getting up; his teeth chattered and his overtaxed heart thumped away in his chest. At every beat he felt like bursting. Now and then gusts of wind and snow buffeted him alarmingly. He began to realise the extreme danger of his position, marooned as he was in the middle of the mountain face, balancing by some miracle on a fingerhold and a few bootnails above a drop of 700 metres, with night racing on. The chimney ended ten metres above his head; would he have the strength to get up? His knees were hurting and his frozen garments, rigid as any suit of armour, chafed his exhausted limbs.

So Georges thought he had better go down again. One idea obsessed him. Nothing was lost – no, nothing was lost, he could easily save his own skin! Never mind about the client. He had only to lash him to some rocks and leave him to his fate. Georges knew that if he climbed down alone he could save hours and hours of antics with the rope: he might even manage to avoid the risks of a bivouac and reach the Charpoua hut. Yes, that was it. He had only to slide down again, tie up the loony, leave him what was in the sack, and get away! Get away from the storm, from this damned mountain, from the body of Jean Servettaz that perched away up there and scanned with its frozen eyes horizons that no living man had ever seen.

This prospect filled Georges with new hope.

To cut loose would spell a return to the moraine, the pastures, the woods, the valley, and the wooden chalet set among the orchards. But if he went on, he would be done for, he would come off the rocks in this infernal chimney; or, if he got down again, he would simply die of cold beside the American. Ah yes – the American … the other plan was forgotten: he had to bring him down. Bring down your client? Of course, that was your job, but that didn't make it fair, my God, it wasn't fair at all! For it was all through that obstinate fool's doing that Jean was stiffening up here in the snow; must he perish as well, all for the sake of bringing down a madman?

Georges turned over all these conflicting thoughts as, still wedged in the crack, he eyed the few metres of desperately exposed climbing that still had to be done. His lapse lasted only a moment. A second later, he was overcome with shame. He shuddered at himself. Imagine him, the leader, giving up! After Jean, at the moment of death, had tacitly entrusted the client to him! He must have lost his senses like the American, if he were thus also losing his pride and self-respect. No, he would try to free the line at the risk of coming off himself, and after that he would do his best to bring the client down. They would both die – or both win through.

Having accepted the idea of such a sacrifice, Georges felt a new strength. He forgot that he was only a poor little manikin stuck on the great face of an inhuman mountain, and he promised aloud, 'Don't worry, Jean, I'll bring him down.'

For a long time he inspected the top of the crack down which tumbled a torrent of hail and snow. Then he got to grips with the mountain, and was locked in a desperate hand-to-hand struggle; sometimes his feet slipped, but he held on by his right arm fast in the crack, all his weight on the elbow jammed in like a bolt, swallowing mouthfuls of snow, his whole body in contact with the rock, oscillating over the drop, but with each convulsive movement gaining an inch or two of height.

At long last he reached the upper edge of the chimney; it was deep in snow and he had to clear a way on to it, sinking up to his waist, before he could feel the security of the rock ledge and straighten himself up slowly. He was nearly blown from his perch by a terrific gust of wind and snow; just in time he found a hand-hold to cling to. Icicles hung from his eyelashes, encircled his mouth, and the strands of hair that straggled from under his beret stood out stiff and white, like glittering spikes of diamond.

Without wasting a minute Georges pulled up the line, that had been frozen into a cranny. He took off the rope-ring, and shook out the two ends of the line for a minute or two to make certain that he would be able to pull it down this time without a hitch. There was no question now of braking his descent in the approved manner, by passing the line around his leg and shoulder; it was too wet and stiff. He had to run the risk of descending the twenty-five metres by sheer strength of arm. Georges pictured the moment when he would be dangling at the end of this thin hemp line and shivered at the possibility that his frozen fingers should fail him, but this moment of weakness did not last. A superhuman will actuated him, directed him, confirmed him in his own idea: to bring down the client. He shuddered and cursed himself for having, even for an instant, dreamed of shirking his duty. Anyway, what the hell did it matter if he should let go; no one could blame him for *that*. In this sort of situation, all return – or none.

All went well to begin with. He could still steady himself with his legs against the rock, but soon he felt space begin to yawn beneath him, and his own weight came on his hands, and compelled him to accelerate. He clutched the line grimly, and gripped it between his big nailed boots, but this extra pressure did little to brake his descent, and the cruel pace reopened the bleeding sores on his hands.

Georges landed on the platform. Without a glance at Warfield, who was still humming away half-buried in the snow, he at once busied himself to see that this time the two ends of the rope had not got entangled. He felt a slight pull, and let out a great sigh; the line was coming! Slowly, carefully, he coaxed it down, trembling when there was any hitch, overjoyed when it ran freely. Then, when there were only a few more metres to come, he gave a violent jerk to bring the end of the line through the rope-ring above. The line fell with a whizz on to the platform. Heaving a sigh of relief the porter coiled it up carefully, then turned his mind to the next stage of the descent.

Warfield was now dozing. Georges shook him roughly, brushing off the snow that made him look like a shapeless ghost, a real snowman, with nothing alive about him except the two dark eye-sockets and a little round ice-encrusted hole for mouth, through which his breath came in puffs of steam.

'Get a move on, Monsieur,' said Georges, 'I've unhitched the line.'

He spoke in as matter of fact a voice as if he'd done something entirely ordinary, and he all but added, 'Sorry to have kept you waiting.' Of the double struggle in which he had engaged, with the fury of the elements and with himself, never a word. Such things are best kept to oneself.

Chapter XI

The two climbers set off on the next stage of their descent. Warfield moved like a sleepwalker, mechanically obeying the porter's commands, empty-headed and vacant-eyed. He moved more and more clumsily, slithering rather than climbing down the narrow snow-filled chimneys. Again and again Georges felt him come on the rope, checked his fall, then planted him firmly on a stance while he verified the line of descent.

The snow became colder and more compact, and Georges reckoned that it would soon be dark. Where was he? He could not exactly tell. He felt played out; he had had nothing to eat or drink since five that morning. Suddenly, a stronger gust of wind than usual tore aside the mist, and revealed the whole face of the Dru, a fantastic sight. It was plastered all over with new snow, caparisoned in ivory, and the enormous columns that soared unbelievably upwards to lose themselves in a sea of silver cloud might have been hewn from purest marble.

There were fewer cascades of snow now, crumbling into a light dust before they reached the glacier. A clearing towards the east showed the dome of the Aiguille Verte, pink in the setting sun; the wind, which now came from the north, blew a streak of iridescent snow off the top. The fine weather was coming back; and so was the intense and biting cold.

Night fell quickly: in an hour Georges would not be able to go any further. He could make out, still far below him, the first contours of the Shoulder which starts just under the Flammes de Pierre and plunges down towards the glacier. If he could reach that spot, they might yet be safe! For just there lay the rocky cave known as Straton's Bivouac, after his great-uncle the famous Charlet-Straton, who spent several nights out there when he made the first ascent of the mountain.

From now on Georges concentrated all his powers on his single goal. He must reach the bivouac. He shook Warfield out of his torpor, pushed him out again on to the face, paying him down like a sack on the end of a rope. The mere possibility of safety made him feel ten times as strong. They certainly weren't done for yet! They had night and cold in front of them. 'Bah!' he thought. 'We may get a touch of frostbite in our feet, or hands, but we mustn't be fussy.'

As they reached the last chimney the mountain turned purple as if caught in the beam of a coloured spotlight. Only for a minute or two; the streamers of cloud, that danced wildly over the depths, turned silver, and seethed over the valleys. In a clearing to the west rose Mont Blanc, crowned with purple, queening it above the opalescent clouds. There was only the briefest of twilights. The climbers had just time to cross a dangerous couloir down which avalanches rumbled, and reach the entrance of the cave under a great sloping slab. It was hung with stalactites, and looked like the sharp-toothed jaws of some fearsome monster, perhaps one of those fantastic dragons with ivory teeth that are painted in such meticulous detail on lacquered screens of the Ming period.

The two were swallowed up in the monster's maw.

Georges fixed up the bivouac properly, making a little wall of dry stones on the windward side, blocking up the cracks through which the wind whistled with a handful of wet snow that froze at once, more effective for the purpose than cement.

'There you are, Monsieur. Now we've only got to wait for morning,' he announced when this was done.

Warfield didn't answer; huddled in a corner, he looked at his rescuer with bewilderment. Now and then a shudder ran over his whole body; he started up suddenly as if he meant to go down.

'Gently now, gently ... All we've got to do now is to keep off the cold. Did you see the sunset? No, of course not – nor the north wind blowing the snow off the Verte? I can promise you it'll be a fine night with the snow sparkling like diamonds – and the cold biting into you, worse than a red hot iron on your skin.'

But never a word from Warfield.

'He's had a pretty bad shaking,' thought Georges, pity for his companion making him forget his own suffering.

He undid the string of his sack, a job that took him a long time, for his clumsy fingers could not cope with the knots. He wanted to eat but he had soon had enough, and was satisfied with a few biscuits soaked in wine from his gourd; they would not go down, and he munched without managing to swallow a crumb. Warfield would not take a thing; his face was purple, and he hiccupped.

'He'll be having pneumonia next!' cursed Georges. 'That'll be the end.' And scooping up great handfuls of snow he briskly massaged the American's face till it turned the colour of a shrimp. He then managed to force a drop of spirits between the clenched teeth. Slowly Warfield came to life – only to start up again with –

'If you like a ukulele lady … '

'You've got that tune on the brain,' growled Georges, simply for the sake of saying something.

At first he hadn't been conscious of the cold, but as night wore on it became more and more intense, cutting through their jackets, already sodden and stiff, shooting its icy darts right through their bodies, contracting their pitifully frozen faces. Through the opening of the little cave a few stars could be seen shining in an extraordinarily clear sky; the whole mountain was still. Everywhere the snow held the stones fast in the gullies and no sérac broke off and fell. The wind had dropped, but an icy breath played round the bivouac.

Soon the cold became unbearable. Even Georges, hardened as he was, couldn't keep still; in spite of the overwhelming exhaustion of the day he twisted and turned, always on his guard against sleep, now and then beating the rock with his fists to restore the circulation to his numbed fingers. Warfield had fallen into a sort of torpor punctuated by awful groanings, and Georges had to shake and thump him to keep him awake. His boots were bent out of shape and stiff with ice, and occasionally Georges gave them a few smart taps with the shaft of his axe. The result convinced him that Warfield had lost all feeling in his extremities.

Georges remembered that he still had a candle, the one from the lantern. He put a match to it, and the tiny wavering flame dimly lit up the cave, and flickered on the stalactites of ice. The young man filled his mug with snow, melted it over the flame, and thus managed to get a few mouthfuls of tepid liquid: the hardest part was to force it between the lips of his client. Then he did the same for himself.

Then ensued a terrible vigil.

The barbarous music of jaws that chattered and clashed seemed to fill the cave. The noise rose in a crescendo like a mad rattle of castanets inside their heads, then receded only to be replaced by a grinding of teeth like the scratch of mice in the wainscot. It was strange music, inaudible from outside, but dazing and deafening to those who made it. More than once Georges, overcome by exhaustion, all but fell asleep; by a superhuman effort he just managed to keep awake, waiting for the daylight that would not come, sometimes crawling as far as the threshold of the cave; it was almost flush with the edge of the cliff, and away below shone the Charpoua glacier, far lighter than either the pale sky or the ink-black wall.

Slowly night receded, and the faraway summits were streaked with light which then spread over the sleeping world. Georges thought of his chalet down in the valley, of his little room with its wooden walls, so snug in winter, of his mates who would just be starting off on their expeditions; then he found himself thinking of Jean Servettaz. He shivered (and this time it wasn't the cold) at the thought of that icy phantom keeping watch, up there, 600 metres above them. Poor old Jean! And what a fearful blow for his wife. She would have to hear the news tomorrow … But would tomorrow ever come, would this ghastly night ever end? Would he have the strength to go on trailing that walking corpse of an American after him?

A deep burst of laughter drowned the dreadful concert of chattering teeth. Warfield again! The laughter came from deep down his throat, in short convulsive bursts, interrupted by a fresh chattering of teeth that went on and on. Georges could not help shrinking back into the furthest corner of the cave.

At last day broke, pale and icy. Georges, his resistance sapped by this fearful night's exposure, would gladly have dropped off in a comforting torpor, but the will to live was stronger, and he got up, shaking off the momentary weakness. Yes, they must start down, and at once. He stepped outside and, on the narrow ledge above the abyss, forced himself to do some exercises. Little by little the blood came back to his numbed and senseless feet; when he felt sufficiently limbered up, he dragged Warfield out from the bivouac.

The American moved with difficulty in his frozen garments. Georges massaged him roughly, seized him round the waist and pummelled him on back and chest; this strange boxing match went on for some moments, till they had warmed up properly.

They were still roped together. Georges tested the snow with his foot, and showed his relief in a broad grin: it would hold! The lower layer, which was inclined to be soft, was covered with powder snow; in such conditions it would be possible to climb straight down the gully, which would save time, for the rocks were impassable. Georges coiled the rope round his shoulder, leaving only a few metres between Warfield and himself; then he gave a long careful look at the slender couloir that narrowed almost to nothing halfway down, and that, owing to the convexity of the slope, seemed to disappear into space a few hundred metres below.

'It'll go all right, as far as the rocks,' he said. 'After that – well, we'll just have to see. Now, Mr Warfield, down you go.'

The American, though still in a daze, seemed to understand the guide's gesture, and set off uncertainly down the slope of fifty degrees.

'On your feet, Monsieur, on your feet, and face outward,' ordered Georges.

In an excess of caution he came down just behind his client, holding him with only two metres of rope between them, ready if necessary to grab him by his belt should he show any sign of weakness. The snow was good, and at every step they sank in up to the knee. Georges cheered on Warfield, who was clearly at the end of his tether and staggered about like a drunken man.

'Come on, Monsieur, we'll get down all right! Just you walk straight down – look at me, you can dance in a place like this!' And Georges pranced down the couloir to show how firm and confident he was, coming as easily down this snow slope as down a mule track. A little above the barrier of rocks, Warfield suddenly fell on his back, and Georges held him only just in time; he realised that the lower layer must now be ice, to which the powder snow no longer adhered.

'Ice underneath! Careful, we'd better go up a bit.'

Yesterday's storm and avalanche had transformed the rocks into a sheet of ice. The two partners in misfortune climbed up again a few metres, and Georges took to the wall on the right of the couloir. Among these broken rocks it would not be possible to fix an orthodox rappel, but neither could they get down under their own steam.

'Never mind,' he said, 'now we can afford to leave the rope behind.'

He took out the line, made it fast round a big block, and let it run down the wall; using it as a handrail the two men climbed down, making what use they could of the holds and irregularities of the face.

Before starting on the next pitch, Georges gave a last regretful look at the line.

'A nice piece, quite new,' he sighed, 'fifty metres long, and so light too, we'll have to come back for it. Anyway, we're lucky to have got away with it like this.'

The couloir went on down towards a second barrier of rock that fell directly on to the glacier. On the far side the Charpoua hut was already discernible, perched like a sentry on its island of rock and overlooking the lower cliffs. Below, the Mer de Glace, a vast frozen stream striped with darker markings, was beginning to look like a northern fjord frozen in the arctic winter. Georges began to traverse across slabs which were so deep under snow that only a very experienced climber could pass without starting an avalanche.

The sun reached them just as they set foot on the glacier.

Behind them the Flammes de Pierre glowed and burned like torches, and on the Dru itself, immensely high behind them, the ivory of the snow-covered rocks and the white of the freshly powdered gullies were shot through with purple.

A strange lassitude fell upon them both. Now that the danger was over, they seemed to feel a crushing weight on their shoulders which sapped their willpower and made deadweights of their legs; they trailed their bodies like lumps of lead, laboriously heaving up their feet in the deep snow. Georges had to force himself to take care, for only too often accidents happen just when the difficulties seem to be over, when the misleading safety of the lower slopes imparts a sense of false security. He avoided the frailer snow bridges, and reached by degrees the central rocky spur of the Charpoua. The descent of the moraine put new life into them. They were soon at the hut. Here it was, watching over the wild cirque with truly comforting benevolence, and Georges lovingly stroked the larch walls, all warm in the sun. A trickle of water ran down the granite rock and they quenched their thirst. Little by little Warfield was coming back to life. He could not take his eyes off that vast mountain face where, for thirty hours, they had been engaged in desperate struggle. When Georges tried to rouse him from his reverie, he turned towards the porter and said simply:

'Thanks, Georges.'

But he did not dare hold out his hand.

Georges changed the subject. 'We must get down quickly,' he said, 'for now we've got to break the news to the folks below.'

Chapter XII

After a few minutes' climb down the slabs on which the hut stood, they struck the interminable little path that followed the crest of the moraine and then dropped down to the Mer de Glace. The descent seemed endless, their knees sagged under them, and their movements became more and more clumsy. The pains which stabbed through them every time they put foot to ground drew from them small groans which they could not suppress.

'My feet must be frostbitten,' thought Georges, and shuddered at the mere notion of taking off his boots.

The noise of a waterfall leaping down the last rocks heralded the end of the moraine. They were now fifty metres above the vast glacier that stretches so peacefully between its high snow-covered walls. Over to the north, where the river of ice falls down to the Chamonix valley, they could see the buildings of the Montenvers, and safety.

Ever since the sun had caught them up, they had had to endure an additional agony besides the effect of frost and cold. Their eyes, as a result of their exposure to lightning and mist, had begun to discharge. When they reached the glacier this new pain became unbearable. They saw the landscape as in a clammy fog, through a film of discharge which clogged their lids, while a thousand needles stabbed their reddened eyes.

Georges, himself stumbling at every stone and irregularity in the way, took Warfield by the hand and led him like a little child. Luckily the porter knew each crack and fissure on the Mer de Glace, and he proceeded slowly and surely past the gaping crevasses. Once across the glacier he struck the goat track on the left bank, with its iron railing and steps cut in the rock, that leads to the Montenvers hotel. The silence was broken by a shrill whistle.

'The 8.21 train,' noted Georges.

The last steep slope up to the hotel was one long agony. They toiled up so slowly that the tourists disgorged by the rack and pinion railway turned and looked back at them: they were tactless and inquisitive and made loud comments.

'Look! Real climbers!'

'They look pretty well done in.'

'Poor fellows.'

'You're sorry for them, Madame. I'm not, no one forced them to go climbing.'

This made Georges and Warfield more than ever conscious of their own particular burden. They forced their way past, their stricken eyes fixed on the path in front. Georges, exasperated, shouldered his way through the crowd of gapers.

'Shut up,' he growled, 'we aren't on show.'

'What a coarse fellow,' tittered a lady with Louis XV heels, who was selecting picture postcards from the stand at the kiosk.

A little platinum blonde, who was posing for her photograph in front of that majestic and unchanging background (Me and the Mountains) went so far as to grab the porter by his sleeve.

'Have you been up there?' she asked naïvely.

'We've certainly been some way,' Georges brought himself to answer.

On the station platform swarmed the usual fine weather crowd. A group of guides, leaning against the parapet where the glacier path begins, watched the two men come up. There was old Jules of Benoni des Plans, Paul Boutet, Napoleon Roveyaz, Michel Terraz, Georges and Antoine Lourtier, all waiting their turn at 'pirating'; they were there to accompany such tourists as wanted to venture on to the glacier, or even to cross to the other side, to the point where the Mauvais Pas path begins. They were called 'pirates', or sometimes the 'sharks' of the Mer de Glace. Every fine day in the season a group was told off for this job by the Guides' Office; they came up by the first train and went down by the last, and rendered a service which, if without danger and without honour, was not without profit; ten crossings of the glacier at fifteen francs apiece brought in just about as much as an exhausting expedition.

'Look at these two,' remarked Roveyaz, 'they're walking pretty queerly.'

'It looks like Clarisse's Georges. Yes, it's him all right, and that's his client, the big American. What on earth's the matter with them, they look as if they'd had a drop too much.'

'Can you see Jean Servettaz?'

'No, he's not with them.'

'Looks as if something has happened.' They moved nearer.

The mere sight of the burned eyes, the frozen boots, the lined and ravaged faces, was enough to arrest the guides – above all the strange look in the eyes of Georges and Warfield, who bore the unmistakable marks of men who have walked very near to death.

The guides took charge of the sacks and escorted the climbers in by the path that leads to the hotel.

'What happened, Georges?' asked Michel Terraz.

There was no answer from the porter. Old Benoni, cutting Terraz short, pointed to the inquisitive crowd that was beginning to gather. They sensed a drama, and were already agog for a story that could be told when they got home; a real accident, what a piece of luck!

'Not here, not in front of all these people, Michel, wait till we get inside.'

The group passed into the low-roofed guides' room with its massive granite columns.

Georges and Warfield slumped down on to a bench, the others clustered round them and the waitress, more out of habit than anything else, began to mix some grog. For a moment nobody spoke, and the older men, in an agony of suspense, let the young fellow get back his breath, and search for words that somehow would not come.

'So Jean's gone, has he?' said Lourtier, to help him get out what he had to say.

'Struck by lightning on the Dru,' gasped Georges. Then, shaken by sobs, he bowed his head in his hands, his broad shoulders heaved, and the tears from his reddened eyes coursed in grimy channels down his ravaged face.

His comrades let him weep in silence.

'It's the reaction, just leave him alone, it'll do him good. Don't speak to him, and don't ask him any questions,' advised Benoni. 'For the moment let's see what we can do for the other chap.'

He shouted through the open door that led into the office.

'Jules, Jules, come here quickly.'

The hotel manager did not need to be told what had happened. Disasters like this were an old story to him.

Benoni pointed to Warfield, motionless on the bench, his eyes far away, and his head nodding on his shoulders.

'Put him to bed, but don't touch his feet. Tell the doctor and the Guides' Office. We'll look after Georges.'

The manager took Warfield by the hand and conducted him up the staircase of the hotel.

The guides were alone with their grief. But they could still catch the shouts, the cries and noise of the crowd, so Michel Terraz got up and shut the door.

Then Georges told his story.

'The storm caught us just under the summit,' he began.

But old Benoni was not listening: he was cutting the frozen bootlaces with his knife, and trying to take the porter's boots off. They were still covered with ice and hard as iron; he had to cut away a great piece of the upper. When he'd removed the thick grey woollen stockings, the feet showed swollen and blue, with jet black toes. 'It's too late,' thought the old guide, 'they're done for.' The instep was already streaked with purple.

Georges went on talking, never heeding the sighs and sobs which punctuated his story. The guides were deeply moved, and from time to time one of them would furtively wipe his eyes with the back of his hands.

The 9.17 train whistled, summoning the crowd of shouting, pushing tourists who pressed in to the carriages. The first batch had gone down again.

Chapter XIII

Chamonix-Mont-Blanc lay asleep. Its massive hotels, comfortable and impersonal, built without semblance of style or grace, were wreathed in the light mist that rose from the noisy Arve, spread over the town, and put a film across the sky. Beams of milky light, penetrating from above and seeping through the mist, made the streets look like the naves of a mighty cathedral. The atoms dancing in the shafts of light, and the million frost-crystals sparkling on the roofs, showed that it would not be long before the sun came right through. It was extremely cold, and although only the beginning of September it felt more like Michaelmas.

Everything was quiet up in the square: the onion-domed church kept watch over the cosmopolitan crowd asleep in the palatial hotels. The professional loungers, who had only gone to bed a few hours ago, would never know the exquisite freshness of such a morning. The lamp behind the square face of the church clock was still on, so that the dial, haloed in light, glimmered through the mist. Above it, the copper dome reflected a stronger light, and began to gleam in the sun.

There was nobody about in the square this morning. Gros-Bibi was opening his little café; he was in his shirt sleeves in spite of the bitter cold. Although it was only six o'clock, Fabien the scavenger was already on his second round; he cursed away as he pushed his barrow and scooped up his little piles of garbage. A group of five or six elderly guides – sacks on back, axes in hand – were chatting together with an occasional word for Fabien. Everyone knew everyone else here, and the humble scavenger could join in a conversation along with the most considerable proprietor. If you were a native of Chamonix (and this was the indispensable condition) then you needed no further qualification to discuss public affairs or to be given your chance to run them. It was a privilege not everyone could hope to have.

Along the lane leading to the Majestic, and on the gate of the Hotel du Mont Blanc, the streamers abandoned by last night's revellers added their bright colours to the piles of fallen leaves.

Fabien grumbled away: 'They make enough work for me, with their dances! I've twice my usual to do this morning. Just look at that! As if the road were meant for rubbish! These confounded playboys, always drinking.'

'Not all of them, Fabien, not all,' broke in one of the 'pirates'. 'Lucky for us there are still a few to go climbing, or else we'd be looking for our bread in some other place. Let 'em all come! You know that we get something out of all these gents who leave their money in the valley. We can't be young forever. It's their holiday, after all, and it can't always be much fun for them in the towns. Let 'em have their good time here. What's more, good or bad, they all end up somewhere on the mountains. At first they come out of – what's the word? – snobbery, that's it, so's to be able to brag about it; then out of vanity, to impress the girls in the evening at the bar; and then it gets hold of them and puts everything else out of their heads! But those are the ones *you don't* see, Fabien. They sleep up in the huts, they come back tired, they rest, and start off again. They're the real climbers!'

A tinkle at the corner of the Rue Joseph-Vallot heralded the approach of something – a stray goat perhaps – ding, ding, ding.

'Here comes the Chief: you could tell him a hundred yards off by that bell of his.'

Round the corner came the Chief Guide, perched on an old-fashioned high-wheeled bicycle, with handlebars that curled up like the horns of a Camargue bull. He stopped by the pavement just opposite the Bureau des Guides and put one foot to the ground. With his hands on the brakes, he hailed the company:

'Morning all. Drinking already?'

'So long, Chief, see you soon!'

'It's mighty cold this morning, but it's quite clear at Les Pelerins, and in an hour the mist'll have lifted. You should see the snow!

It's right down; and the Aiguilles are all covered. No more mountains for a while. It'll take a week of fine weather to clear it off, and in a week there won't be as much as a cat in Chamonix. Confound it! There were still so many clients wanting to do another climb. Well – *ça fait mé pi pas pi!*'

'*Ça fait mé pi pas pi!*' An odd dialect phrase, in constant use among guides, and practically untranslatable. It means: Clearly, everything's not for the best, it *could* be a good deal better, but as you can't do anything about it, you must just put up with it. *Ça fait mé pi pas pi! All* the mountaineer's philosophy is contained in that little phrase, and its sound conveys its meaning well enough.

Jean-Baptiste Cupelaz unlocked the office which opened directly on to the road, took a broom from the back, and set to work at once to tidy the premises. His big clumsy fists looked as if they would be more at home with an ice-axe than a broom.

Jean-Baptiste was a strong man in the prime of life. Unfortunately, a piece of shrapnel in the pelvis – a souvenir of Verdun – had cut him off for ever from serious climbing. So he'd been appointed to this post of Chief Guide, which, in fact, meant never guiding at all, but keeping the office books, making a list of visitors' projected expeditions, deducting the provident fund dues from the guides' fees (five percent on the tariff for an expedition), seeing that every man got his fair turn on the roster, and summoning guides whom clients had asked for by name. It took a good deal of honesty and a good deal of tact as well to handle the inevitable difficulties that cropped up during a season, when, for instance, a guide – usually not one of the best – would make out that he had been badly treated by another who had been luckier with his clients.

There were two things about his job that worried the worthy Jean-Baptiste: the telephone, to which he could not get accustomed, and white wine, to which he could get accustomed only too easily. All day there was a coming and going – to the greater profit of Gros-Bibi – from pub to office, office to pub, and back again. Every guide who came in after a climb considered it a point of honour to pay his dues and then stand his round of drinks; every guide who set out for a stiff climb offered Jean-Baptiste a parting dram. For those who were going out or coming back it did not matter much, for the days of abstinence and hard going quickly dispelled the effects of the alcohol. But the Chief Guide never left his sedentary job, where he ran risks far greater than those he had faced on his most dangerous climbs before the war, or even in the storm of fire and shell at Verdun.

'Another two or three seasons and you're done for,' warned the doctor.'

'All right, all right, but I can't start being standoffish with all the chaps.'

'Just you look out, Jean-Baptiste, you'll have a nasty surprise one of these days. Can't you try saying No?'

Jean-Baptiste forced himself to follow the doctor's sensible advice, and when the 'pirates' asked him over –

'Come on, Jean-Baptiste, just a little one!'

'Later on,' he would answer, 'at present I'm busy with the roster. Come back in an hour, so that I don't have to rout you out of all the cafés in the village.'

And he would settle down limply at his table.

The Guides' Office was a poorly furnished place and looked more like a lawyer's waiting room. It was square and high, papered with a hideous striped paper, faded and yellow, and with a floor of broad, knotty pine planks. A big table covered with black oilcloth, littered with papers and bills – the sort of thing you see in any country *mairie* – stood in the middle; there were five or six cane chairs for visitors. The pipes of a round stove added to the ugliness of the room, and an old jam tin had been hung on a rusty piece of wire under its upper joint to catch the drips. All the same, this shack that might have been the setting of any little nobody of a clerk contrived to have a soul of its own, because year after year its humdrum walls had served as backcloth to the never-ending epic of the Alps.

The place was rich in memories. The drab walls were hung with relics that the guides, without thinking much about it, had stuck up just when they happened to receive them. A signed portrait of Whymper hung next to an old yellow photograph of the visit of

Féliz Faure: beyond it, in a small frame, was a picture of the King of the Belgians on his return from the Dru. All the great figures of mountaineering had left their mark here: Cunningham, Freshfield, Mummery, Tuckett, Emile Fontaine, Vallot, Gos, Tricouni, Dunod, Mieulet, Durier, Janssen, and others, and their photographs rubbed shoulders with maps, sketches, geological charts, drawings and rare old coloured prints that would have warmed any collector's heart. A relief map of Mont Blanc, in a glass case, assisted the Chief Guide's explanations. Collections of minerals – hyalin quartz, smoked crystals, protogynes, mica-schist, gneiss, lumps of asbestos – gathered dust on a cupboard on the wall. At the back an enormous glass-fronted bookcase, given by some Senator or other, displayed its scanty collection of books, most of them too abstract or too difficult for the guides, who never bothered to open them.

But the real soul of the office was in the back room: a dark hole behind a partition and overlooked by the town jail. Somehow, it contained two atmospheres: the stuffiness of the office and the bracing air of the heights. Ropes were hanging all over the place; there were ice-axes of every age and every make, crampons and lanterns – all the gear dumped by guides between climbs. At the very back, stacked up like a folding screen, a stretcher of stout grey canvas waited ready for use. A newer stretcher with an aluminium framework, and altogether of more modern design, hung from a metal joist in the ceiling. It completed the rescue apparatus which – together with a large first aid box marked with a red cross – was a silent reminder that this den could on occasion become the antechamber of death.

A narrow granite-paved alley separated the Guides' Office from the local Information Office, a much more up-to-date affair, with its wide counter separating customers from clerks, and its deceptive air of being a travel agency.

Through these two offices passed all the life and all the seasonal activities of Chamonix-Mont-Blanc. The Information Office welcomed the visitors, advised them, found them rooms; while the Guides' looked after those who were attracted to the heights.

Jean-Baptiste Cupelaz opened his register, wrote down the names of the 'pirates' for the day, then cast an eye over the list of proposed expeditions. It was not a long one, for the bad weather had deterred most climbers. The Chief Guide shook his head.

'Well, this snow means the end of the big stuff.'

The big stuff – that means the really stiff climbs, the difficult expeditions that are only attempted by the small and skilful minority, and that not all the guides will take on. Doing the big stuff means being ready to tackle anything – perhaps the Verte, or the Aiguilles, or one of the major ice and snow climbs; it also means a lot of money – and a lot of risk. The Chamonix guides have never accepted the classification of first- or second-class guide. They find their own level, by refusing to take on any climb that they consider beyond their powers. In this way only a small élite, thirty men at most, share the risks and profits of an exacting trade. For the rest, Mont Blanc – which has been purposely tariffed rather high – is the limit: they stick to it, and it is not unusual for them to go up it a dozen times in the course of the summer, while the better guides prefer to make for the harder climbs.

The Chief Guide completed his list, and called to the 'pirates', who set off nonchalantly up the station road, axe under arm, to catch the train to Montenvers.

A few minutes later Cretton, the hall-porter of the Carlton, came in to ask about a guide.

'Somebody steady, one of the older chaps who doesn't go too fast; it's for a diplomat who wants to go up to some of the huts; no need for a top-notcher, but give us a chap with a bit of conversation, who knows all the yarns; he'll do very well out of it.'

'I'll let you have old Jules Rebat, he'll tell him all about his travels in America.'

'Fine! Tomorrow I think I'll have a young fellow who wants to go into training for the big stuff – got anyone for him?'

'Wait a minute while I have a look at the roster.' And Jean-Baptiste read out several names in the order in which they'd been put down.

'It's always the way,' he grumbled, 'the good 'uns are off on climbs, and they let their turn go, because they've been specially picked by a client. But I'm expecting Jean Servettaz down tonight, he's due back from the Dru; that's right up his alley, I'll leave word for him.'

And off went the hotel porter.

Two big Germans appeared.

'A guide, *ja bergführer!* For Mont Blanc. How much?'

'Five hundred francs, and another 350 for the porter.'

'We don't need a porter, we can carry our own gear.'

'It's the rule, Monsieur, it's for the safety of the party.'

'*Ja, ja!* Tell them to meet us tomorrow at Couttet's Hotel.'

'*Ja, ja,*' answered Jean-Baptiste, to the manner born.

They went off, leaving the Chief with two or three of the older guides who sat and smoked in silence. He got up and went to the door for a look around.

'Look! It's clear now – but what a lot of new snow! Just look at those chimneys up on the Charmoz: they're like rivers of ice! We're done for now; might as well shut up shop.'

The mist had cleared, and the mountains shone white above the moraine. The line of sunlight was creeping down the trees below the Brévent; above it, all was warmth and radiance, while lower down the woods and meadows were bathed in filmy blue light. The sunlight slowly descended from its invisible source; it shone above the Aiguilles, left one side of the valley in shadow, and touched the sleeping rocks to ardent life. The great ice flows of the Dôme du Goûter, the Bossons and the Taconnaz, were scarcely touched as yet; here and there the patches that caught the light emphasised the grim darkness of the rest of the glacier.

The first motor buses were arriving from lower down the valley, bringing up their usual contingent of day trippers who scrambled out and rushed for the postcards and souvenirs.

A sunburned guide turned up, his empty sack flapping from his shoulder by one strap.

'Back again, Etienne?'

'Yes, I got in last night: I've come to pay my due.'

'Have a good trip?'

'Too much snow, we were held up under the bergschrund on the Charmoz.'

The guide paid his due, started to go out, then came back. 'Aren't you coming? We'll just go over for a quick one, to clinch the matter.'

'Good enough.'

The two of them crossed to the café opposite, the Chief Guide leaving the door of the office open behind him so that he could see who went in. The square filled up: visitors, guides, hotel staff bustling about their business, local dignitaries animatedly discussing the affairs of the day. Politics, especially local politics, seemed to be the major topic of interest.

The girl at the café at once brought over a small, longnecked glass carafe, engraved with a line and cross to measure off the portions; no customer here would ever let himself be served with wine from bottles not so marked, or take it in one of those deceitful tankards that they use in the South of France. The Chamoniard wants exactly what he has asked for, and his stolid nature does not take kindly to any fanciful variation.

'Finished your engagement, Etienne?'

'Yes, with the Englishman, but I'm starting again in three days for Corsica with a climber from Berne; there's too much snow here now. You know, Jean-Baptiste, I think you've got to travel when you're a guide; if you nose round, there's always some range in Europe where you can get some climbing. The great thing is to get your clients.'

'You're right, that's the main thing.'

Chapter XIV

Into the café came a tall man, to be greeted with respect and deference by the drinkers at the tables. Actually, with his extremely well-cut suit, Homburg hat, and immaculate town shoes, he seemed rather out of place in this haunt of guides. He had a cigar between his lips, and his slightly blotchy complexion revealed a man who lives well, eats and drinks rather too much, but keeps in pretty good trim. He came straight over to a place beside the Chief Guide and Etienne, and genially hailed the waitress.

'Bring some more of these, my dear.' Then, by way of making conversation, he asked:

'Any news of my nephew, Jean-Baptiste?'

'They should be on their way back, Monsieur Dechosalet.'

The Chief Guide called him *Monsieur*, just as if he were a client. For since boyhood Paul Dechosalet had made his way successfully through life, and was now sole proprietor of the Hotel des Voyageurs – the oldest inn at Chamonix, 117 bedrooms, fifty bathrooms, as the advertisement has it. Success had not prevented him from remaining a proper Chamoniard, completely at home with those who had remained guides or peasants and had not made their fortunes. All mountain folk are like that; even when they have made their pile they keep their simplicity and lack of side. In this valley where the feeling of equality is so deeply rooted, people are never judged by their bank balances, but by their character; and if it is the better-off among them who are chosen to run local affairs, that is because they can best hold their own with the gentry from outside who want to have everything too much their own way. Hence Paul Dechosalet wore with some regret, but with quite an air, a faultless collar and a well-cut suit. But that was only for the summer season; as soon as the visitors had gone he changed with relief into his old corduroy shooting jacket and nailed boots, and put on a deer-stalker cap that, in proper country fashion, never came off, not even at meals.

As a sidelight on his character, some years before he had built himself a magnificent villa, expensively furnished and with every modern convenience. He had lived there exactly a fortnight, and had then come rushing back to the old family chalet in a neglected corner of the garden of the Hotel des Voyageurs that had once been the orchard. He felt more at home in low rooms, with bare wooden walls and a huge china stove, than in the luxury and comfort of his fine new establishment. He did not like being called Monsieur, and he could not bear any kind of formality from his contemporaries.

'Monsieur, Monsieur,' he grumbled, 'I'll trouble you to lay off all these Monsieurs. I wish you'd just call me Paul and be done with it. As if you'd forgotten how we used to fight as boys – and the days when we went chasing after the girls, as far as Servoz!'

'All very well, Paul, but a man of your position … '

'Come on, drink up. Same again, dearie.'

The three men emptied their glasses and got up.

Paul Dechosalet set off for a stroll through the streets, with a nod and a word for his many acquaintances, while Jean-Baptiste went back to his place at the office.

Etienne, with nothing special to do, leaned up against the door and smoked a quiet pipe as he surveyed the coming and going in the square.

A big fair young man went in and, speaking fairly good French, asked for a guide for Mont Blanc. He was still in travelling clothes, with light shoes and a straw hat.

'Have you done any expeditions before, Monsieur?' inquired the Chief Guide.

'What?'

'Done some climbs?'

'No, never; I'm a Swede, on my way back from college in America; I want to climb Mont Blanc before I go home to Sweden.'

'You've never been on a mountain?'

'Never, but I'm a very good walker.'

'You'll need a guide, and a porter.'

'That's all right by me; but I'd like to start today because tomorrow evening I have to catch the train for Geneva. They told me I could sleep at the hut – the Grands – what's its name?'

'The Grands-Mulets.'

'That's right. And I want to rent boots and an axe and anything else that's needed.'

'Here's a piece of luck for somebody,' thought the Chief Guide. He called Etienne over.

'Are you off again in three days?'

'Yes.'

'Do you want to take this gentleman up Mont Blanc? Knows nothing about it; I'll give you a good man as porter.'

'I'm ready to try, but this snow won't give us much chance of reaching the top; we'll have to make fresh tracks in the new stuff.'

'You can always take a crack at it.'

Five minutes later the fair young Swede, fitted out from top to toe by the Chief Guide, set off towards the téléferique of the Aiguille du Midi.

Jean-Baptiste buried his head again in his accounts.

He was interrupted by the ringing of the telephone – an old-fashioned model with a handle, on the wall of the back room.

Next to drink, the telephone was the Chief Guide's main worry. He couldn't get used to speaking down this silly little tube, or talking normally to a person he couldn't see. Usually he made one of the other guides answer; the young chaps always enjoyed using it. He himself much preferred messages brought by cyclists, loungers, or hotel porters.

Awkwardly he unhooked the receiver.

'Hello,' he shouted, 'Chief Guide here ... Yes, it's the Guides' Office ... Yes, sir ... Oh, it's you, Jules, is it? Where are you? Montenvers ... Hello, can't hear you ... What's that you're saying ... My God ... It's not true ... *Jean*, d'you say ... Struck by lightning ... Really dead? – *Can't* be true ... Georges's feet frostbitten ... What about the client ... Nothing much wrong with him … That's something … Yes, of course, I'll let them all know, but give me time to turn round, I'm all knocked sideways … Wait a minute, ask Georges how much snow there is on the Dru … Right down to the glacier … They won't be able to go up yet, at that rate … Is it fine up there … Grand day … and cold. Right. Thanks, Jules, yes, everything's all right here, thanks.'

Jean-Baptiste hung up the receiver: it took him some time to collect himself. His face showed his consternation and grief.

'What a thing to happen! Never heard anything like it,' he told the others. 'Jean's been killed on the Dru, and Georges's feet are frostbitten. We must send a rescue party out! If I understood him rightly, he's stuck up just under the summit; it'll take some good men to bring him down!'

'Couldn't the chaps at the Montenvers go up?'

'They certainly couldn't; nothing but older men up there today; they're all past it. Trouble is, all the younger men, or nearly all, are out; I've just sent Etienne Davet off to Mont Blanc. You wouldn't be ready to go, Maxime, would you?'

Maxime Vouilloz was a good fifty or over, but he was always in good training and had been a first-class rock climber.

'Of course I'll go; and Jacques Batioret too; he's digging up potatoes. I'll tell him.'

'That makes two. We must have eight at least. Six to bring down the body, two to carry the ropes and back up the others, and fix the rappels.'

A group of young porters came into the office to hear what all the talk was about, and were given the news. They were probably all between eighteen and twenty-two years old, but the daily struggle had left its mark on their faces, and they looked considerably older.

'Why shouldn't some of us go?' said Fernand Lourtier. 'I've been three times on the Dru. And Boule here has done all the big climbs.'

'I'll go,' said Boule, a rubicund young fellow, clean-shaven and never without a smile. His debonair bearing, so unlike the weather-beaten aspect of his friends, concealed a really remarkable agility.

'I'm no ace,' said Paul Mouny, 'I wouldn't offer to go first, but I can always back the others up … and you see Fernand and I are friends of Pierre's, so the least we can do is to bring his father down.'

'And where is Pierre, anyway?'

'He went down to Courmayeur with Red Joseph; we'll have to telephone the Chief Guide over there to tell him.'

'We'll also have to break it to Marie, poor Jean's wife,' said the Chief Guide abruptly. 'Who's going to take on that job?'

'Suppose we asked her brother to do it,' suggested Fernand Lourtier.

'Paul Dechosalet? I had a drink with him not an hour ago, run and fetch him here.'

'I'll just look in at home on the way and tell Aline to go along too. Pierre would like to know that she'd been up to his mother.'

People had already begun to assemble outside, for the bad news had travelled fast through the town, spreading consternation on every side. In no time at all a small crowd was shooting off questions without respite. They were sincere enough in their sympathy, but a nuisance at this particular moment when the guides wanted to concentrate on rescue operations.

'Don't lose any time,' said the Chief Guide. 'Well, that's settled, anyway. Maxime, you'll lead the party. I'll write down the names, shall I? With you goes Jacques Batioret … '

'That's right, and I'm letting him know.'

'Then the young men: Fernand Lourtier, Boule, Paul Mouny.'

'All here.'

'Now we need three more.'

'I'll come,' put in a big red-haired man, Armand Rosset, from the village of Mont, 'if the rest of you will have me.'

Rosset came from a different village from the others, and guides tend to go by families, villages, clans. Rosset did not belong to them.

'Of course we'll have you,' Maxime assured him, 'but I still need two others.'

'There's Michel Lourtier,' suggested Paul Mouny, 'he's young, of course, only sixteen, but he climbs like a monkey, and he could take the ropes. Like to come, Michel?'

'Where to?'

'It's a stiff job. To bring down Jean Servettaz, who's been killed on the Dru. There'll be plenty of ice in the gullies!'

'Poor old Jean,' mused the boy; then added unhesitatingly, 'of course I'll come.'

'I'll make up the number,' announced a solid young fellow who had just come in. 'I don't belong here, but we're all friends up there on the mountains. I was going back to St Gervais this evening. Will you ring up the office there so that they can leave word at home?'

'Certainly, Jean Blanc, and thanks.'

Jean Blanc was a guide from St Gervais, certificated by the French Alpine Club. There is naturally a certain amount of rivalry between the old established Corps of Guides at Chamonix and guides elsewhere, who have been appointed by the Alpine Club, which is a younger organisation. The former were incorporated into an independent company over a century ago, and have jealously guarded their prerogatives ever since. But in times of trouble like this, quarrels and rivalries were forgotten and everyone worked shoulder to shoulder.

The first shock over, Jean-Baptiste was once more the organiser and commander-in-chief. He resumed:

'Be off and get ready, you young fellows: take two pairs of mittens, for it'll be cold; no need for crampons, they're no good in that soft snow and would only be something more to carry. As for the ropes, I've got fifty metres of eleven-millimetre rope here in the office, it'll do for bringing down the body; for climbing ropes, you'll have to draw on your spares. You'll need at least three lengths of line for the rappels, and don't forget the rope-rings. Maxime, you must have some odds and ends of rope that would do for rings up in your loft?'

'Surely I have. All we need now are lanterns.'

'Here are two big ones for you; that'll be enough with your own, and Batioret's. Now let's see about the stretcher. If I were you I'd just take the six-metre aluminium rod. It knocks down into three pieces: it's the handiest thing to tie a body on to. And anyway, there's a stretcher up at the Charpoua hut, the Alpine Sports Club had one taken up two years ago, after the accident in the Mummery couloir.'

'What about the sacks?' asked Maxime.

'Right you are, we've got to think of everything. If I were you, I'd take a blanket from the hut – there must be some old ones – and then I'll give you four sacks. Here, Michel, run to the Co-op and ask them for four big corn sacks; the manager will let you have them as soon as he knows what they're for.

'Now there's no time to lose. You must catch the 11.30 train; that'll get you to the Montenvers at 12.15, and you'll reach the Charpoua in time for a good night's sleep. And indeed,' went on Jean-Baptiste, turning to the leader of the party, 'if I were you I'd make a reconnaissance as far as the bergschrund, then you'll have the trail made for tomorrow.'

'You're quite right, Jean-Baptiste, don't worry, we'll manage.'

'I've just one more thing to say to you, you young 'uns, mark my words. Poor Jean's been killed, and that's enough. That makes two of our men this summer. Just because you're bringing down a dead man, I don't want you to do anything silly. I know you well enough – I've been young like you – I know what you'll say. We can't leave poor Jean stuck up there on the rocks like a scarecrow to frighten off the jackdaws, we can't bear the thought of it, and there's his widow to think of and his son ... I know how it is ... At Verdun, if one of our mates fell, away out in no man's land, we'd risk anything to bring in his body. It's natural enough; I can't get rid of the feeling that he must be cold up there, poor Servettaz ... But you *must* be careful, it wouldn't help anybody if there was another accident – like that day when three men got frostbite on Mont Blanc when they went to bring a body down. Be careful, the rocks seem to have had a lot of snow on them. Maxime will decide what to do. If necessary, stay a day or two at the hut – but above all, don't run any unnecessary risks. Is that clear?'

'Quite clear, Chief.'

'All right, get off, and be back at eleven o'clock. I'll go and see about breaking it to the family.'

Shortly afterwards Paul Dechosalet appeared in the office. He still bore traces of deep emotion, and was out of breath after rushing straight over from the hotel. His eyes were red, and he looked as if he might burst into tears at any minute.

'Tell me, it's not true what they're saying?'

'Only too true, my poor fellow; whoever would have thought of that happening to Servettaz! Just the other day, when he came back from the Lötschenlücke, he seemed so sure of himself. "Four hours steering a compass course on the Aletsch glacier!" he told me. "I thought I was walking in a circle back to the Concordia Platz, but I managed to find the hut. I wasn't fifty metres out in four hours' going! The mountains haven't got me yet!" And now he's gone.'

'What a dirty game it is! It's easy to see why he didn't want his son to be a guide. He's going to take it hard, is poor Pierre; anyway, I'm here to keep an eye on their affairs.'

'Yes, they're lucky to have you, Paul, they all look to you for advice.'

'Has the rescue party started?'

'I'm expecting them shortly, they went off to get ready.'

'I'll be back again; must get them a few nips to take up with them, it'll be cold up there. Anyway, I'd like to see them; don't you think it's a bit dangerous going up with all this new snow?'

'Of course it is! But you wouldn't want us to leave one of our own men up there, unburied, at the mercy of a wind that might easily blow him off the face to be lost forever in a crevasse? People like to have their dead near them; I think nothing ever pleased my father more than when he spotted my grandfather's body in the ice forty years after the accident. It had come from near the top of Mont Blanc, almost untouched, preserved in its shroud of crystal, down to the lower plateau of the Bossons glacier. Grandfather was a young man when he was killed, much younger than Father; his hair was untouched and his face pink and fresh, but frozen so hard that his eyes were hard as agates. Fancy, forty years moving down in the glacier. And all those years, we never knew where to go and pray on All Saints' Day. Father used to look up at Mont Blanc, up there by the Rochers Rouges where the accident happened, and it worried him that we didn't know where Grandfather was. His place was all ready in the cemetery – all they had to do was to put him in it; it was just as if the family had all foregathered at last. Wasn't Father pleased! "Now," he told me, "now at last we're all here!" What struck me most was seeing Grandfather as a young man of thirty. I was only a little boy then, and I couldn't think of a grandfather who wasn't old and white-haired. I'm telling you all this to show that we'll do our very best to bring him back before it's too late.'

'I quite understand, Jean-Baptiste, but I don't want them to do anything rash.'

'I'm a bit worried, for I only managed to get some young porters; there'll only be three guides, but Maxime Vouilloz is a wary old fox.'

'I'd trust him all the way.'

'They were all anxious to go, you know, down to that little Michel whom I included against my will; sixteen's a bit young, don't you think?'

Shortly afterward eight men with all their equipment met in front of the office, and apportioned out the food and the spare gear. Paul Dechosalet came back carrying a little brandy. Michel, the last to arrive, filled his pack with the four corn bags in which they would wrap the body. The bundles stuck half out of his rucksack: he looked like one of the itinerant cloth merchants that occasionally come over from Piedmont. Outside, the crowd grew bigger and bigger. Everyone was agog to get the news.

The eight members of the party turned their backs on the bystanders with their silly, irritating questions. They refused to answer and nursed a silent resentment against people in general, against the mountains that had taken one of their friends, against the weather that was spoiling their plans, against the new snow that would hinder their work of rescue. Soon they had everything ready.

'Go on, Maxime, you've just got time to catch that train,' advised the Chief Guide.

'Come on, boys. So long, goodbye!'

'Goodbye.'

'*Fera mé pi pas pi*,' called out Boule, with a smile, as he slung his sack on his shoulder. Boule was always cheery and his expression was that of a confirmed optimist.

The party marched down the road to the station, and passersby, intrigued by the three cylindrical rods on their shoulders, turned to look back at them. They walked on steadily, ignoring the barrage of questions. Young Michel came last; in spite of everything he could not help feeling a little proud at having been picked for such a tough team, and when a tourist came up to ask him where they were going, he couldn't help answering, and pointing with his axe to the snow-sprinkled Dru, the top of whose terrific pyramid showed behind the Montenvers.

'Up there, Monsieur, and take it from me it's not going to be an easy job.'

He might have had years of experience behind him.

They were given a compartment to themselves on the mountain railway, and were soon eagerly discussing routes, chimneys, cracks, and so on, as if they'd forgotten the object of their journey and were bound on a routine climb.

At La Fontaine-Caillet they passed the downward train; they were just able to see old Benoni in the last carriage. He was bringing down Clarisse's Georges – a sad and battered Georges, with a look of intense suffering on his drawn face. He gazed at them without saying a word, and his grief was so patent that it struck the rescue party to the heart. Maxime threw Benoni a look of inquiry.

'Yes, feet frostbitten,' the old man laconically replied. 'He's been in great pain for this past hour.'

And then both trains were off again, the one taking Georges – now temporarily suspended from the Corps of Guides – down to hospital; and the other, just crawling on to the big viaduct, taking the dead man's comrades up to their dangerous assignment.

They did not pause at the Montenvers; Jules had come down to the station to give them the latest news, and without wasting a minute they proceeded down the path to the glacier, overtaking the importunate tourists, and only slowing down a little past the cliffs of the Pont, where the crowd usually stops.

Once clear of these encumbrances, they resumed their normal gait, and Maxime Vouilloz went on ahead to set the pace.

In three hours they were up at the Charpoua hut.

Maxime Vouilloz, Michel Lourtier and Jean Blanc went off to make the trail and inspect the rocks. Boule unpacked the provisions, lit the stove, and prepared their evening soup. The others spread a blanket on the table and began a game of tarot, the wine bottle at their elbows; they marked the score on a greasy bit of paper torn from a notebook. They made themselves forget the drama that was being played out above, in which tomorrow they would be cast for leading parts. They put down their cards as carefully as if they'd been at Gros-Bibi's or Breton's at Chamonix.

Only when it began to get very cold did they close the hut door; no one gave so much as a glance at the magnificent sunset that gilded Mont Blanc and glittered on the light powder snow on the doorstep of the hut.

From time to time Boule, with the inevitable smile on his face, left his pots to watch for the return of the other three.

He came back shivering, but still with a smile on his lips:

'Lord, it's cold! Grr, there's a bite in it! You haven't seen the Dru; it looks like marble. We're going to have some fun tomorrow, believe me!'

And he resumed the stirring of the soup – a nice thick mess into which everything had been thrown: sausage, potatoes, macaroni, beef extract, soup cubes, cheese.

'With that on your stomachs, my hearties,' he declared, 'you won't feel empty for a long time.'

In a big bowl at the side he heated snow, a little at a time, and gravely supervised the melting process; then poured the water into the big crock hanging from a hook just behind the stove.

Voices outside announced the return of the reconnaissance party. They kicked their boots against the hut walls to rid them of snow, then came in one after the other with snow on their puttees and frost on their moustaches. Young Michel, his eyebrows all white, seemed at least ten years older.

'There'll be no going up tomorrow,' announced Maxime, 'there's at least fifty centimetres of snow under the Shoulder, and already it's melted and frozen again!'

'We'll see what tomorrow brings, it's all the same to me!' said Boule. 'Come on, you there, put away those cards.'

They ate hungrily, then taking off their boots and stuffing them with old newspaper to dry them, they laid themselves down side by side on the long shelf, with the rescue stretcher slung just above their heads. It, too, was waiting its turn to help.

Boule washed up the dishes with Michel's assistance; and when his friends were all well settled, he slowly went outside.

It was a starry night, and so cold that it was best to keep one's mouth shut. Boule walked round the hut, looking long at all the familiar peaks; hands in pockets, a half-smoked cigarette dangling from his lips, he stared for some moments at the Dru.

All alone at night on the mountains, Boule suddenly became very serious; he was no longer smiling. He shook his head gravely as he looked at the rocks and their armour of ice.

'We'll have to see,' he said aloud, 'we can't just leave him up there.'

He turned back into the hut, blew out the candle, and lay down beside his friends.

The wind moaned on the mountaintops, and made the hut walls shake and crack. Then silence fell on the night with its load of sorrow.

Chapter XV

Up the steep and stony track to Moussoux slowly climbed Jean-Baptiste Cupelaz, Paul Dechosalet and the Mayor of Chamonix.

They were on their way to break the news to Marie, Jean Servettaz's wife. The Mayor, who ran the affairs of the district as judiciously as he ran his big and prosperous hotel, had not even stopped to change. He had come just as he was, his tailcoat and thin pumps according ill with the rough track that mounted up between stone walls. It climbed steeply up the side of the Brévent, serving both as a path and as the bed of a torrent. They had left behind them the hamlet of Moussoux, comfortably perched on the gentle slopes of the dejection cone of the Roumna Blanche – the terrible gully down which the big avalanches dash like tidal waves, in the depth of winter and at the melting of the snows. The country folk turned round to look at the three of them. 'What are they doing here?' they wondered. 'What's made the Mayor come up at this time of day? And Uncle Paul, and the Chief Guide?'

'There must be trouble up at the Servettaz.' And the old women crossed themselves apprehensively.

Behind them, the great amphitheatre of peaks, pinnacles and radiant domes of snow, spires and white fingers, turrets and knife-edged spikes, was sharply outlined against a sky of dazzling blue. The glaciers, freshly white after the storm, crawled their creaking way towards the valley with cracks and groans, elbowing aside, in their age-long course, the woods where the burnished gold of the autumn larches stood out against the dark green swell of the spruces. Cars were hooting down in the valley, and a blue-and-white train, neat as a toy, jolted its two old wagons along the narrow-gauge line with a noise of grinding axles that mingled with the monotonous hum of the electric engine.

The three men climbed up through the last thickets before the 'Moëntieu' of Moussoux.

'It's the last house, Mayor,' the Chief Guide reminded him. 'You can see it now, that new-looking chalet against the spruce plantation. It wasn't always so big. That was Jean's doing; he took quite a few years over it; he did it all himself – or nearly all. It's a fine piece of work.'

'He was a worker, was Jean, and a real good 'un. I counted on him more than on anyone – such a frank, friendly chap … it's a big loss to the valley. And what a terrible blow for your poor sister!'

'Left with three children, too; it's cruelly hard. Thank God, Pierre's a sound young fellow,' answered Uncle Paul. Then panting, he added, 'What about a breather, Mayor? We're almost there. Better get our wind.'

The three of them sat down on the grass at the edge of the path and went on talking with barely a glance at the marvellous view that they had known from their earliest days, and with never a look at the Aiguille du Dru, sparkling under its new snow. Paul mopped his brow; he had found the steep climb too much for him. The Chief Guide could not help noticing details that a layman would have overlooked. Seated astride a hummock of grass, he inspected the chalet of Moëntieu.

'I'd have thought twice myself before building on that site,' he said. 'The Servettaz's chalet is right on the track of the Brévent avalanche. And yet it's never been touched – the old chalet stood there for 300 years. Our grandfathers knew the ways of mountains better than we do. Do you see, Paul, how they reckoned on that big boulder standing by itself over there, to split the avalanche into two streams? The right hand branch would come to a stop a little above the house; occasionally it reached the thick protecting wall they built in the old days: it's never been known to go further. On the other side, just a hundred metres away, there's the Nant-Favre torrent; they worked it out to a T! It must be peaceful up here. And they get all the sun; in winter, it reaches them more than two hours before Chamonix, and that's something worth having!'

Ten years ago, the Moëntieu of Moussoux had been no more

than a modest chalet nestling under its big stone-tiled roof, with a lower storey of stone, broken by a few small iron-barred windows, and above it a loft of great wooden beams. The walls were thick, and lined on the inside with larch planks; windows, ceiling and floors were likewise doubly faced. The space between the two walls was packed with sawdust, which provides excellent insulation against the cold. It was also the haunt of mice, who found it a convenient winter dwelling. On the south side was the *outa*, a sort of courtyard on to which all the rooms opened: the huge kitchen with its wide chimney (its opening controlled by a movable panel) up which you could see daylight; the long low communal bed-room, with its big squat beds and billowing quilts and knitted blankets. On the other side opened the stable from which, in winter, came warm smells of cattle, litter and dung; and, at dead of night, an occasional tinkle from the bell of some bored cow. Fifty yards away, beside the stream and the cattle trough hewn out of a fir-trunk, stood the barn, built in the style peculiar to the Alps. It was a small building, as wide as it was high, with a roof of shingles, constructed throughout of thick larch planks carefully squared and jointed together, black with age. The opening was right in the middle of the front – nothing more than a hole, rectangular at the bottom, and semicircular at the top, with a door thick as your fist and a massive iron lock that exactly fitted it. This little building stood on wooden logs cut square; to keep out rodents, a round boulder that no mouse could climb had been wedged between each log and the barn itself. The building thus appeared to be balanced on its stone foundations and wooden corner posts.

All the family valuables were kept there for safety: Sunday clothes, huge cowbells with their copper-studded collars of stamped leather, stores of corn, rye and oatmeal, crocks holding sausages and hams encased in fat. Here too were hung great quarters of dried and smoked beef. On the floor and in the chests were piled up the family's relics, all those trifling objects that are never discarded, for they represent the past, and are handed down from generation to generation with no other purpose than to keep memory green. The chalet itself might go up in flames, but most of the family's goods would be saved, their irreplaceable treasures preserved intact.

A stone's throw above the chalet stood a thick V-shaped wall, built of huge blocks of granite, ten feet high and nearly twenty feet thick: it was a protection against avalanches, and the final, dirty downflows of the great spring avalanches would slow down and come to a stop against it.

Today, instead of the old Moëntieu, stood a new chalet, more than one storey high, but otherwise incorporating most of the features of the Savoyard style of building.

It certainly was most pleasing to the eye. Its walls were faced with panels of dark wood, its window frames were of lighter wood, there were gay, well-kept window boxes; it had an air of prosperity. It was the great achievement of Jean Servettaz, who had all of a sudden taken to building.

He had first felt the urge shortly after the Great War. He'd been travelling around a lot that year, and found himself one day at Zermatt with his old friend Lochmatter, who was just opening up his new house. The famous guide had converted it into a small family pension for the convenience of his regular clients, who preferred the peace of a real mountain home to the sophistication of the big hotels. And Jean had said to himself, 'Why shouldn't I do the same? Luckily the wife's enterprising; she'd have to do a little more cooking, and it would always help us to get through the slack season when there's nothing coming in.'

By autumn Jean had made up his mind. He was well respected in the valley, and could easily have raised a loan. Uncle Paul had been only too willing to help. But the mountaineer's stubborn pride forbade him to ask help of anyone. 'I'll do it myself,' he declared. 'Haven't I got two arms, and plenty of guts, and six months of winter to turn to account?' Marie had been a bit alarmed to begin with. She did not relish the prospect of such an upheaval in her daily life, and the idea of having gentlemen in the house to look after bothered her a good deal.

'How do you expect me to cook for them? I've never had lessons.'

'You'll give them cheese *fondue,* and thick onion soup, and plum stuffing, and *potées,* and apple cobbler, and mushroom omelette. The girls will go out to the woods and gather all the different kinds of mushrooms for you, just you wait and see! I tell you that's the sort of thing the gentry like to eat, and not these sauces and made-up whatnots they get served up on silver platters. Don't worry, wife, you can do it. I know you can. Give them anything as good as the soups you give us and they'll be only too pleased.'

'This'll run us into debt.'

'Not at all. We'll take five years to do it, or ten, but we won't borrow a red cent. We've got wood at Praz des Violes, and the stone's there for the taking: we just have to fetch it from the screes of the Roumna; we'll get the sand from the Arve, and I'll make the furniture myself in the winter.'

'Well, if that's how you're going to go about it,' conceded Marie, and there was no further discussion. The matter was settled.

The following autumn Jean had gone up with Red Joseph to the Praz des Violes, a little flowery glade at the upper edge of the wood with a view over the whole valley. The earth was already hard, the grass creaked underfoot, and old footprints of nailed boots were stamped on the clay of the path. The guide owned some dozen fine larches up there, and a few spruce. The two of them had brought up some cold pancakes and a gourd of wine: all day they made their choice among the forest giants, marking the best and least knotted with chips of the axe. The following week Jean took up six hefty men, of the same stamp as himself, and cut down the trees, which fell with a crash of tangled branches, making windows in the forest through which filtered the pale autumn daylight. Great care was needed; the slope was steep and the ground hard, and the men's boots were caked with frozen snow and pine needles. But these mountaineers moved at ease in the steep wood, occasionally steadying themselves with a pick as if it were an ice-axe.

The snow came in November that year, and the woodcutters profited by it to send the stripped and resinous trunks shooting down the gullies. They kept themselves warm with great fires of bark and brushwood, and the straight columns of smoke above the treetops signalled their presence to all the valley.

The logs shot down the gullies and their crashing and snapping re-echoed in the dry cold air: they tore up great clods of earth and stones that bounded down the slope and came at last to rest in the snow. The woods resounded with the slow, rhythmical chants of the woodcutters at their work. Indefatigably, time and time again they toiled up beside the gully, now and again stopping to jack up a log with the pick, or to free a larch that had caught on a projecting rock, or to shove on a log that had slowed down and lost way, as if it did not relish the big drop that lay ahead, over which it would rush madly towards the valley.

At the foot of the mountain the gully fanned out, just above the little wooden bridge of the Paradis des Praz. The logs' final lap was down a frozen waterfall, about fifty metres high; after hurtling through the air in several bounds, they came to rest in a heap, the late arrivals overlapping the rest. From above, it looked like a pile of matches suddenly spilled from their boxes on to the snow. A few took a line of their own, started down wrong end first, left the gully, and from that point their headlong, unpredictable course was fearfully dangerous to the men. When this happened Servettaz blew his horn to give the alarm.

From top to bottom the gully was scored with red and ochre, littered with new bark and brushwood, as if the blood of all the trees felled up in the clearing were oozing down the hillside and trickling down through the snowy forest.

When the pile was big enough Jean harnessed the mule and hauled the logs along one by one; they were hitched straight on to the swingletree by a big iron quoin hammered into the head of the log. This primitive contraption made its way along narrow cart tracks to the sawmill at Gaudenays. It was a tricky route, and at the sharp bends the supple ends of the spruces swished in the snow, while the mule trotted forward in a shower of snowy crystals. Jules Balmaz at the sawmill undertook to turn these into fine beams, floorboards, and wood for making furniture.

Then all Jean had to do in order to collect the resin and pitch in the springtime was to get out his big haycart and bring the stuff back to his barn, where it was carefully put to dry in the open air.

But this was only a beginning. He opened a quarry in the big Roumna stoneshoot where he could pick out to his liking fine square stones which piled up in his orchard to await the arrival of the masons and cutters.

He needed good, straight-granite blocks for corners, windows, and the slabs of the courtyard; and he set to work to get it from a great erratic block stranded by quaternary glaciers on the hill-side. All this stuff accumulated at the old Moëntieu waiting its turn to be used.

Then came summer: and never before had Jean been known to drive himself so hard, to do so many climbs, to choose the hardest – and highest-paid – expeditions, with never a thought of danger or exhaustion. In that and the following seasons he would stay up at the huts for as long as six weeks without once coming down, averaging three hours' sleep a night, absolutely tireless! Only his cheeks, drawn taut under their sunburn, betrayed something of the strain. He made up for it in the autumn, when he shut himself up from morning to night in the barn, where he had installed a carpenter's bench. There he planed, jointed and assembled his furniture; he made tables, chairs, bedsteads, and even a handsome wardrobe with three carved panels. He was happy as a king, and sang all day long.

Now began the real heavy work. The massive roof of the old chalet with its 300-year-old framework had to be removed all in one piece; it was so well put together with big wooden pins that it made an indestructible unit. Several men came up from the valley to lend a hand. Jacks were placed at the four corners of the building and under the instruction of Canova, the measurer down at Michaud's works who came up here in his spare time, the roof was gradually raised. It came up a few inches every day, and at the same time the masons were working on the walls. The job was begun in spring and finished in autumn. Jean had now got his four walls in place. He next had to plan the layout of the five bedrooms he had in mind, and the big living room that would replace the old sleeping quarters. He had also to build the inside staircase, and put the window frames, doors and cupboards in place. Finally, he had to furnish them with the simple, practical chairs and beds that he had made after a good local design that fitted in well with the look of the whole building.

After working at full steam for six years, Jean had built his house.

Early in the summer with which this narrative is concerned, the Moëntieu of Moussoux was ready to receive visitors. Its conspicuous woodwork, charming carved gallery and massive cornerstones of Mont Blanc granite gave it great dignity. The five bedrooms were not empty for long. First to arrive was a Paris manufacturer, whose idea of rest was to spend whole days roaming the lower slopes of the mountains and to bring back handsome contributions to the commissary in the shape of mushrooms, strawberries, blackberries and raspberries. He often took with him Suzanne, the younger of Servettaz's two daughters – occasionally also the elder, Alice, who was nearly fifteen years old. He taught them how to distinguish the different kinds of edible fungi, and to read the face of nature like an open book. Some years before he had given up doing big climbs, but the pleasure he still found in the pastures and woods was more than enough to justify three months' holiday at a stretch.

A young climbing couple occupied another room. They were always off on expeditions, sometimes away for as much as five or six days, and then back for a week in the valley before setting off again for fresh conquests. They were ideal clients for Servettaz, who in days gone by had guided the young woman's father. He considered Alain and Christiane Bardes almost as his own children, and primed them with good advice every time they set out.

Two other rooms were occupied by a couple of Englishwomen. They had come with a recommendation from a famous British climber who knew Servettaz intimately: they were quiet, divided their time between reading and walks up the mountainside, except when bad weather kept them indoors with their knitting. The last room had been taken by Hubert de Vallon of the Groupe de Haute Montagne, who had learned his climbing from Servettaz before launching out on his own and becoming one of the best guideless climbers in Europe. He kept the warmest feelings for his old mentor, and Servettaz could never find it in his heart to reproach him for preferring to be first on the rope, rather than spend his life following a guide, no matter how brilliant. On this point Servettaz rightly estimated the current tendency. 'Our job,' he used to say, 'is to train youngsters for the mountains, and the greatest satisfaction I can get is to see one of my old pupils taking his turn at the head of the rope. Then I know that my teaching has borne fruit.'

Marie had risen early that morning to make breakfast, get the household going, and look after the thousand and one little jobs that demand the good housewife's attention. As she opened her window she glanced at the peaks across the valley and murmured, 'What a lot of new snow on the Aiguilles!' And immediately she thought of her son, who had now been away for several days; and also, a little, of her husband – but without worrying about him. A guide like him was never rash. The morning sped quickly by; there was the stove to make up, vegetables to be picked in the garden, bedrooms to do, and, in the new stables adjoining the chalet, the cattle had to be seen to. There were five cows and a mule, not to speak of a very fine flock of poultry.

Marie was an active woman, glowing with health. She was finely built, with features that did not lack delicacy, and she would have been almost beautiful if continuous hard work had not made her old before her time. Certainly, her black hair was drawn tightly back from a severe part into a knot at her neck; but how can you expect a woman who is on her feet from morning till night to have a minute for titivating herself?

Suzanne had gone off to gather bilberries; Alice, who was made after the same pattern as her mother, was helping her in the house. The two bustled about, forever busy, and grudging no effort. Christiane Bardes came out to join them, and gaily offered to lend a hand:

'Let me help, Madame Servettaz; it's an off day for us, and Alain's having a lie in. Have you seen the mountains this morning? They look marvellous with all that new snow right down to the tree line:

absolutely marvellous!'

'Christiane, my dear, you and I will never see eye to eye on that subject. When it's all white like that I can't help thinking of all those who may still be up there, and I say to myself, Pray God nothing happens to them. Certainly I don't worry about Jean; he always knows when to turn back, you'd almost think he felt the bad weather before it came. But I can't help being a bit anxious about Pierre ... '

'But isn't Pierre with Red Joseph? And he has even more experience than your husband – '

'Of course it's silly of me, but I can't help it. My husband's done everything he can to put the boy off climbing, and I keep on telling myself, "Pierre mustn't be a guide, we must stop him climbing" – as if it could be any use! Climbing's the one thing he thinks of whenever he comes home, and I truly believe that being sent away from Chamonix just made him all the keener. Where is he now? He *was* going to do Mont Blanc, and go down on the Italian side – it takes several days, and I couldn't say exactly where he might be now. So you mustn't be surprised if I'm a bit anxious.'

'There's really no need, Madame Servettaz. For one thing, Pierre isn't going to be a guide – he's promised you that, and he's going to run this place for you later on. And for another, he's an absolutely first-rate climber. No matter what you say, you won't stop him climbing; he was made that way, and if he doesn't do it for a living you won't stop him doing it for fun. Come on, and put your mind to beating up this cream; the sight of it's making my mouth water!' Christiane put in the tip of her finger and licked it with relish. 'Tell me,' she went on impulsively, 'when you've turned this place into a proper hotel, what are you going to do with your present guests? That's what worries me: it's so heavenly here just as it is. I can't see myself wandering as I please into a huge kitchen with a regiment of pots and pans and imposing *chefs,* or putting my nose into the office where you will preside like queens ... If *I* were Monsieur Servettaz, I'd keep the house just as it is now.'

'There's nothing I'd like better,' sighed Marie. 'I can't abide all these plans for still more new buildings, and if it weren't for

Pierre ... ' Her son's name sent Marie off into another state of contemplation.

'What on earth's the matter with you this morning? I've never seen you fret like this before – and you a guide's wife!'

'Of course I learned to control myself, but don't think it's always easy. You think you're hardened to it, you see your man go off every day on climbs you've never heard of – there are so many of them in the district. But gradually you begin to know them, and always through some disaster: an accident here, an accident there, that's all you remember about them. Whenever you speak about them to your husband he has some excuse to justify the danger ... "What, *him?*" he'll say. "Oh, he was always a careless fellow. That business? Oh, it was pure bad luck" ... And so the years go on. At first, you used to kiss him when he set out – now, you hardly like to say *au revoir.* You just put up his bait, and your man says "So long," as if he were just going down to Chamonix – and it seems quite natural for him to be gone. And you never hear of the narrow escapes except through other people. Jean's never talked much about his climbs, and it's from the wives of his friends that I get to hear how he was nearly caught in an avalanche, or got hit by a stone in a gully, or how his client came right off – but as it's always past and gone, it slips out of your mind, you get used to it, you stop fretting – except when horrible little thoughts make their way into your head, like today ... '

And Marie heaved a deep sigh, and looked embarrassed at having said so much.

'But there, that's enough,' she went on, 'I've got a lot to do, Christiane, there's all the washing to hang out yet. If you really want to help, take a fork and beat up the eggs – I want the whites beaten separately. Alice, take the washing basket and come into the garden with me. Now, young lady, remember you're the hostess, and if you don't produce a delicious pudding for us, I'll tell Alain that it's all your fault.'

'Don't worry, Marie, I'll follow your instructions.'

Alice and her mother went out with the big basket of washing. Their drying green was under the stunted plum trees – the only fruit that would grow at this height. They began to spread the washing out carefully, and did not at first see the three men who climbed slowly and hesitantly up the winding path between the hawthorns, brambles and wild raspberries. Jean-Baptiste headed the procession: the nearer he came, the more apparent was his hesitation, the more pronounced his limp. Then the Mayor, self-contained and silent, followed by Paul Dechosalet, still wheezing and grunting. Alice saw them when they reached the little ash grove that separates Moëntieu from the village of Moussoux.

'Mother, there's some men coming up to the house. It looks like the Chief Guide – I know him by his walk. The second's a very smart gentleman, and behind him – hello, it's Uncle Paul. What on earth are they coming up for?'

Marie raised her head quickly and, without knowing why, let fall the pile of washing she held in her arms. Her legs gave way under her, and she felt her heart would burst.

'The Chief Guide coming to *our* house?' she whispered. 'And Uncle Paul? Lord have mercy upon us! Something terrible must have happened.'

'But, Mother,' said Alice, 'the Chief Guide's often come up before to tell us that Dad's off on another climb and isn't coming back yet.'

Marie wasn't listening to the girl, she was looking terror-struck at the three men, for something told her that they were the bearers of bad news. They came up slowly and unwillingly, driven on by an irresistible force, walking like automatons under the burden of their terrible secret. They moved at the bidding of some higher power, as if the mountain wind, fresh from the snowy peaks, had driven them up from the valley towards the chalet, saying: 'Go and tell them what you know. I bring you the dying man's last breath; you must go up; they're waiting for the news up there.' And Jean-Baptiste walked more slowly, more miserably, the closer he came; and Paul looked more than ever like collapsing. Only the Mayor, alive to the painful task before them, controlled his features lest he should break down at the last minute.

Marie waited for them in a daze, at the edge of the orchard, the girl close by her side. The washing lay scattered on the grass. Not one of the actors in the drama had eyes for that wonderful view of airy peaks, not one had ears for the rumbling of the Arve in the valley below. Marie shuddered; if Jean-Baptiste had come up by himself, she would never have given it a thought, for it was his business as Chief Guide to inform her of her husband's movements. But seeing him come up in the company of the Mayor, and of Uncle Paul too, whose feelings showed only too plainly in his face – that showed it must be something really serious.

Rooted to the spot, and ready for whatever might come, Marie awaited the expected blow. Her forebodings had not deceived her; there had been an accident to Pierre. But still the others said never a word. Then suddenly she flung herself on her brother in a frenzy; he looked at her with compassion, and tried to find the right words to break the fatal news.

'I knew it,' she cried, 'it's Pierre, isn't it – answer me, can't you! He's hurt himself, hasn't he – it's all my fault, I should have kept him at home, I should have stopped him going ... Pierre, my little Pierre ... Tell me, Jean-Baptiste,' she entreated, 'what's happened to him, for mercy's sake. You don't say a word, he must be badly hurt. Monsieur le Maire, for the love of God ... '

'You must be very brave, Madame Servettaz,' the Mayor's words came slowly.

'Oh, you don't mean to say he's – ' interrupted Marie, and without finishing the sentence collapsed on to the grass. There she stayed, shaking her head from side to side, and gazing at the three men bowed over her. They found it hard to proceed.

'Jean's had a terrible accident,' went on the Mayor; then, realising that nothing could be worse than this awful suspense, and that he might just as well tell the whole truth, he added hoarsely, 'he was struck by lightning on the top of the Dru.'

'Struck by lightning – by lightning,' echoed Marie. She pushed back a wisp of hair that had fallen over her forehead, and stared at them, wide-eyed and open-mouthed, not taking the news in, and indeed not wanting to take it in. Alice collapsed in sobs at her mother's side, and hugged her in her skinny arms. The men stood by in silence, respecting their sorrow, and waiting to be asked how it happened. At last Marie managed to whisper:

'Was it – *Jean*, did you say Jean? My Jean? Struck by lightning on the Dru? It can't be true. No' – her voice rose in a shriek – 'it can't be true. Nothing could happen to *him*, do you hear, he told me again and again, nothing could happen to him. Are you sure?'

'I'm afraid it *is* true, Marie,' answered Paul.

'Ah,' she shuddered. Then, moving like a sleepwalker, she got up and said, 'Let's go into the house.'

She stooped in passing to pick up the washing scattered over the grass and put it in the basket. She was about to carry it in, but Jean-Baptiste got hold of it first and – 'Take the other handle, Paul,' he said.

She did not open her lips again till they were all settled in the kitchen. Christiane had been startled to see them come in with Marie as pale as if she were on her way to the condemned cell. She summoned up enough strength of mind to refrain from asking questions, and to push forward a chair. Jean-Baptiste took her aside.

'Jean's been struck by lightning on the Dru, Madame Bardes.'

Very gently, Christiane made Marie sit down and stayed beside her without saying a word: she was calm and resolute, and ready to give all her loving sympathy once the men had gone. In the meantime, they let the full import of their news sink in. Marie's grief was dumb, and not one tear trickled from her poor staring eyes.

Her brother Paul looked sadly at her, his hand on the shoulder of his niece, who stood shaken by sobs. He forced himself to speak some words of comfort.

'Don't cry, little girl … try to be calm … Alice, dear, you must try to be brave … look at your mother and what she's going through.'

At long last Marie seemed to wake up from a hideous dream. She tried to speak, but the words stuck in her throat and she felt like suffocating. Finally, she got them out in a monotonous chant:

'I knew that something terrible had happened, this morning,

when I saw the new snow on the tops. It was Pierre I thought of at once; I don't know why, but I've never been anxious about his father, never; he was always so sure of himself, so sure … So when I saw you coming I was terribly afraid … You won't understand … it was because I was afraid that something had happened to the boy … and what you've just told me is so appalling, I never thought it could happen. Oh, my head! – but – but' – here her voice rose to a cry – 'if Jean's been killed, it's because it really *is* dangerous; and he knew it, and never wanted his son to be a guide. I'd hardened myself to the dangers *he* risked every day … I'd stopped believing in them … Oh, Jean, Jean – after all he'd been through – the war – and all those climbs – and all his work bringing down these logs when the gullies were frozen – and then to be killed like that – and on the Dru! He used to tell me, "The Dru, that's the climb for me … I like that sort of thing – it's difficult all the way, but the rock's good and solid, and it's a real mountain, with a glacier on it, and it's got height – it's a thousand times better than any of those short rock climbs, however difficult they may be, that are all the rage just now. Whenever I can I take my clients up the Dru."' She stopped, afraid that she might have said too much; then resumed listlessly: 'But what's going to happen now? The three children … and this place to look after – Paul, it's too dreadful.'

'You've got Pierre, Marie, he's a man now; he'll take his place as head of the family,' comforted Paul. 'You can thank God you brought him up as you did, you and Jean. He'll know who to turn to and help you.'

'Where is he? And how can we tell him?' wailed Marie.

'I telephoned Courmayeur,' went on Paul. 'They'd already started up for the Col du Géant. So there's no need to worry, the storm can't have touched them. They're almost sure to hear the news on their way; in any case, I'll try to meet them.'

'And, Jean – my man,' groaned Marie.

'The search party's already gone up. In spite of the new snow and frost, they all volunteered to go and bring him down,' said Jean-Baptiste.

'Oh, that's very good of them all. But you must tell them to take care – tell them I beseech them to be careful ... There's been enough trouble. But surely Jean would never have allowed anyone to go off with all this new snow about; can't they wait for better weather – for it's all over, anyway, it's all over,' and her sentence ended in a sob.

Just then Alain Bardes came down the staircase. One look at the group of red-eyed men round the stricken Marie, at Alice's prostration, at his own wife, was enough to make everything clear to him.

It was a tremendous blow to him, for he had loved the guide as a father. He drew his wife aside, spoke for a moment with her, and rapidly decided what was to be done.

'Christiane, you go and look after the other visitors, I'll see what use I can be here. Someone'll have to tell Suzanne – where is she?'

'She's out for the day with Monsieur Dupuis: they went off to the woods. It's all right, I'll see to everything.' And taking Marie's arm, Christiane gently propelled her to her bedroom. 'Come on, Marie, don't bother about the house; you leave it to me. Alice, will you stay beside your mother?'

'I can stay too,' said Uncle Paul.

'No, I think you'd better go down with the others; my husband can see to all the formalities with you; I'll deal with everything up here.'

The Mayor, the Chief Guide and Paul took their leave: there was nothing more they could do up here. The homestead that had but lately been so gay and welcoming was now given over to grief and sorrow.

Jean-Baptiste gave a long look at the chalet in all its newness.

'Poor Jean, he didn't have long to enjoy his handiwork.'

With long strides the three men descended the stony path towards the valley. The Dru was more dazzling than ever under its mantle of ermine.

'God's mercy,' muttered the Chief Guide. 'Beside mountains like that, what poor little creatures we are!' But he did not shake his fist at them; it might have been a sacrilege.

A little further down they met a young neighbour, Aline Lourtier, climbing quickly up the path. She wore a kerchief around her head, her eyes were red, and marks of fresh grief were still about her.

'Going up yonder, Aline?' asked Paul.

'Yes, I thought they'd need me. I heard the news from my brother. Poor Jean Servettaz – and Pierre – does he know yet?'

'He'll know soon enough. Go on up, my dear; you'll find Madame Bardes in charge, but you know more about the house than she does. You hurry up to them.'

And he added, when she was out of sight:

'There's a sort of understanding between her and my nephew. She's a good girl, plucky and straightforward. A proper mountain girl.'

They came down by the Mollard path, and landed in the square, which was noisier than ever. Jean-Baptiste went back to the Guides' Office, where some clients were awaiting him. He took a note of their needs, fixed up guides for them, made out a list of 'pirates' for the Montenvers and for the Bossons glacier.

In the afternoon the guides he had named set off, pack on back, for the mountains. People questioned them as they passed.

'Weather going to be fine up there?'

'Yes, it'll be very fine, very fine indeed. We're in for a splendid autumn.'

Chapter XVI

Towards daybreak, everything was uncannily quiet. Nothing fell in the couloir, where the new snow held the stones fast. Even the séracs broke away with a sound that was no louder than a sigh, and the fall of the débris was muffled by the thick layer of snow on the glacier. In the silent hut, the guides were still asleep.

Awakened by the trilling of his alarm watch, Boule got up well before the others. He lit a candle, then moved gently about the hut, lighting the stove, breaking the firewood, laying out the provisions. Soon Michel Lourtier hopped off the shelf to help him, tousled and sleepy-eyed, but inquisitive as ever.

'Will we be able to go up, Boule?'

'We've got to. I haven't put my nose out yet. Here, go and fetch me a bowl of snow for the tea.'

Michel had a struggle with the door, which was stuck fast by frost: it opened suddenly on a sky of stars, and let in a great blast of cold air. The sleepers on the mattresses groaned, turned over, and curled up again under their blankets. Raising himself up on his elbow Paul Mouny yelled at the boy: 'Shut that door, for God's sake, you're freezing the whole hut.'

Once outside, Michel hacked out blocks of hard snow with his ice-axe, brought them in and put them in the pan. Boule set it on the stove. The snow was long in melting: the porter kept on stirring, to hurry it up; soon it turned into a sort of transparent, icy paste, then into water. He poked up the fire to bring it to a boil.

Boule smiled as he worked, while the others, enjoying their last minutes of rest, snuggled down under their blankets. It was perfectly natural to them that Boule should get up first. There seemed to be an unspoken agreement between them: the others would never have dreamed of depriving him of this unwelcome job.

He did it without ostentation, and without humiliation. For Boule, life consisted in making yourself useful, in doing your best, without pushing yourself forward. Often, when a guide had taken him on as porter, he had found himself at the head of the rope when the difficulties began, simply because he assumed that that was his place, that he was stronger than his companion and was certainly not going to let the other man run unnecessary risks. He could have been a guide, but had no wish to. He preferred to follow, and knew how to obey much better than how to command. He would always be a porter.

Awakened by the bustle in the hut, the guides one by one got off the shelf, stretched, yawned, slowly put on their big nailed boots, carefully fastened up their short gaiters, pulled heavy sweaters over their flannel shirts. One after the other they got up to look at the weather.

'Fine day,' said Maxime Vouilloz, 'pity there's so much snow.'

'It's going to be cold, we'll have to put socks on over our boots if we don't want our feet to get frostbitten,' said Jean Blanc, who'd lost a toe on the Dôme in 1922 and was still sensitive on this point.

'You're right, we'll have to put on all we've got. The sun won't be on the mountain before nine o'clock, and there'll be some powder snow to get through.'

Carefully they pulled their big glacier socks over their boots.

'I'm against going,' suddenly burst out Jacques Batioret. 'It's crazy. Do you realise how much snow and ice there is on the rocks? It'll be hard enough work to reach the Shoulder, and after that … '

'I'm with you,' answered Maxime, 'but at least we should make a trail to the foot of the rocks and see how things shape up: we can decide what to do then.'

'Tea's ready,' called Boule. 'Pass me the water bottles.' They filled their aluminium bottles with the tea, very sweet and piping hot, and each man rolled his bottle carefully in a blanket to keep in the heat. Then, as they ate, they divided up the loads.

'Better have three ropes,' said Maxime Vouilloz. 'We'll take turns breaking trail as far as the rocks; after that, I'll go on ahead. Who's coming on my rope? I need two good men, as we'll be first;

then Jacques Batioret will lead the second rope, and we need another hefty lad to take the last one.'

'You take Fernand,' suggested Batioret, 'he knows the Dru well.'

'All right, I'll go with Maxime, and Boule, you come along with us: there's no one like you for giving a leg up!'

'Good, I'll go wherever you like,' answered Boule.

'And you, Jacques? Who's on your rope?'

'Give me Armand Rosset and Jean Blanc; and then Paul Mouny, who's the oldest of the young 'uns, can take the last rope; we'll give him Michel, *he* won't be much of a weight to haul up.'

'Listen,' burst in Michel with great indignation, 'do you think I need any hauling? Just you wait!'

Having settled the matter, the eight men tied on to their ropes at fifteen-metre intervals, each taking a few coils of spare rope around his chest. Then, putting on their gloves and woollen helmets, they passed out in single file, each man holding a neat coil of rope in his left hand and his ice-axe in his right.

By lantern light, they climbed up the steep spur of the Charpoua, wading through snow up to the knee; but breaking trail was easy work, for the snow was light and powdery. All the same, the cold was fierce. As they proceeded, the great walls of the cirque stood out more sharply in the half-light; already the sunrise was striking the ghostly dome of the Verte. A long white line, the Mummery couloir, linked the summit to the upper basin of the glacier, dividing the mass of shadow into two.

They were soon on top of the spur, and from there traversed horizontally to the foot of the great wall of the Dru, just as the top flushed a pale pink. The cold seemed to have accumulated down in this hollow, and the guides only breathed in through the woollen helmets which covered everything but their eyes. An icy blast penetrated the wool, and condensed into rime. Their eyelashes stuck together, and the cold stung horribly on that little piece of the face that they had dared to leave unprotected.

'It's worse than winter,' growled Maxime, 'we'll never get any higher.'

'We said we'd go as far as the rocks,' Boule reminded him.

Every ten minutes another rope took the lead and made a long furrow in the snow. There was every need for caution, for the crevasses were masked by snow bridges, thick enough, but fragile. Once, Jacques Batioret's foot disappeared through the snow, and he saved himself by his elbows, above an unfathomable blue-green abyss. Jacques swore, and Boule laughed; he found it amusing, and couldn't help making his crack: 'Deserting us, Jacques?' But at the same time, to temper this sally, he jumped over the hole and helped his friend out of his painful situation.

The approach to the rocks was extremely difficult. Snow had fallen the night before, the rocks glittered like glass, and there was a big granite slab to be climbed, covered with verglas. Maxime set to work with great energy, swinging his ice-axe and hacking out great chunks, and his companions followed in silence.

At the first halt on the rocks, they paused for a rest and a word.

'It would be madness to go on,' murmured Paul Mouny, and everyone thought he was right; but Michel begged, 'Let's at least go up to the Shoulder; if we take it in turns, it'll go easily enough.'

'Shut up,' Maxime Vouilloz interrupted him sharply, 'you can give your advice when you're asked for it. I'm in charge of the party, got that? Well, I say we should turn back, and it isn't certain that we'll even be able to go on tomorrow.'

'And if the bad weather starts up again the day after tomorrow,' put in Boule, 'then you can say the Dru's finished for the season. All the same, Maxime's right: it would be crazy to go on.'

'Let's wait and see what the sun does to the rocks today: sometimes a south wind clears everything up.'

'If we're going to turn back, there's no use hanging around here any longer: we're getting frozen for nothing. Get a move on! Down to the hut! We'll leave a fixed rope here to get us down the slab: it'll come in handy tomorrow.'

Paul Mouny chipped the ice off a corner of rock and carefully fixed a twenty-metre rope round it. They slid down it to the glacier and rejoined their upward track.

An hour later, they were back in the hut. They shook out their snowy gaiters, ate some food, and stoked up the fire in the stove.

At last the sun reached the hut and everything became pleasant. The day was evidently going to be unusually warm, such a day as you often get in September after a spell of bad weather.

'Just as well,' grunted Maxime Vouilloz, 'it'll melt things quickly today.'

The guides set about killing time until evening. Some of them took out blankets, and stretched themselves on the granite slabs, face downwards, like marmots on the watch. Paul Mouny carefully uncoiled the wet ropes and hung them down the little rock wall, to make them dry more quickly. Then they lit their pipes, and as they smoked they looked out at the unbelievable circle of mountains, the Géant, the glaciers, the peaks, all this prehistoric landcape strayed right into the middle of contemporary Europe.

Inside the hut, Boule was busy at the stove, getting the soup ready for dinner, carefully peeling the potatoes, pipe in mouth, elbows on knees.

Young Michel darted from one group to another, scrambled about the rocks, practised roping down, never still for a minute. He had all his wits about him, and not a thing escaped his notice – neither the fleeting shadow of a cloud on a crevasse nor the swoop of a jackdaw on the moraine; and he heard the distant music of the torrent, borne up by the wind, and carried off on the breeze.

He was the first to see, far away below, three figures climbing slowly up the Charpoua moraine. They were outlined against the glacier, and their gait proclaimed them to be guides. One came up more quickly than the other two, gaining ground every minute: when they halted for a moment, he kept steadily on his way.

The guides watched his progress with the keenest interest.

'Who's that ahead?' asked Fernand Lourtier. 'He's increasing his distance – at this rate, he'll be at the foot of the rocks in twenty minutes.'

He yodelled high and clear to attract the attention of the unknown climber, who however made no sign of response. But once the last echo had died away, there came up an answering yodel from one of the other two behind. The guide immediately recognised the shout –

'That's Camille coming up.'

'That's him all right; but who's with him?'

The next hour was spent in speculation. Boule appeared from time to time to inquire with a smile if they'd be up soon. 'We can't start without them; I've got something ready for them too.'

'They must be coming to give us a hand,' said Fernand soberly.

The leading climber was lost to view under the slabs in which the hut stood. A quarter of an hour later he appeared on the level ground in front of the hut, and the guides recognised Pierre Servettaz. He was out of breath after his fast climb and came towards them without saying a word. They all rose to their feet at the sight of him.

'God bless you, Pierre,' said Maxime with deep feeling.

One by one, on the narrow platform by the hut, the hardy fellows gripped their young companion by the hand. His appearance had brought them back to reality with a bump, and at sight of the son, thoughts of the father up above came sharply back into their minds.

'Give us your sack,' said Paul Mouny.

Pierre sat down on a boulder; he was tired, and sad, and couldn't say anything; slowly he sipped the hot tea that Boule brought him out in a mug.

'Where were you when you heard?' asked Maxime.

'Up at the Col, we'd come up from Courmayeur … It's terrible …'

'It was a cruel stroke … Is that Camille with you?'

'Camille Lourtier and Red Joseph.'

'Has Red Joseph come up all this way?'

'Oh yes, he was absolutely bent on helping us.'

Pierre noticed the new tracks on the upper glacier.

'Have you been up already?'

'Up and down,' uneasily answered Maxime. 'Too much snow on the rocks, we'll have to wait a bit. We'd hardly have got as far as the Shoulder today.'

Pierre made them show him the exact place where his father lay. From here it was possible to pick out – high up on the rocky face, apparently almost at the top – the little snowy ledge on which the tragedy had taken place. It was even possible to distinguish the ice hanging down in stalactites: the state of the mountain was anything but encouraging.

'It's not going to be easy,' was Pierre's comment: he could guess what the others were thinking. 'But all the same, we'll go up.'

Maxime didn't answer ... he didn't want to hurt the young man, but in his heart of hearts he believed they'd taken on an impossible job.

Their conversation was interrupted by the arrival of Camille Lourtier, whose axe clanged on the rocks. With a curt 'Good day, all,' he took his sack off his shoulders, immediately subjected the mountain to a most knowledgable scrutiny, and muttered as he shook his head:

'We're not up there yet ... I'd never have believed there could be so much snow.'

Half an hour later Red Joseph appeared. He was plodding up slowly, and looked tired, but did his best to conceal it.

'We're all getting older,' he remarked philosophically, to anticipate any questions. And his drawn face, tired mouth and the sadness in his eyes spoke only too plainly of the grief that weighed him down even more than his fatigue.

'Come in where it's warm, Joseph, the soup is ready,' advised Paul Mouny.

When he'd gone to the hut, Paul took Fernand aside.

'We mustn't let Red Joseph go up tomorrow. It's just too much at his age; he'd stay up there.'

'Well, you make him see that if you can.'

'We should be careful not to rub him the wrong way – especially since he can't get used to the idea he's reached the age limit.'

'Best wait till tomorrow.'

Slowly the afternoon wore on, with hardly a sound from the guides. As time had to be killed somehow, several of them started a game of tarot. Red Joseph, Maxime, Jacques Batioret and Pierre, who were more exhausted than the others, stretched themselves on the shelf and were soon asleep.

Night came on suddenly after a magnificent sunset, which set fire in turn to Mont Blanc, the Géant, the Jorasses and the Aiguilles. To the rumble of avalanches succeeded the calm of evening. Long after the sun had gone, the mountains still reflected a rosy light from beyond the horizon. Then the shadows fell, first on the Aiguilles, then on the great satellites, the Géant, Verte, Jorasses and Mont Maudit. Along the whole length of the range only two points still held the light: the summit-dome of Mont Blanc and a patch on the Dôme du Goûter; but still the shadows crept up, bent on vanquishing the last source of light. Usually the assault went slowly, and the light lingered long on the summit. But this evening it happened with a brutal suddenness; without awaiting the sun's last kiss, the dome of Mont Blanc vanished into darkness. And now the cold, no longer arrested by the daylight, took harsh possession of hollows, ridges and glacier, penetrating everything with icy breath. The mountains shivered in a sudden wind. Then all was finished.

The guides had carefully noted every detail of the sunset.

'Not so good; the sun went too quickly. Let's hope we'll just manage to get up.'

'It's going to be fine tomorrow,' declared Fernand Lourtier. 'Father always used to say: "When the sun disappears all of a sudden, then there'll be rain in forty-eight hours" … forty-eight hours. So you see we absolutely must go up tomorrow.'

'The old 'uns will never want to start with conditions like this.'

'Well, can't we go?' threw in Michel.

'But the old 'uns will be right,' reasoned Paul Mouny. 'However, we've said all we have to say, so let's turn in and have a bite and then go to sleep … it's getting cold out here.'

Supper, by the light of a single candle, was a sad and silent affair. Pierre asked no questions; he was completely master of himself, and he ate with deliberate resolution, obviously determined to be on top of his form for the effort that tomorrow would call for, when they tried to bring down his father's body from the mountain.

Michel Lourtier, who didn't much care for silence, had ventured to ask:

'Shall we be on the same ropes tomorrow?'

'Tomorrow's another day, and you'll have all the time you want then to settle it,' Maxime snubbed him, but there was a note of anxiety in his voice. The brief sunset, the state of the rocks, the tiredness of Red Joseph, did not seem to forecast any good.

The lad took the reproof as a matter of course, and when the meal was over he was the first to climb into his bunk.

By eight o'clock they were all lying down, and their rhythmical breathing filled the hut. Now and then a sleeper turned over and the creaking of the shelf sounded absurdly loud in the dark. Towards midnight the hut was shaken by a terrific gust of wind that made every board creak and groan, while strange whistlings and wailings drowned the breathing of the sleeping guides.

Paul Mouny turned over and listened to the noises outside; then, noticing that Fernand also was awake, he whispered:

'The wind's rising, d'you hear it?'

'I think it'll hold up all day – but after that we're done for, the bad weather'll start again. And this time it'll last.'

'We simply must go up.'

'We simply must.'

Not another word, after that, till the order to get up.

Boule had the tea all ready, and they ate and drank in silence. Sacks were fastened and each man, muffled up against the cold, waited for orders. As the senior member of the party, Red Joseph took the decision:

'I'm coming with you. Camille, you'll go first, then me, then Pierre.'

Then, as the others looked like starting off immediately, he added:

'There's no use starting so early. You've made the trail, and there's no point in getting your fingers frozen on the rocks.'

A little later they set out, following yesterday's tracks, and as far as the rocks they climbed up slowly, steadily and in silence. They moved with bowed heads, overwhelmed by the vastness of the cirque and the inhuman scale of the walls of the Dru, and oppressed by thoughts of the death that lurked up there in waiting for them. Maxime, who was leading, looked back from time to time, and realised that Red Joseph's rope was making heavy weather.

'It's no good – Joseph shouldn't have come. It's not right for a man of his age. And he hasn't had any real sleep for a week. Well, it's his own funeral, I suppose; we'll wait for him at the fixed rope.'

The rope in question was frozen hard and all but soldered to the rock. Maxime shook it violently and freed it; then, grasping it firmly, he quickly climbed up the pitch. Down by the bergschrund, the others waited with upturned faces for him to reach the stance. Then, one by one, up they went in turn. The tracks stopped here.

Now Jacques Batioret took over the lead from Maxime. He climbed steadily and with decision up the snow-filled chimneys, sometimes sinking in up to his waist. In the shadow, the snow was powdery and blew about in icy dust, but where the sun had struck it, a light crust had been formed, not thick enough to bear the weight of a man, but too hard to be broken merely by a step. It was exhausting work climbing up under these conditions, and Jacques Batioret gave up his place to Paul Mouny.

In spite of it all the guides gained height quickly, with never a false move, helping each other and taking turns in going first. A steep couloir brought them up to the barrier of ice-covered rocks, and as they were wondering how best to tackle it, they spotted the length of line left behind by Georges. It was thick with rime, and trailed in the wind.

'That's a piece of luck,' exclaimed Boule, 'it'll save us quite a bit of time.'

All the same, it was a tricky section. Camille Lourtier went up with an assurance that astonished his companions, clearing the holds with his axe as he went. Down rattled the fragments of ice, tinkling like broken glass on the granite slabs. Once or twice Camille stopped in mid-career and clapped his hands to warm them; then took off each of his gloves and blew on his blue fingers before proceeding with the climb. Red Joseph followed him at an interval of fifteen metres, climbing with caution and perfect confidence, and displaying all the resources of a technique which it had taken a quarter of a century to perfect. He was obviously tired: that was evident from his excess of precautions, his many halts, and his laboured breathing. He had hardly reached the upper limit of the barrier of rocks before Pierre was at his side, having come up in one continuous movement. He never troubled to look and see if he were safeguarded, and moved as if impelled onward by some all-powerful force.

'Don't do that sort of thing, Pierre,' Camille reproached him, 'there are enough of us to give each other a hand, and only one man need risk the exposure. When there is a rope, you should use it.'

Above this point, the couloir continued, and they resumed their laborious upward progress. At every step the leader broke through the frozen crust and sank up to the thigh in powder snow, swearing like a trooper. Occasionally, to avoid sinking in altogether, he had to move on knees and elbows; it was strange to see men like these on all fours above the fearful drop, exhausted but still making progress. At last they reached the foot of the great wall.

The sun, slowly climbing down the rock face, came at last to warm them; it was a wonderful morning and everything pointed to a splendid day, when all of a sudden a warm wind followed the cold.

'The föhn,' muttered Maxime. 'Let's hope that the weather holds for us.'

'We're all right today, but I don't like to think about tomorrow,' grumbled Jacques.

'By tomorrow we'll be down,' stated Pierre.

The föhn, the south wind, was now blowing over the whole mountainside, softening the surface of the snow, starting up avalanches, and sapping resolution and willpower with its languid breath.

The guides halted for a few moments, and once they were rested they turned their attention to the great wall of the Dru. It was not a sight to encourage them. The slabs were free of snow, whereas the cracks were choked and stuffed with it, and all the stances well covered.

'Well, boys, it's going to be hard work,' announced Camille.

'We'll take it in turn to lead,' Pierre insisted. 'We're all capable of leading. Each of us will lead one of the chimneys, and we'll manage fine that way. We must go up now; I'm sure the bad weather's coming soon. We can't leave Father any longer up there; if the föhn gets any stronger, and the storm starts up again, we might never find him.'

'Don't worry,' Boule assured him, 'we're all with you.'

'It's easy to see how young you are,' Maxime grumbled, 'you overlook all the difficulties; don't they, Joseph?'

'We'll never get up today. Better wait a while,' he answered; he was sitting in the snow, quite exhausted by the ascent, and he scrutinised the mountain with the eyes of experience.

'Listen, Uncle! I quite agree with you: it's going to be difficult, and you shouldn't go on. The couloir was too much for you, and it's us younger men who should go right up. We're certainly going on, but you should stay here and wait for us, you really should.'

'I never meant for a second to burden you with the job of getting me up there. I'm not feeling too good; I'm too tired and out of sorts, and I was just going to tell you that if you go on, I'll wait for you at the Shoulder.'

Fernand Lourtier put in his word. 'Staying here for hours and hours isn't going to do anybody any good. And it isn't going to be so simple, anyway. Of course, we'll get up there, but if we can get the body down as far as the Shoulder, that's the most we can hope for; there aren't enough of us to do anything more. Two of you will have to go to the Montenvers to ask for extra help. Maxime, you ought to go down with Joseph.'

'Can't possibly. I'm responsible for the party: if you mean to go on, then I come with you. I agree I'd better not be in the lead; I'm getting old too. I don't give the Dru a second thought when it's dry, but it's a different matter with verglas on everything. All the same, I must come with you. Send Michel back.'

'But I want to go on … can't you send someone else?'

All the guides refused to turn back. Red Joseph, realising that not one of them wanted to quit his post in the hour of danger, spoke his mind.

'To my way of thinking, it's the best men who ought to stay. And the best means the youngest and spryest and the chaps who are best on rock, for it's going to be a hard climb. You'll have Jacques Batioret with you, and I've brought you Camille, who ought really by this time to be a guide. Maxime, you'd better just come down with me. I honestly don't feel at all well, and I need a good man to safeguard me down the couloir. The young 'uns are going to manage fine, I know them; when we were their age we'd have spoken just the same way.'

'But man, I can't leave them … '

'I'm older than you, Maxime – so I can give you orders. For one thing, you have to be young for all the manoeuvres that will be needed up there; for another, I'm just a burden on you, and since I have to turn back, I must have you to see me down. Fernand's quite right, we must send them up some more help. But mind, you others,' and Ravanat's voice took on a note of severity, 'be careful, and change leaders often. Now, off with you! We'll stay here a minute and watch you go.'

Chapter XVII

Jacques Batioret set to work on the first chimney. From below, Maxime and Red Joseph could see him gain height slowly, dislodging the snow with his body, hacking away with his axe at the lumps that hindered his progress. It was gruelling work, but he did not take long to reach the top.

Soon after Boule took over the lead; then Fernand relieved him, then Camille. Michel was the only one not to take a turn.

'Keep back, Michel,' ordered Boule, 'you're too young to lead; you're lucky to be here with us at all.'

Red Joseph and Maxime slung on their sacks, stood up in the snow, and craned their necks to follow their young friends' progress on this particularly tricky ascent.

The three parties went up at a good pace. It certainly looked like a fairly normal climb; but, in fact, it was extremely dangerous, and it was only the climbers' skill and training that made it appear easy.

Ravanat was reassured by what he saw, and gave the word to be off.

'Let's get going, Maxime, while the snow's still good.'

They set off slowly down the couloir, Maxime coming last, and kept on looking back half regretfully to see how the climbers were getting on. They had reached a point high up in the great wall when a rocky rib finally hid them from view.

There was no truce, up there, in the pitched battle with the mountain. The higher they climbed the greater the difficulties they encountered. Luckily the warm breath of the föhn wind softened the snow and enabled them to get warm when halting for a moment on a stance between two difficult pitches. Then off they would start again on the same old round – clearing the cracks, fighting their way up, with now and then a spell of cutting hand-

and footholds in hard ice.

'Call this a rock climb,' muttered Boule, 'you'd think this was a winter ascent!'

'We've seen nothing yet,' cursed Jacques, 'it's only just beginning. Did you ever in all your born days see such awful conditions as these?'

They reached the foot of a wide, high chimney; the sight of all the ice in it made them hesitate. Pierre, who was warming to the struggle, wanted to go up first, but Boule waved him back. 'Stay where you are – it's my turn.'

What Boule did not say was that this pitch was too dangerous for Pierre to be allowed to lead. So up he started himself. He made slow progress, and sometimes he did not seem to be mounting at all. Little by little, however, he gained height. Carefully he tested every hold, calculating each slightest movement and avoiding any unnecessary effort. He kept up a sort of running commentary, audible to the men below.

' … some verglas, this, my boy … here we are, no more hold … hang on, Boule, hang on … good God, man, what a sweat.'

Halfway up he was brought to a stop by an icy bulge. Still looking upwards, he yelled out:

''Fraid this looks pretty hopeless. However, send me up the hammer; if I can make a few nicks … '

'Hold on a second,' shouted back Fernand, 'I'm coming up.'

Fernand clipped the hammer, two karabiners and a piton on to his belt, and in his turn started up the chimney. In spite of Boule's good work in clearing it of snow and ice, he found the going terribly hard. As he climbed, he gave vent to his admiration.

'How on earth did you get up? Confound you, Boule, with that everlasting grin of yours! My God,' he yelled, with his body half jammed in the angle, 'there just isn't a single hold – there's ice in everything. Make sure that rope's well belayed, you down there – it's—'

'Come down, you idiots,' bawled Paul Mouny.

'Come down this minute,' ordered Jacques Batioret, 'it's not good enough … You'll only break your necks by going on.'

Boule was still laughing, up there under the overhang, but now there was a note of apprehension in his mirth. With one arm and one knee jammed in the angle, he was tiring visibly: his eyes were on Fernand climbing upwards. But neither of them was in a position to help the other.

'Hurry up, Fernand, if you possibly can – I've got cramp,' Boule gasped, for his friend's ear only.

'Hold on just a second, I'm coming.'

Boule felt his fingers slowly losing their grip, and his muscles were stiff with cramp.

'Come on, quick,' he begged.

With positive anguish the men below followed this crazy struggle between the two guides and the mountain. They watched in absolute silence, and with desperate anxiety, only too aware of their own powerlessness to help.

'It's absolutely crazy. How in the name of God did you get up there,' gasped Fernand. 'I thought I could climb pretty well, but I'd never in a million years have managed to get up.'

'Shut up, and keep your breath.'

With a final effort Fernand heaved himself up till he was just below Boule's feet. It was high time, too.

'Wedge yourself in, quick,' snapped Boule. 'It's only for a second, but – I've got cramp in my arm, I must shift my position or I'll let go.'

Fernand wedged himself in the crack and was able to take some of Boule's weight on his shoulders. The latter gave a great sigh of relief; the strain faded from his face; once again, he radiated cheerfulness. Danger and exposure were all forgotten and his one thought now was to hurry on.

'If you hadn't made that stretch,' he chuckled, 'I'd have come right off, sure as death. Hand up that hammer and a piton.'

Very slowly and carefully, so as not to disturb the balance of the human pyramid, Fernand passed the tools up.

'You've got to support me till I get this piton knocked in,' Boule instructed.

'Right, go ahead.' Up on their fantastic perch they talked to each other as nonchalantly as if they had been sitting in two armchairs.

Boule rested for a moment on Fernand's shoulders. The big tricouni nails dug painfully into Fernand's flesh; but he bore the weight without flinching. Although the veins in his neck swelled visibly under the strain, he gave no sign of it except to whisper, so that the others couldn't notice anything:

'Be as quick as you can, Boule – you're heavy.'

Using one hand, Boule placed the piton in a tiny crevice, then hammered it right in up to its head. Then he fastened one of the snap-links to the ring, and passed his climbing rope through.

'Give us a bit more rope,' he ordered the men below.

He was now safeguarded.

Fernand hauled in – first with one hand, then with his teeth – a few feet of rope, and handed the slack up to Boule, who duly safeguarded him by passing it through the snap-link. They both let out a sigh of relief. From below Paul Mouny and Jacques Batioret, appalled by the fearful struggle taking place before their eyes, set up a shout.

'Give it up, for God's sake, and come down. It's too risky.'

Pierre Servettaz was watching the proceedings in a fever, and he could not help showing what was in his mind by yelling:

'Can you make it?'

'We'll have a shot at it.'

Fernand Lourtier now embarked on a highly daring manoeuvre. He climbed up Boule, who had belayed himself to a rock and was now crouching on the piton, and managed to raise himself up on the other man's shoulders. He performed this acrobatic feat extremely slowly, all his faculties bent on not dislodging Boule from the chimney. For if *he* wavered for even a fifth of a second, then it was goodbye to both of them. Boule endured his partner's weight, and his nailed boots, with stoical fortitude; he even managed to crack a joke, for all that his big round head was squashed down on his shoulders.

'Hi, you up there – you must have kept on your crampons … what d'you take me for – a fakir?'

Once up on his partner's shoulders, Fernand did not lose a

second; he had to act quickly, for this was his last card. Very carefully he made a few small handholds in the ice that lined the back wall of the chimney, and then (to the immense relief of Boule, who at once felt that he had gained at least four inches in height) he continued cautiously upwards. The tiniest slip might easily prove fatal. Fernand concentrated all his willpower and nervous energy on avoiding the least mistake; a few more feet, and he was beyond the glazed overhang and could proceed more easily. At long last he stood on the top of it. He was completely exhausted and his fingers were dead after their prolonged contact with the ice; but his first thought was to take in the rope and safeguard Boule as he in turn climbed up.

They both sat down on the tiny platform and let their feet dangle over the precipice.

'What d'you think of it?' said Boule.

'If there's any more of this, we're done.'

Boule turned and looked up. They were perched on a slight projection on the great wall of rock, the only break on a subsidiary ridge; and below them the rock fell away steeply on the Charpoua side. The only way up led over a great slab, tilted at an angle of seventy degrees and encased in verglas and hard snow. It looked hopeless. After that came the big snow-covered ledge, just under the chimney with a piton. They could not see it from here; but by craning their necks they could just catch sight of a bluish-looking bulge that glittered in the sunlight. This was the famous overhang where Georges's line had jammed. What would the crack be like today?

'We'll never get past that slab today,' opined Boule, 'and as for the bit above it – I'd rather not think about it. We'd better tell the others.'

'Hi, you down there!' shouted Fernand. 'It just gets worse and worse. We'll never manage it.'

'Can't you let me come up at least as far as you've got?' begged Pierre.

Boule made fast the rappel line and flicked the ends down. One by one the others climbed up to join him and Fernand on their airy platform, and there they held a council of war. As senior, Jacques Batioret advised caution.

'We've done all that we possibly could,' he declared. 'You both risked coming right off that pitch, and it'd be worse further up. Surely that's good enough. And you won't take it too hard, will you, Pierre? You know your father would never have let us go on. Isn't that so?' he appealed to the others.

But they were uneasy, and did not answer. They did not doubt for a minute that Jacques was perfectly right, and ever since the night before they had felt in their bones that the Dru could not possibly be climbed in its present icy condition. But then neither did it seem possible to turn back without having gone to the furthest limit to bring down Servettaz's body, before the wind could send it hurtling down into the icy depths. Boule turned round and, putting a rough hand on Pierre's shoulder to hide his feelings, spoke out:

'You've got to see reason, Pierre. These pitches that Fernand and I led – we wouldn't climb them again for all the gold in the world. We only did it for your father's sake – and yours – but we can't face any more of it. Anyway, we're both absolutely all in, I've got no feeling in my arms, they might be lead as far as my shoulders ... Honestly, I can't go up another inch.'

In the long silence that followed they could clearly hear the cannonade of stones which the föhn wind had loosened in the Verte Couloir.

'I know you've done all the work so far,' answered Pierre; 'but it's my turn now. After all, he's my father; so it's certainly my business to fetch him down, and stand the risk. I'm going to get up that slab, you see if I don't.' He stood upright on the narrow ledge, with a quick, nervous gesture took up a few coils of rope, and faced the slab as resolutely as a wrestler squaring up to his opponent.

'Stop, Pierre,' yelled the others.

But he had already flung himself to the attack and Michel had only just time to get his rope clear so that it should not catch and pull him. Face to face with this new difficulty, nothing could have made Pierre leave off. He certainly astounded them all. Never before had they seen him climb with such dash, such assurance, and such superb technique. He found holds for a bootnail on wrinkles only a fraction of an inch wide; he pulled himself up by one finger, moving with certainty and precision, and in this way reached the lower edge of the verglas.

'Look out, Pierre, you're almost on to the verglas,' Paul shouted.

'Very good climbing, I must say – very good,' muttered Jacques Batioret to himself; 'reminds me of his father when he was thirty.'

When Pierre reached the crucial point, he stopped and looked down.

'Boule,' he ordered, 'send up the hammer, this ice is like armour plate.'

Boule tied the slender steel hammer to the rope for Pierre to pull up.

Now followed a fantastic piece of work. With the end of the hammer Pierre chipped out some little holds in the sheet of ice. It sounded quite hollow, and the men below hardly dared to breathe, for fear that a slightly stronger blow would detach the whole layer.

'Go easy, Pierre, easy; it'll all peel off ... you can tell it's hollow,' entreated Boule. 'The whole sheet'll come off, and you'll come with it.'

'It's *got* to hold,' bawled Pierre.

The hammer blows no longer rang out clear, as they usually do on ice; they sounded dull and muffled, as if Pierre were hammering at a piece of cardboard.

For a whole hour he cut without a pause, sometimes taking ten minutes over a single hold, oblivious alike to the yawning gulf beneath his feet and to the chill in his fingers; then he passed out of sight, swallowed up in the vast mountain face. The rope ran out very quickly, then checked. From above came the triumphant cry:

'Done it!'

And then, after a minute or two:

'Come on.'

Once again, the line came whizzing down to them; and, mesmerised by this astounding display of willpower, the others braced themselves to join him.

Fernand was first up.

'A fine piece of work, Pierre. Your father would have been proud – a grand job. Not one of us could have done it – '

But Pierre was already eyeing the next pitch.

It was not an encouraging sight that met his eyes. The overhang was topped by a cornice of ice; verglas was on the holds, and the rock looked like blue glass. There were enough difficulties in those twenty metres to daunt the stoutest heart; and a shudder ran through the others as they watched Pierre, who was calculating how best to proceed. They no longer dared to voice any protest, for they realised that no power on earth could make him stop. And had he not just proved himself fit to tackle any obstacle and overcome it? But then this particular one was beyond the limit.

After a moment's reflection, Pierre gave Fernand his orders.

'Give me a rope-ring, two pitons and the hammer. I want your gloves, mine are frozen. Boule, look after my rope. Just leave this to me.'

'I wish you'd give it up, Pierre. You scare me stiff.'

'Don't you worry, Paul, I'll get up ... We're going to have our revenge on the Dru. If I remember rightly, the worst's over after the crack – or nearly over; if I get up, we'll be all right. So I will get up – you wait and see, my boys.' And up he started.

The crack was horribly narrow and overhung an immense drop. Pierre was soon involved in its difficulties. They could hear the scrape of his bootnails on the granite, a rasping sound that contrasted with the clink of the pitons and snap-links tied to his belt.

With prodigious effort he climbed up fifteen metres, then had to stop for a good look at the next stage. His breath came in laboured gasps. The ice-covered rocks offered not the slightest friction to his clothes. Imperceptibly he recoiled a fraction; his heart was pounding like a sledgehammer, and his chest felt like bursting.

'D'you see the piton?' shouted Fernand.

'Two metres further up,' gasped Pierre, 'and thick in ice; I'll have to free it with the hammer.'

Boule had instinctively belayed the rope round a block of granite; but his eyes were fixed on the cliff on which Pierre was battling, and never left him for a moment.

With furious energy Pierre continued upwards. Every effort gained him a few inches' height, but then he lost ground again as his fingers slipped from the icy holds. Each successive effort took more out of him; he wedged himself into the crack and clung to the rock; the hoarse sound of his breathing, the frenzied pounding of his heart, were an agony. 'You've got to get up, get up,' he kept muttering. 'If you reach the piton, you'll be safe.'

He was not to know that it was at this very spot, but under better conditions, that the porter Georges had also been engaged in an equally grim struggle. All his willpower and strength were concentrated on one goal: to get up, to remove his father's body from its rocky ledge, and bring it down.

He realised well enough that the only possible hope was to keep his body outside the crack, and climb up by the sketchy holds on the edges, balancing as delicately as a tight-rope walker.

Of course, it was risky – but all the same he was going to have a shot at it.

He wriggled his body out of the crack and worked himself up another metre. Beneath his questing fingers he felt the polished dome of verglas that enclosed the piton; he tried to scratch it with his nails, but it was no good. It would need the hammer.

Balanced on one bootnail, his body hugging the cliff, he willed himself not to slip: then slowly withdrew one hand from its hold and lowered his arm. He groped with his fingers for the opening of the snap-link that would release the hammer from his belt. All of a sudden he felt in his legs the nervous trembling that is brought on by exhaustion. Quickly he tried to recover his handhold, but he was already tottering. His fingers clawed fruitlessly at the granite and he fell backwards without a cry.

With a last reflex action he jumped clear, his arms outstretched like a crucifix, his eyes distended. He could clearly distinguish his friends who stood rooted with horror to the little ledge, then with a final look he took in the frightful abyss where he was going to crash. His fall seemed to last for centuries. He didn't feel at all frightened, but remarked to himself with some surprise, 'So I'm going to die.' His thoughts turned first to his mother, then to his father. Later on, he was to describe it: 'I thought I was done for, and I found myself thinking of all sorts of things, of the family, of Chamonix. I figured I'd crash on the slab below. It's strange, but I was more startled than frightened. But how can you see so many things in so few seconds?'

He dropped right on his feet, legs stiff as ramrods, just as a cat dropped from a height lands on its claws. He fell right on to the snow-covered slab: it broke his fall; then like a ball he rebounded off into space.

Boule had not lost his head for a minute; he put every ounce in his body into holding the rope, only praying it would not snap under the imminent shock. When that came, he was ready for it; firmly planted there, he took it, and felt that somewhere down below the fall had been checked. Praise be, the rope – an eleven-millimetre hempen rope – had held.

Everything had happened so quickly that the guides were still standing there open-mouthed as if they had not half taken it in; and it was Boule who first plucked up courage to call out hoarsely:

'Pierre, are you hurt, Pierre old man?'

Hearing no answer, he called again, louder this time: 'Pierre – Pierre.'

Anxiously they craned over the edge and saw the inanimate body spreadeagled below, suspended like a broken puppet at the end of the rope.

Jacques Batioret had uncoiled the rappel line, and he threw it down towards the injured man. Without waiting for orders young Michel Lourtier took hold of it and, not bothering about any kind of a safeguard, boldly slid down at full speed towards the body. The others bombarded him with questions.

'Is he badly hurt, Michel?'

'He's not stirring – he's bleeding from his nose and ears.'

'That's bad – we'll have to get him down at once,' swore Paul.

'We'll chuck you a rope, and you lower him to the foot of the slab.'

They threw a rope down to Michel, who lifted the body with a strength unbelievable in such a youngster. Boule paid out the rope very gently as Michel slid down over the slab. As soon as he had reached the ledge below, he laid Pierre out on the snow and called to the others to join him.

The guides crouched round the injured man and waited for him to come around. Paul Mouny had slipped his hand inside Pierre's sodden windjacket: to his huge joy and relief the heart was still beating. Not till he had actually touched the warm flesh with his fingers could he stop fearing the worst.

At last Pierre gave a faint moan, then opened his eyes; at first he could only make out some shadowy forms bending over him, but he recognised the voices of friends. 'I'm alive,' he thought; then memory came back, in disconnected fragments, like a jumble of striking but unrelated scenes from a film. Ah – it was coming back to him – his hand slipping … himself falling … but he'd never seen the end of that fall.

With a great effort he tried to stand up. The others supported his body, and staunched his wounds. 'Hello,' he thought, 'blood on my jacket … I must be damaged somewhere.' He tried to speak, but couldn't get the words out. Some of Uncle Paul's brandy was forced down his throat. It took effect at once. He seemed to come out of his stupor and in a voice that sounded very far away, he asked wildly:

'What happened? Tell me, what happened?'

'You came off, Pierre; Lord, what a fall! Thank God you're as nimble as a cat and you landed first on the snow, or it would have been all up with you. Thirty metres, you fell – you've certainly got a charmed life.'

There was only one idea in Pierre's head:

'Does this mean we have to give up? All the same, we can't leave Father up there.'

'We'll have to wait a while' – there was brotherly feeling in Fernand's voice: 'You take it easy, Pierre: we'll be up again as soon as possible. But our job now is to get you down, and that's not going to be any picnic. How d'you feel?'

'I've got a splitting headache; sort of shooting pains, and then everything spins around.'

'And the rest of you?'

Painfully, Pierre moved his arms and legs; they all seemed to work.

'It looks as if you were only bruised; that's something. It was falling on that snow that saved you.'

Jacques Batioret examined Pierre at length: his skin was terribly grazed; he was bruised all over; and blood flowed freely from a scalp wound. But what worried Jacques was the thin continuous trickle from ear and nostril. He took Boule and Fernand aside.

'I'm afraid it may be a fracture of the skull. I once saw the same thing happen on the Grépon; it doesn't look much, but it gets far worse within forty-eight hours ... we must get him down just as quickly as possible. We'll have two lines at each rappel. Boule, you'll go down side by side with him, ready to hold him if he shows the least sign of needing it. Blanc and I will see you down from above. Paul will go ahead with Michel, the others can safeguard Pierre's ropes.'

He turned back towards Pierre.

'Ready? Shall we start? If you don't feel up to it, just say so, and we'll carry you; but we must get down as quick as we can; we don't want to get caught out at night up here.'

Mechanically Pierre arranged the line round his body, and slid down its full length at breakneck speed. Boule, coming down beside him on the other line, on the watch for any sign of weakness, was hard put to it to keep with him. And so the descent continued; with an astounding effort of will, Pierre went on down, only speaking when they paused on the ledges for the others to fix the line and make the rappel ready. In a fever of impatience he begged them to hurry.

'Quicker, can't you – my head's worse every minute.'

It was more like a tumble than an orderly descent, as this bunch of men, all tangled in their ropes, came pell-mell down the cliff.

But it was a controlled tumble, with every one of them knowing exactly what to do, continually on the alert, always keeping an eye on the injured climber. Coming down last, Jacques Batioret kept on muttering under his breath, 'If only he lasts as far as the glacier … if only.'

And Pierre, paler with every minute that passed, grabbed the lines, flung himself at the pitches, hustled on the others, and entreated them, 'Quicker, can't you, quicker.'

Confusedly he realised that if he couldn't reach the foot of the rocks under his own steam, if the others were forced to carry him down the rest of this dangerous and ill-starred descent, then the time they would lose would make a bivouac inevitable. And he knew enough about mountains to realise that a man in his condition could not hope to survive the rigours of such a night out. Occasionally despair got the better of him, and his poor bandaged head lolled helplessly from side to side. But such weakness was only momentary; he soon mastered himself and continued his furious descent. In face of such courage, the others were speechless. They fixed up each pitch for him and young Michel was everywhere, tirelessly swarming up and down the ropes like a monkey, freeing the line, clearing a stance, putting a rope-ring in position.

They reached the Shoulder at last, but Pierre did not pause for a second; with Camille, Fernand and Boule to hold him, he set off in great leaps down the soft and heavy snow of the couloir.

With the föhn blowing stronger every minute there was considerable risk of the snow avalanching; they were well aware of the possibility, but snapped their fingers at it. If a miniature avalanche knocked one man off his feet, then the others drove their axes in up to the head, held on to them grimly, checking the slide. And so the descent continued.

Pierre was rapidly losing strength. He took an eternity to climb over the last rocky projection, and came down the last rappel in an uncontrolled slither. The short crossing of the glacier was agony; he stumbled and staggered in the snow like a drunken man, and had to be held up by the arms.

He only began to revive when he felt the rough boulders of the moraine under his bootnails, and saw the hut a few hundred metres off: 'If I can get there, I'm safe – safe.'

He could not: his strength deserted him, and he reeled over as if someone had struck him a great blow on the back of his head. For some time past Boule had foreseen this moment, and his arms were ready to receive Pierre as he fell.

They heaved him up on Camille's back; his arms dangled and his head lolled as the guide descended with the utmost care, feeling for the loose pebbles of the moraine with his foot. With mounting anxiety the rest of them watched the growing trickle of blood from Pierre's ears.

For all their exhaustion, the guides did not stop to rest at the hut. Pierre's bandages were changed, the stretcher unhooked, blankets rolled round him, and the mournful caravan was on its way once more.

Poor Pierre groaned at every jolt; he had lost consciousness and muttered incoherently.

Down the endless moraine they carried him, and did not stop again until they reached the Mer de Glace. They had the queer feeling of having passed out of a peculiar world where everything was vertical; they hardly knew how to walk on this flat, crevassed glacier. The heat stifled them; arms and legs were weighted with lead; the sky itself seemed to press heavily on their shoulders.

Engrossed as they had been in their tricky work of rescue, they had not bothered about the weather, and were startled to observe that the Dru, where they had been such a short time ago, was clouded over. Not just mist, but those long grey streamers that denote bad weather, dishevelled comets that fastened on to the Aiguilles, twisting and twining, obscuring the tops, and then came lower in successive stages until they formed a continuous cloud ceiling around the 3,000-metre level. A few drops of rain fell.

They decided to go straight on.

'Go ahead, Michel, and warn them at the Montenvers. They must break the news gently to Marie ... It's more than a mother ought to bear. And get a doctor up to the Montenvers.'

Michel set off at a run, making a beeline down the glacier,

taking the crevasses in his stride; before long he was only a black dot, difficult to distinguish from the boulders thrown up by the ice.

The cortège continued on its mournful way down the Mer de Glace. They proceeded steadily, relieving each other at the stretcher without even putting it down, carrying their wounded comrade over the green depths of the crevasses. Speed was their chief weapon against the death that stalked beside Pierre and threatened him with the increasing flow of blood from his battered head.

Just as they reached the place known as the 'angle', where a sketchy track follows the left bank of the Mer de Glace, they spotted the second rescue party which Red Joseph had sent up, coming quickly to meet them. There were no explanations: the fresh climbers, newly arrived from the valley, relieved the exhausted guides at the stretcher, and the augmented cortège continued on its way.

There were crowds at the Montenvers, and a rush of inquisitive tourists as soon as they were sighted on the path.

Boule walked ahead, solemn, tense, impatiently brushing aside the tourists who leaned over for a better sight of the figure on the stretcher.

'Make way – make way,' he shouted. 'All right, and if it *is* the second, what about it. What'll we do next? That's *our* business – we'll see to it later on.'

Down in Chamonix two women, with kerchiefs on their heads, sat sobbing on the wooden benches of the station waiting room. Marie moaned, piteously as a wounded animal, but her cries were dimmed by the deep wind-borne roar of the Blaitière torrent as it scattered foam on the mountainside. It was no use telling her that this might not be anything serious; she was deaf to all such words of comfort, and it was Aline who still managed to keep a glimmer of hope despite her sorrow.

Marie sat with her head between her hands; now and then she stretched her arms out towards the mountains in a gesture of hatred and despair.

'My man and my boy – the mountains have taken them both

from me – both husband and son. If my poor Jean could have known!'

Not far off there were others waiting, guides and various officials. Their eyes were red, and they kept slipping out to the platform to escape the agonising cries. Then a whistle screamed from the scrub-covered hillside down which serpented a thin line of smoke. The superintendent of the Montenvers line braced himself to announce:

'They'll be down in five minutes.'

The ambulance waiting in the station yard backed up till it was nearly touching the platform.

The mountain train drew into the station at a walking pace, almost as if it were holding back out of consideration for the precious burden it carried. The first to get down was the doctor; he gave instructions to clear the waiting-room. Casual onlookers were ordered out; then with infinite precautions, the guides carried in the stretcher. Michel was last off the train; he carried several sacks and an armful of axes.

As Marie was about to throw herself on the body that lay swathed in its blankets on the canvas, the doctor held her back.

'No, Marie, you mustn't touch him; you'll see him tomorrow all right. We're going to pull him round, I promise you. Aline, take her home, won't you? Then you can come back to the hospital for news.'

Uncle Paul and the Chief Guide came over to the doctor; but he would not say much.

'Skull fractured on the rock, I take it. A bad business, but we'll pull him through. We're still in time to operate; but it beats me how he managed to come down that face by himself.'

'You must save him, Doctor, you must,' entreated Uncle Paul, 'or else his mother will go mad.'

And the ambulance drove off, taking Pierre to hospital.

Night came on, and with it a thin cold drizzle of rain. Chamonix was shrouded in mist; the wet streets glistened in lamplight. Sorrow was abroad in the town; yet up in the centre, by the square, the electric signs of the bars and shops glowed from every twinkling letter. On the terraces violinists with numbed fingers played halfheartedly to the last of the season's tourists.

The rescue party arrived back on foot, going very slowly; they passed through the town without speaking to anyone. The guides walked awkwardly; occasionally someone's nailed boots would slip on the asphalt. Everybody turned to look at them, but their grave faces discouraged questions. They stopped at the Guides' Office, stowed their sacks inside, then repaired to Gros-Bibi's opposite. They took seats in the darkest corner, where Jean-Baptiste Cupelaz soon found them. Only now did they break silence.

'You must have had a horrible day,' said Jean-Baptiste with deep feeling. 'For that to happen, it must have been really bad – bad and dangerous.'

'A little too bad,' answered Boule. 'We'll have to wait for good weather before we try again.'

'I'm going to take you off this job … I'll collect some other boys … you've all done everything you possibly could, you deserve a rest.'

'No, we've made up our minds to go up again, the whole bunch of us. It's our job, don't you see, to get him down. We promised Pierre we would, and after all that's happened, we're certainly going to. We'll bring him back, and if we don't, it'll only be because we've come to grief ourselves.'

'Have it your own way, it's all the same to me,' agreed Jean-Baptiste. He realised it was no good reopening that particular question.

It was pitch-dark in the valley and the cold rain glistened on the close-shaved autumn fields. The wind whirled the dead leaves off the poplars and ash trees; water dripped off the tall spruces, and their sodden branches bowed down to the earth in prayer. The deserted bathing tents beside the Casino pool flapped in the wind, which whipped the water and drove the ripples across the surface till they vanished in the shadows.

And in Chamonix itself the visitors fled to bars and hotels for shelter, hugging the walls to avoid being splashed by the overflowing gutters.

Clouds filled the valley, but above the 3,500-metre line the highest peaks floated like islands on a billowy sea. Waves of mist broke against the granite tips, revealing, as they receded, dizzy couloirs that plunged towards the darkness.

Up at Moëntieu the village women had gathered to pray for the dead guide; they knelt on the hard floor of the living room, chanting their prayers in a loud monotone as they held their beads. Marie, prostrate in a big armchair, shivered in spite of the enormous wood fire that crackled on the hearth. She sat still and dry-eyed, gazing with sorrowful intensity at the figure of Christ on the wall – carved in larchwood, with a faded sprig of box as crosspiece.

Meanwhile, high up above the clouds unrolled the splendid pageant of a mountain sunset. A last ray of light flushed the highest point of the Dru. Great black birds croaked and circled, swooping down to the floor of clouds, then up again to perch on a narrow ledge, like seabirds on a wreck. Yellow-beaked jackdaws quarrelled, flapped and fought under the feet of a human figure. Could it indeed be human, this corpse clad in hoar-frost, whose mummified hands still gripped the rock? The dead man's face looked towards the valley; but what once had been Servettaz's clear and twinkling eyes were now two black and bleeding holes. The corpse, a motionless sentinel, kept watch to all eternity; facing the great peaks and gazing out beyond the burning sunset towards the farthest limits of space.

The summit outlines grew blurred, and were soon lost in the ascending darkness. A strong wind rose and flapped the red scarf knotted round the dead man's neck. Down in the valley cars drew up at the brightly-lit Casino. It was the last dance of the season, and every time a guest in evening dress swung open the door a gust of warmth and music escaped into the street.

In the hospital, a man with a bandaged head cried out in delirium.

Warm once more in their own chalets, unconscious of the rain lashing at their windows, Boule and his companions were deep in dreamless sleep.

The scene changes to Geneva, early in October. An icy wind from the lake made the water swirl and eddy against the piers of the low-arched Pont du Mont Blanc. Yellow leaves from the plane trees chased each other along the pavements. Steamboats at anchor puffed away peacefully down by the landing stage. Gulls clustered and swooped, open-mouthed, now skimming the waves, now wheeling high overhead before diving down on their prey.

Boule, Paul Mouny and Fernand Lourtier were walking awkwardly up the deserted highway, lined with villas and gardens, that leads to the heights of Eaux-Vives. It is a quiet and peaceful part of the town, out of hearing of the noisy business quarter.

Awkward in their Sunday clothes, and in shoes far too light for feet that had worn nothing but climbing boots for the last three months, the three mountaineers progressed very cautiously, stopping at every crossroad, and frequently pausing to consult a scrap of paper in Fernand's hand.

Their way took them along by a high wall of red brick that bounded a charming park with many a pleasant walk and quiet alley; they finally halted in front of a big gateway that opened on to an avenue lined with plane trees.

'Here we are,' said Fernand.

But they paused for a moment before going on, intimidated by the calm of the great park, the regularity of the avenues, the bourgeois opulence of the buildings set among the trees.

'I'd rather go back to the Dru,' admitted Paul Mouny.

'Come on, they won't eat us.'

Nobody did eat them. They were greeted on the doorstep of the luxurious nursing home by a nurse with a most charming smile, who put them quickly at their ease.

'You must be guides from Chamonix,' she said; 'and I expect it's Georges you've come to see. He *will* be pleased – follow me, it's this way. Poor Georges, he had a very bad time, but he's over the worst now. I know exactly where the accident happened' – here she blushed a little at her temerity – 'you see, I've climbed the Dru too; I spotted you by your badges; every Saturday I go off to the mountains.'

The three guides picked their way cautiously behind the nurse along the linoleum-covered corridors, tiptoeing as if they were in church. She threw open a door, and announced cheerfully:

'Some friends to see you, Georges.'

Georges was sitting in a cane armchair with his feet in a basin full of amethyst-coloured liquid; he was pale, and his formerly bronzed face had taken on the sallow look of a town dweller.

'Boule – Paul – Fernand! It's awfully nice of you three to look me up here.'

They looked at each other and could not think of a single thing to say. Finally Boule brought himself to ask:

'Well, how goes it?'

'You can see for yourselves,' answered Georges sadly.

He took his legs out of the basin and displayed his poor frost-bitten feet; all the toes and part of the foot next to them were dead, shrivelled and blackened as if they had been burned; there was no flesh left on the bones. It was a dreadful sight. The guides tried not to show their feelings.

'Poor old Georges. Has it been pretty bad?'

'Awful,' said Georges. 'I thought I was going to lose both feet. Luckily for me, Warfield's been a real brick; he got me in here, you know. I'm having the most expensive treatment – I could never have afforded it myself. The doctors tell me that it's all over now; one fine day my toes will fall off by themselves, and the wound will heal up … Yes, I'm nicely fixed up here.'

'What are you going to do?'

'Why, start off again. I'll be able to climb all right, in special boots; I'm going to train myself all over again, just you wait and see. Of course, I can't think of doing any big expeditions, but they might take me on as warden of a hut. Catch me settling down in the valley for the rest of my days!'

'But even after all you've been through?'

'All I can think of is getting back to the mountains. Here, look out of that window.'

Through the open casement could be seen the cliffs of the Salève in the foreground, and then, above the jagged lines of rocks, a great diamond glittered in the distance: Mont Blanc.

'You see – I'm looking at it all the time, and the more I look the more I want to go back.' He sighed deeply.

'By the way,' said Boule, anxious to change the subject, 'we've brought you some cigarettes.'

'Aline gave me a cream cheese for you.'

'And Uncle Paul sent you these two bottles of red wine.'

They put their presents down on the little table by Georges's bed. Then they all fell silent for a minute or two. Georges put his feet to soak once more in the basin, saying by way of explanation:

'It's the only way I can stop them hurting; if I don't, I feel the pain right up to my head.' Then, lowering his voice, he asked:

'What about Pierre?'

'Oh, he's all right! They trepanned his skull, he's convalescent now. Like you, he talks of nothing but climbing again. That doesn't go down well with his family.'

'And how did you get Jean down?'

'You know about Pierre's accident, of course. Well, we waited till the snow had melted a little, then we went up a week later. There was still some ice around, but it wasn't too bad. We found him in the same place, but frozen so fast to the rock that we had to use a hammer to free him. We wrapped the body in the grain sacks. There was one arm that was raised above his head and stiff as an iron bar – it stuck out of the bag, with its fingers clenched and it bothered us a lot. Thank God it got broken after one or two rappels, and we were able to tuck everything away in the bag; it looked better that way. Everything was clear sailing down to the Shoulder; but just when we got there, a rope suddenly broke. It nearly pulled Fernand off, as he didn't want to let go. We just couldn't bear to lose the body. But we did lose it, all the same. It crashed down the whole height of the Shoulder and bounced on to the glacier. It must have fallen more than 400 metres! We were ages looking for it; at last we found it at the bottom of a crevasse forty metres deep, just below the bergschrund. We put it back in the sack – but it was a good deal lighter this time. When we started off it must have been nearly six feet long, but down at the Montenvers it all went into a small sack ... Anyway, we put him in his coffin straightway – we didn't want Marie to see him like that ... We could all breathe more easily when it was all over and done with. We gave him a fine funeral – people came to it from all over the place – even a Minister turned up. By the way, they gave us all the medal for life-saving ... a lot of good it'll do us! But they've given you the Gold Medal and a special mention ... But that's not going to get you back your feet.'

The visit came to an end.

When they had gone, Georges dragged himself to the window. It was here that the nurse discovered him, lost in a sad reverie; there were tears in his eyes as he gazed eastward, where the chain of Mont Blanc dazzled and shone.

'Now, Georges, you mustn't give in – you've always been so brave.'

'I want to go back up there, Nurse; say what you like and do what you like – and I'm not forgetting what you *have* done for me – I can't breathe down here. It's just too low down for me.'

PART 2
THE MAKING OF A GUIDE

Chapter XVIII

Six months had gone by since the accident, and winter had brought its healing gift of resignation to stricken hearts. Life up at Moëntieu had resumed its usual rhythm. On returning from the hospital Pierre had kept to his room for a long time, watching, from the window that opened wide on to the mountains, the coming of the snows. Every extension of the thick white coverlet seemed to increase his sense of inner peace.

He was seldom down in Chamonix that winter. Occasionally he put on his skis and ran down towards the town in a silken flurry of snow, but he was home again by sundown, for his exertions brought a heightened colour to his cheeks. Then Marie Servettaz would quickly bring him a huge bowl of piping hot tea, with milk in it; and he would sit quietly by the huge china stove, daydreaming, smoking his pipe, or reading. He liked sitting in the big central room, so warm and well-lit, decorated by himself in such excellent taste with superb mountain photographs, signed portraits that famous climbers had given his father, and a few unpretentious pictures from the brush of well-known mountain painters.

Meanwhile Marie did her best, though without much success, to interest him in the coming season at their little pension. He answered all the letters of inquiry promptly, but rather because his correspondents asked for news of the mountains than out of any eagerness to obtain their business. To him they were old and valued friends, especially Hubert de Vallon, for whom he felt a real affection. Hubert wrote of his plans, asked Pierre for information about the state of the snow and the rocks, discussed possible expeditions, and wanted to know all about the new climbs people were planning. Pierre read his letters with a sigh, and freely unburdened himself in his answers, knowing that whatever he said would be sympathetically understood. Aline often came up to see him; they had been friends before they became sweethearts, and their relationship still kept an easy, friendly note. He liked to have her near him, and she spent many hours up there, knitting away beside Marie and his sisters.

After those tragic September days Marie had bravely taken up her work again; she considered herself lucky to have snatched Pierre back from the mountains, but she shuddered at the idea of his returning to them again. There could be no question of that right away, he was still far too weak; the main thing was to keep him from thinking too much about it. Whenever he went down to Chamonix she felt a pang of jealousy; she knew only too well that he would foregather with the three inseparables, Fernand, Paul and Boule, and that they would talk mountains the whole time. With Fernand in particular it had become almost an obsession, and some of his climbs had already won him a reputation for skill and daring. So Marie would take Aline aside and plead with her:

'Fernand shouldn't go filling his head with all this everlasting climbing talk – he really shouldn't. Of course your brother's a fine young man and doesn't see any harm in it. But if he goes on talking about the climbs he's going to do in front of Pierre, how can we expect him to stay with us? We must stop him from going off again; and you must promise to help me, Aline.'

'I'll help you all I can, Marie, but honestly I don't think I have a better chance of being listened to on that subject than you have. All the same, I'll do what I can.'

There was one thing that bothered Pierre: a succession of severe headaches, which left him feeling that his head was quite empty, yet heavy as lead. Since these recurred at regular intervals, he decided to consult the doctor.

He called on him, without previous notice, one fine spring morning.

Dr Coutaz was very highly thought of, especially by the guides and country folk; in winter he was the only doctor who would cheerfully spend several hours on skis, in any kind of weather, to visit patients who, as often as not, could not afford his fee.

He went mainly out of a strong sense of professional duty, but also from a deep feeling for the mountains and the people who live among them. So Pierre had no hesitation in going to see him. The diagnosis was rapid.

'That crack on the rocks has left you with some trouble in your ears, Pierre, and that's causing the headaches; but I'm inclined to think that with time they'll disappear. But you've got to take care. And no funny business. You're liable to have attacks of giddiness, it's the usual effect of an injury like yours; so I'm warning you to look out for it. But you'll know all about it the first time you find yourself looking down into space.'

Pierre turned rather white, but managed to hide his distress at hearing this verdict.

'Come on,' he said with a smile, 'that's not going to stop me going on the hills.'

'Of course not. My warning applies only to big expeditions; there'll be no harm in easy climbs, or snow expeditions, provided you've got a good man with you. But you mustn't think of leading; you might let go suddenly without a word of warning. In the meantime, take it easy up at Moëntieu. By the way, are you having visitors again this summer?'

'Not till May, Doctor. But from then onward we're full up for the whole season.'

'That's one more reason, my boy; there'll be plenty of work up there, and you must do all you can to help your mother; that'll keep you busy and stop you brooding too much about the mountains.'

'Trust me to do that, Doctor, but I'd rather not make any promises; indeed, I'll go so far as to bet you that in less than two months I'll be taking you up the Grépon!'

'Don't talk nonsense, Pierre; vertigo's a serious business. Do what I tell you.'

But Pierre's thoughts were not exactly happy as he walked away from the doctor's.

'Can't believe it's possible – that I'm through with real climbing.' Then his face cheered up and he blamed himself for being so dense. 'What an idiot I am! Of course, it's a conspiracy – Mother must have spoken to the doctor and told him that she was afraid of me starting off again – and perhaps Aline too – perhaps – oh, of course there's Uncle Paul, he plays bridge every evening with the doctor, he'll be in on it too.' His face hardened and he spoke out loud. 'So they think they can stop me from going back – we'll just see if they can!'

There was a deserted look about the square at Chamonix. The Guides' Office was shut, and so was the shop where they sold mountain crystals; in Gros-Bibi's there were exactly two customers who, with the help of a good deal of gesticulating, were concluding some sort of a bargain.

Spring was in the air. For the last week a warm wind had blown through the Chamonix valley. Coming up from the Italian side, it blew down the long trough of the Mer de Glace, broke against the steep grassy slopes of the Aiguille à Bochard, then fell back in warm gusts on the narrow meadows beside the Arve. And there, after one short night, its mild breath had opened up the miraculous flowers of the Alps. Every day last winter's snow receded a little further up the mountainside, first as far as the high pastures, then up to the gullies and glaciers. This advance of spring could be traced, step by step, as nature staged its full-scale attack on the mountains. Woods left tawny and russet by frost and storms put on their green again with the new shoots, but further up, on the 2,000-metre level, everything was still dried up. Snow beds melted away, leaving rusty stains on the face of the landscape. They looked rather like wounds that had not properly healed; like scabs that had been pulled off to reveal the lighter skin below. Then these wounds too began to heal, the high pastures turned green, and the close turf high up on the hillsides added its tone to the fresh harmony of the mountain landscape.

There was water everywhere: in the swollen mountain torrents; in the Arveyron, rising higher every day as it carried off the overflow from the melting glaciers, sweeping down water dense and milky as whitewash, really a sort of fine mud composed of sand, granite and water.

Soon the föhn wind would drop; its characteristic rumble, as it played round the Aiguilles with a curious snoring sound like a steam boiler at high pressure, could be heard no more. And with the dropping of the wind would come the rain, those heavy spring rains that make the grasses sprout up thick and dense in the swampy hollows. Yet the higher slopes would still receive their daily powdering of new snow. And the glaciers, their surface smooth and even, every crevasse stuffed to the brim with the winter's avalanches, would offer a superb playground for the last of the skiers.

But on this particular day the föhn was still blowing, and the pine trees on the steep hillsides swayed as one in the gale. It played on man and beast and caressed them with its warm breath, so sweetly intoxicating after the winter's dry cold.

Up above the plant line, capercailzies, blackcock and ptarmigan croaked on the last of the snow; the cock birds sang in triumph as dawn flushed the sky, leaving their mossy nests in the undergrowth to perch on the larch trees. The chamois were coming up from the depths of the Diosaz towards the glaciers and peaks where they would place their young in safety on inaccessible ledges.

Down in the valley the cattle were slowly and heavily emerging from their winter quarters, dazed after their long imprisonment. Their heavy bells had been replaced on their necks, and now from every meadow and forest the gay music of the lighter cowbells chimed clearly over the deeper vibrations of the bronze, and the solemn note of the greatest bells of all – a dull, mysterious note that sounds like a muffled hammer beaten on a copper gong.

And Pierre, standing there in the middle of the square, felt his blood run more warmly in his veins. He undid his collar, breathed in great draughts of air and took a few steps over to Gros-Bibi's.

'Any sign of the others?'

Gros-Bibi needed no further explanation. 'The others' were the three inseparables, Boule, Fernand and Paul.

'Fernand must be working in the fields,' he said. 'Paul went up to lend a hand at La Tour; they've spread the snow, and cleared the mule track.'

Paul lived at La Tour, the last hamlet in the valley, 1,500 metres up. The snow was so deep up there that they had to clear it away by hand without waiting for it to melt. In autumn long five-metre poles were driven in at intervals to mark the boundary of each field; then in March, following a centuries-old practice, the surface was spread with earth and cinders to make the snow melt faster – it lay at an average depth of two metres.

Snow melts quickly in places which have been 'spread' in this way, though all around it may lie undisturbed. Next, paths are dug out so that carts and plows can pass from one field to another, and work begins again. The unsuspecting stranger may suddenly behold with surprise the pointed ears of a mule sticking up here and there on the wide snowy meadows, barely visible above the high banks that border each field.

Pierre came out of Gros-Bibi's and wandered rather aimlessly through the town. The doctor's words troubled him, and he kept on turning them over in his mind; he felt he must unburden himself to a friend. He walked down the road to the station, crossed the Montenvers footpath, and found himself among the bushes at the foot of the Blaitière alp.

Swollen by the rapid melting of the snows, the torrent frothed and tumbled down 600 metres of hillside to the valley.

Still obsessed by this business of vertigo, Pierre started along a little path that wound up among the fir trees at the side of a big avalanche couloir. The air was sultry and oppressive, and he sweated freely, but did not slacken his pace; he had taken off his jacket and now carried it on his shoulder, chewing a blade of grass, and absorbed in his thoughts. The notion that he – Pierre Servettaz, a guide's son – could be liable to vertigo absolutely appalled him. With all the callousness of youth he used to scoff at it as 'nothing but funk', and, whenever occasion offered, he would make fun of the timid creatures who hesitate on the edge of a precipice, clutch the rock, or shut their eyes to keep out the horrid vision of the drop. When this happened, Pierre would be firm. 'Use your willpower, for heaven's sake,' he would order them, 'vertigo's a thing you can easily control. Up with you, now. Get on, and you'll find it'll pass off.' And now here he was threatened with this very same weakness, for the doctor had told him plainly enough that medical science was so far powerless in face of this particular disability.

So Pierre kept on up the hillside, gradually quickening his pace; occasionally he paused to let his thumping heart calm down a little, then darted off once more at a dog trot up the zigzags of the woodland track.

The Blaitière torrent hurls itself in one bound over a cliff that is more than fifty metres high. It is a particularly impressive sight when the stream is in spate; the water hurtles down with an infernal roar, rebounding from the side of the gorge in iridescent spray; wraiths of mist hover over the fall and weave in and out of the twisted roots of the larches leaning over the abyss. It would certainly have been classified as a 'sublime horror' in the epoch of crinolines, but in our day the sceptical tourist has seen plenty of others and is not to be easily impressed. Only a few unambitious ramblers, attracted by the nearness of the place, come to drink in huge draughts of fresh air, and to enjoy mountain honey and new milk in the little chalet perched aloft like a bird's nest.

Pierre made straight for the fall. He had made up his mind: he was going to find out to his own satisfaction if the doctor had been right or wrong.

Yet this crucial experiment frightened him, and as soon as he heard the roar of the still invisible waterfall, he unconsciously slackened pace; the path now ran on the level, and was really nothing more than a narrow ledge on the steep wooded hillside. He walked along calmly enough, as if he were somehow being protected by the silvery trunks that rose so straight in the shadow, concealing both sky and valley from his eyes. But it was not long before he felt the cool touch of the spray on his cheeks, and heard the deep rumbling of waters in turmoil. He sat down with his head in his hands, and gave himself up to thought. Twenty yards further on, he knew, the wood ended and the sheltered path was abruptly transformed into an airy balcony overlooking space, a unique belvedere from which to view the abyss and the wild gorge down which the torrent hurtled. A few steps would bring him to it. He pictured himself leaning over the frail handrail, bending further and further over, reading his fate in the seething waters below. If he could withstand the fatal fascination of space, that siren call from the waters below, then the test would be conclusive. If he couldn't – if he couldn't – ah, he could picture that too, the wretched scrap of humanity collapsing against the cliff face, clutching the rail, eyes shut tight to keep out the dreadful scene. In that case, his fate would be plain enough. It would mean giving up the mountains, going back to the valleys and becoming one of the vast crowd of plain-dwellers, of people who spend their lives sitting down. It would mean giving up the free and adventurous life of a guide; the exhilarating struggles with granite cliffs, the long descents down icy couloirs, coming steadily down from step to step. It would mean giving all this up.

He took a few hesitating steps, saw the clearing where the path left the wood, and shrank back helplessly. He just couldn't go any further; for a long time he stayed listening to the deep, enticing voice of the torrent that called to him, 'Come to me, come to me, don't be afraid.' He trembled with impotence and despair, he tried to forget his trouble, and like a doomed man who begs for respite, he refused to walk any further. Abruptly he got up, turned his back on the light, then sped off down the deserted path, hurtling down the shortcuts, stumbling against tree trunks, slithering on the pine needles, catching on the branches. He never stopped till he reached the mossy glade just above the meadows, where at last he could breathe more easily. He sat down on a big boulder, and lit his pipe; then let his thoughts wander, watching with abstracted eye the ascending spirals of blue smoke.

The föhn was still blowing up aloft, still puffing like a blacksmith's bellows among the Aiguilles. Its warm breath reached down to the valley and gently fanned Pierre's perspiring face. He slowly mopped himself with his scarf, got up, and continued on his way, wandering aimlessly along some rather sketchy paths. Finally, he came to a decision, skirted a thicket of alder and birch, crossed the stoneshoot of the Grépon torrent heaped up with the earthy debris of an avalanche, and came down on the hamlet of Mouilles.

An old woman was scouring out iron pans under the spout of the water trough.

'Good day, Madame Lourtier,' Pierre greeted her. 'Is Fernand around?"

'Oh, it's you, Pierre, is it? How are you feeling, poor lad? And your mother? I should be going over to see her myself, but I'm getting old. Now, is it really Fernand you want, or Aline?' she added with a twinkle.

Pierre blushed. 'Both of them, Madame Lourtier.'

'Fernand's cutting down brushwood at Biollay beside the Arveyron, on the plot of ground we got from Grandfather, and Aline's out yonder with the cows – she can't be very far off. You know the way. Don't lose any time – goodbye!'

'Goodbye!'

Pierre hurried along the track that led into the bosky wood of Bouehet, and on its further side stepped out into the little meadow enclosed by stone walls where the Lourtiers' cattle grazed, their cowbells ringing gaily from their necks. Aline was sitting on the grass, a kerchief knotted round her head, a hazel switch under her arm, busy knitting a cardigan of thick natural-coloured wool. Blended with the tinkling of the bells was the deep rumble of the Arveyron hard by, its swollen waters bearing down their burden of snow, and the melancholy whistling of the wind, some 3,000 metres above. Good smells from the reborn earth mingled with the aromatic odours of woods in springtime.

Fernand was cutting down alders and loading them on to an old haycart. The unharnessed mule was peaceably nibbling the meadow flowers; his collar had slipped down on to his head and was only kept on by his long, quivering ears. Fernand left his work to walk across to Pierre; then both of them strolled across the meadow towards Aline. Placidly she watched them approach, and only betrayed her pleasure by the particularly tender look in her fine black eyes with which she welcomed Pierre.

The two lads lay down on the grass at her feet. Noticing that

Pierre seemed out of sorts, Aline asked, 'What's the matter, Pierre? Is anything wrong? Are you ill? Or has something happened to disturb you?'

'It's nothing.'

'Don't be silly, of course there's something, I can see it in your face. Come on, tell us.'

'Honestly, it's nothing at all. I was bored at home, so I came over to see you. Time goes very slowly if you're good for precious little, like me. And this blasted wind gets on my nerves; it brings on my headache.'

'It's only the usual spring wind, Pierre,' said Fernand, 'it'll soon be gone. It always unsettles everybody; just look at the cattle.'

They watched the little herd of ten beasts. The cows came and went, scooping up tufts of grass with their long tongues, tossing their horns, turning around, bellowing. Prominent among them was a powerful creature, jet black but for its tawny back, with truly magnificent horns; it wasn't still for a moment, but pawed the ground with its feet, snorted noisily, and teased the others with the tip of its horns.

'Gently, Lionne, gently,' shouted Fernand.

'Is she your fighter?'

'She is indeed,' put in Aline. 'He took it into his head to make her a "fighting queen" when we go up to the alp. Look at the result – no more milk, and a bad-tempered, quarrelsome animal, just a bundle of nerves.'

'But a grand fighter, Aline. Just look at that neck, as thick as a bull's, and those slender legs. If she can hold her own with the former queens, she'll be champion this summer over the whole alp of Balme.'

'I'd rather she gave more milk, like my lovely Parise here,' answered Aline, and pointed to a fine well-built animal with a swollen udder and veins that stood up on her belly.

Fernand's chief interest, apart from climbing, was in his cattle. Although still young for the job, he had selected the few cows that represented his family's fortune; then, bitten by this peculiar enthusiasm that you find in the valleys bordering the Swiss canton of Valais, he had set his heart on rearing a *reine à cornes,* a fighting cow that cost him a pretty penny without bringing anything in. His sister would not allow this wild, useless creature into the byre, and she was full of reproaches on the subject.

'Don't you agree with me, Pierre,' she appealed to him, 'Lionne's just another useless mouth to feed?'

'Well, Aline,' he replied, avoiding such a delicate topic, 'what with the mountains, and our chalet, and hunting in autumn, and skiing in winter – *I* don't need to ask for anything more!'

'A queer hotel manager you'll make!'

'I never asked to be one,' objected Pierre, 'and anyway, I'm never going to be one – unless'; his face clouded over, he looked listless and sad, and the sentence was left unfinished –

'Unless?'

'Oh nothing, I was talking nonsense.'

Fernand stood up. 'I'll leave you two here ... I've got to go home with the cart. See you later at Breton's, Pierre ... about four o'clock, and we'll have some *fondue.*'

As the cart jogged off, leaving Pierre and Aline alone in the clearing, they drew nearer to each other. Pierre lay for a minute or two without speaking or moving; then, sick at heart, he heaved himself up, put his head on Aline's knees, and gave himself up to thought. Clouds were scudding across the sky, and the leaves still on the trees murmured at every gust of wind, drowning the roar of the torrent and the music of the cowbells. Then all would be calm again. All at once, Pierre felt he must speak.

'The snow's going; look, Aline, the rocks are as dry as in summer. We'll be able to start early this year.'

'Always harping on about those mountains of yours! Try to think of something else for a change.'

She bent over him, and he could feel her breath on his cheek.

Aline ran her fingers idly through his tangled brown hair, while he lay passive as a child. Her gentle touch on his brow soothed his uneasiness and dispelled all troubling thoughts. He had nearly forgotten all about the doctor and his warning. Then all of a sudden it came back to him, and his face took on the hardness of an old marble statue bronzed by many a summer's sun.

Aline was worried. 'What is it, Pierre? What's come over you? Pierre, tell me what's troubling you,' and in a very low voice she added, 'I love you, Pierre, truly I do.' She cupped her hands round his upturned head and gazed tenderly into his eyes. But he turned away with a beaten look. 'Don't you want to tell me your trouble?'

'Yes, of course – only later. Don't ask me more about it, Aline; I love you too, I love you terribly.'

'But you're always thinking about the mountains, aren't you?'

'Would you stop me from climbing?'

'No, Pierre, I wouldn't; but it would give me a lot of trouble and worry.' And her hands stole back to his hair.

'Promise me that you'll only go as an amateur. You could manage – ' then she corrected herself with a smile, '*we* could manage very well on what we got from the pension and the cattle. So why try to be a guide? When you want to go climbing, you can go as an amateur, with Fernand and the others – but never with a client. That's where the risk comes in. Never knowing what sort of a man you're going with – running the risk of being pulled off by a fellow you've never seen before … And if you'd like it, I could sometimes come along with you. I like climbing, you know; when I was just a little girl every time I went with Fernand to the high pastures, I used to go up to the glaciers, to explore that world that took all our menfolk away and didn't always return them. You see how happy we could be together.' And she added in a whisper – as if she were half ashamed of using a word she had only met in novels, and associated with sophisticated love affairs: 'Darling.'

Their faces were almost touching: he had only to raise his head slightly to kiss her tenderly. Their lips met, and parted, but their brows still touched, and her curls mingled with his. Pierre too spoke in a whisper as if he were telling a secret.

'Aline, you're a wonderful girl, and I don't know what I'd do without you.'

'Without me – and without the mountains.'

He did not say a word in reply.

'You know I'm not jealous.'

'It's in the blood, Aline; you mustn't hold it against me. Just remember – Father did all he could to put me off climbing; if I wanted to, I could certainly lead a far more comfortable life. Uncle Paul would help us build a bigger place, and I know very well I could run a big hotel; yet none of it means a thing to me. I only care for that' – and his finger pointed to the jagged line of peaks – 'and that.' His sweeping gesture took in clearing, trees, wood, torrent, cattle; then turning on Aline with a laugh and taking her in his arms, 'That too!'

'Look out, Pierre! Someone might see us.'

'Well, aren't we engaged to be married?'

'Yes, but let's be sensible. It's time to go in. Give me a hand with the cattle.'

They walked slowly back through the bushes, the tinkling herd in front of them. The bells filled the valley with their music. Far off, the deep note of the church bell sounded the Angelus, its solemn voice dominating the others, till it too was cut short by a gust of wind that sent a shiver and rustle through the slender spires of the pine trees.

Chapter XIX

Up at Moëntieu, everybody was asleep. It might have been two o'clock in the morning, perhaps three. Everyone? No, Pierre was awake and restless, tortured by the wretched obsession that had taken so firm a hold of his poor head, and he tossed and turned in vain attempts to sleep.

As there was no one else to talk to, he sat up in bed, looked out of the window, and began talking to himself. It was a strange monologue, punctuated by head-shaking, and cheered by gleams of hope, that were quickly succeeded by the reaction of despair.

'You idiot,' he scolded himself, 'you've got it all wrong … The doctor doesn't know a thing about it.' Then doubt crept in again. 'Well, but why did you hesitate the other day? You could have found out the truth quite easily. You'll have to try again, for you simply must know. You've just got to lean over a big drop … then, once and for all, you'll know.' Once again caution made him hesitate. 'And if you fell? Well, so much the better. Would you rather drag around the valley all your days, seeing your friends going off on their climbs, waiting around for them at the corner of the square as if they were one of the sights of the place? God, no. You're going to find out.'

Brusquely Pierre threw off his bedclothes, got up, put on the light, and dressed himself quickly and quietly. He tiptoed to the staircase, boots in hand. The new door gave a slight squeak; he shivered. 'If Mother wakes!' He felt as if he had embarked on a shameful flight.

Step by step, often stopping to listen, he descended the stairs to the dark kitchen where the smell of food still lingered. The faint glow from the last dying embers was reflected in the iron door of the stove.

Pierre opened the door: it was a frosty night, with a sprinkling of stars. 'A fine night,' he thought, 'a fine night to learn one's fate!'

He went back to the kitchen and warmed up some strong coffee on the spirit stove. He forced himself to eat some bread and cream cheese, but it stuck in his throat. From the larder he took some cold mutton, cheese and eggs. He filled his water bottle with coffee and pushed everything into his sack. Then he unhooked his axe, leaned it against his chair, and slowly pulled on his boots. A sudden noise made him start: was it the floor creaking above him? No; only the various little sounds made by the newly-built chalet as it rested from its labours and, tired of holding up the roof, relaxed with creaks from every joint and beam.

Pierre left the house as stealthily as a burglar. He walked mechanically along the winding path, his feet stumbling against the stones in the darkness. Where was he going? He had no idea; all he knew was that he must climb.

It was not quite so dark on the screes of the Roumna Blanche, which trailed down like a light scarf on the dark surface of the mountainside. Gradually Pierre's eyes got used to the darkness, and he began to distinguish the black silhouette of the tops against the sombre sky. He climbed with his old accustomed stride, head well up, breathing in the freshness of the night, then plunged into the darker gulf of the forest. The path mounted steeply between tall spruce trees. Below, the ground fell steeply away; above, the hillside presented a steep wall to which clung trees with tapering trunks and twisted branches.

Pierre had forgotten his lantern, but it did not seem to matter. He allowed himself to be guided by instinct, and walked on his toes, drawing pleasure from each contact with the ground, all his senses wide awake. From time to time he even shut his eyes the better to drink in the mountain night. Then he would open them again and look up to the top of the clearing, cut through the trees, that marked the track. A solitary star twinkled frostily, and Pierre set his course by it. Sometimes he stumbled against an obstacle, sometimes his foot found no hold; then he would hug the slope more closely. It all seemed unreal to him, and the winds from the great spaces filled him with a wild exhilaration. A lighter shape detached itself from the mass of shadows: it was the Chablettes refreshment hut. The building was deserted. Pierre sat on the step in front of the locked door and shivered; mechanically he undid his sack, took out the coffee and gulped several mouthfuls. Down in Chamonix myriad lights sparkled and shone. A crash echoed across the valley; one of the séracs on the Bossons glacier had broken off, and the noise was answered by the hooting of a great horned owl.

Pierre started up again: a big bird took off from a low bough and flew away on a current of wind; probably a blackcock.

As he continued to mount, his self-confidence increased. This climb by night enchanted him, and he laid himself open to receive every impression that his beloved mountains could give. But the dark curtain of the forest was brusquely torn aside as the path approached the great avalanche track. Far above his head the cliffs of the Brévent bounded the horizon like an unscalable prison wall. The path mounted in narrower and narrower zigzags, here and there crossed by the trail of an avalanche. It was slippery going on the earth that lay thinly on the ice, but Pierre had recovered his assurance and strode along with no hesitation whatever, gripping his axe firmly: night was all around him, but the sky was visibly paler, like an ink drawing that is gradually receiving a wash of water. He came out on to the plateau of Planpraz, well above the tree line. Little gusts of wind blew from the east; an indeterminate light heralded the dawn. He opened his mouth wide to the freshness, and it filled his body with deep content.

Chavanne was deserted, though from the chalet came a faint smell of curdled milk and fermented hay, blown down on the wind. He stopped to rest, for it was still too early to go on. It would take him an hour to the foot of the cliff above, 400 metres high and smooth as marble.

A thousand metres below his feet was the black hole of the valley; opposite him the chain of Mont Blanc, which had seemed to grow higher the further he climbed, had now resumed its normal dimensions. Its topmost dome rested, like the dome of a Byzantine cathedral, on the intricate architecture of the Aiguilles, whose outline was sharpened by distance. They formed a forest of stone where pillars, towers, campaniles and turrets, all decked with snow, crowded together in fine confusion. The Bossons and Taconnaz glaciers, seamed with lateral crevasses, crawled lazily down like enormous reptiles.

It grew colder; Pierre's teeth began to chatter, but he could not tear himself away from the sight of yet another sunrise. In one second everything seemed to take on a new freshness and purity. A tiny pink glow rested on the summit, though its source remained hidden somewhere in the east, where faint glimmers showed in the sky, and as dawn came up the air grew lighter. Pierre could have burst into song; every fibre of his being reached out to welcome this renewal of life. He got up, settled his rucksack on his shoulders, and, walking up in all the freshness of early morning, reached the little corrie under the Brévent. It lay still in shadow, and the boulders on the scree took on queer yet somehow familiar shapes. Up he strode, in a fever of expectation.

With the path to guide him, he threaded his way up under a rickety turret, then abandoned the path for a faint track that led up to the foot of the Brévent cliffs.

This face of the Brévent is a short and easy climb for an experienced cragsman, but it is very exposed. Guides like taking beginners there, also clients whom they want to test before a big expedition; the rock is very flaky and needs extreme care.

Pierre had done this climb several times before; his reason for coming back to it now was because he knew how admirably it would provide the test he needed; a man who suffers from vertigo would never get up the final pitch. His former doubts came flooding back; he dreaded the failure that he half expected, and his confidence deserted him. He began to hesitate. The way to the rocks led across a steep grassy couloir; it could be pretty slippery when the turf was wet with dew. Ordinarily, Pierre would have bounded gaily from one stone to another. Why, then, on this occasion, could he only advance with the utmost precaution, driving the point of his axe into the ground to steady himself, leaning unnecessarily into the slope instead of putting his feet down boldly? Anybody who had seen him from some way off would have thought, with some alarm, that he was a beginner who was not too sure of himself.

He felt horribly uneasy; he turned his eyes away from the downward slope; stumbled, made a false step, and nervously clutched his axe. He clung to the shaft, and his brow dripped with sweat; he was hideously afraid.

Yet somehow he struggled on and, to his considerable relief, set foot on the scree at the base of the chimney; the stones gave way under his feet and showers of gravel rattled down into the open mouth of the couloir below. With some difficulty he reached the foot of the rocks. There was nothing now before him but an interminable sun-warmed cliff. It was split vertically by a gloomy cleft that the sun never reached, set between deep-cut, jagged walls, full of loose stones and dripping with moisture.

Pierre started up. His limbs felt unnaturally heavy; he tested the rock carefully with his fingers before entrusting himself to a hold. Then he shook off his inertia and, summoning up his courage, braced himself for the assault.

The first obstacle was a tower that overlooked the entrance to the gully. Pierre got up easily enough; the cold touch of the schisty rock restored his confidence, and he climbed with dash and elegance, his eyes riveted on the rock before him. Shadows were all around him, and in the narrow couloir he felt himself at one with the mountain. He climbed up quickly; the gully cut deeper into the cliff and every pitch offered a fresh difficulty that he overcame with ease. Confidence once more flowed through him; though he still dared not turn outwards. His fingers tested each doubtful hold, and now and again he had to send down a loose stone before he could go on himself; it fell into the gorge, giving off a smell of burnt gunpowder as it crashed against the rock. After 200 metres of this, Pierre reached the point where the gorge abuts on to the sheer wall itself. He had come to a dead end; an impossible-looking crack that ended in an impassable overhang lay between him and the summit ridge, over which projected a heavy, tottering cornice of snow.

His job now was to reach the broad ledge halfway up and traverse the whole width of the face to rejoin the central arête. Getting out of the chimney, a thing easy enough in itself, demanded care; the holds were big, but none too sound, and he had to make use of odd wrinkles and projections for his hands and feet. With redoubled precaution Pierre started off, forcing himself not to think of the now considerable drop beneath him. A slight effort brought him on to a delightful sunny terrace that overlooked the whole face. A stone dropped there would fall 500 metres before it touched ground; it was a triumph of perpendicularity. This precipice, though on a smaller scale, can be compared with some of the rock walls in the Dolomites where the climber is slung between heaven and earth.

The terrace makes a sort of peaceful haven halfway up the wall; space is all around – above, below, on the right, the left; and from the summit ridge the projecting cornice cocks an inquiring eye on the climber.

With unseeing eyes Pierre gazed at the magnificent panorama of peaks and glaciers from which only the blue depths of the valley and the rumbling stream divided him. He was nervous and jumpy, and kept his eyes on the tiny crack at the far end of the terrace which would take him away from these airy hazards and up to the summit. It was the one tricky part of the whole climb, and it was short; only ten metres at most.

The terrace ended abruptly. To reach the crack Pierre had to make a long stride over the dizzy precipice, and then practically throw himself across to reach some minute holds and get a footing in the crack. It ran like a gash up the face and overhung the precipitous wall. Many a novice has fumbled badly at this point. Pierre knew this very well, and as he moved forward his limbs began to tremble. His whole fate was about to be put to the test. He tried to lean over and reach the other side of this bottomless pit, but felt irresistibly drawn towards the abyss below. From this point, the eye looks straight down on the screes of the Roumna Blanche that plunge towards the valley at an appallingly steep angle. It struck Pierre that if he were to fall, his body would hurtle down 1,500 metres with never a check, down to the highest meadows just below the forest.

Right in the middle of them he spotted Le Moëntieu. From here it looked like a toy chalet; the roof glinted in the sun, and a thin wisp of blue smoke ascended from the chimney. Marie must have noticed his disappearance; perhaps she was even now wandering anxiously around in search of her son.

And he was up there, shivering and hesitating, on the point of shirking the test for the second time. He reasoned aloud with himself: 'What are you waiting for? You've done this pitch at least twenty times. There's nothing to it but one big step, then you lean forward, you grab the hold up there, and it's done. You could do it with your eyes shut. Get a move on.'

He leaned forward, bent his knees, made ready to spring – then at the last minute his whole body hesitated, rooted to the terrace by some occult force. He stretched out his arms, but could not bring himself to take the decisive step; far from it! His heart was in his mouth, and in a frenzy of disgust he threw himself down on the terrace. Flat on his face on the warm rock, he sobbed like a child. He abandoned himself to despair. So it was true! He was no better than an old bundle of cast-off rags, a pitiable object who could not control his nerves and willpower. He screamed in his fury at the crows that wheeled mockingly round him, but his voice was carried off in the wind.

To despair succeeded listlessness. With his back to the mountain he let his gaze play sadly on the scene before him, picking out the various landmarks: Mont Blanc, where he had led the way last autumn; the Dru, tacked on to the Aiguille Verte and looking from here absurdly low; the Grépon with its castellated outline where on one occasion, spurning the ordinary route, he had sprung from block to block, stepping lightheartedly over the most ghastly drops. But this wretched gap that he had to cross now was quite another matter.

'Tie yourself on!' murmured a voice inside him. 'You've got to fight this, Pierre, you've got to beat it – come on, jump!'

Without stopping to consider why he did it, he uncoiled the

rope, tied himself on, just as if he had had a party behind him. Anyone seeing him now would have put him down as crazy; and perhaps, indeed, he was. For he began to speak out loud, as if he were addressing a client, trying to deceive himself into thinking he was once again first on the rope. It was certainly a strange enough dialogue.

'Just stop there, Monsieur, all you've got to do is to watch my rope so that it doesn't get tangled. It's easy, just a step across. The drop below? That's nothing. You just take one big step – a metre – you take steps a metre long in ordinary life, so all you need to do is to imagine you're walking along a pavement, it's absolutely the same. But first of all, you can watch – I'm off! Safeguard my rope. That's right, and now, just watch!'

His words excited him, and he tittered nervously: slowly he advanced to the gap, with trembling arms and quaking knees. Then, terrified that he might once more be going to shirk, he started talking aloud again, putting heart into his imaginary client.

'Keep your eye on me, Monsieur! Bend forward, and – hop!'

Shutting his eyes, he let his body swing over the gap; his hands hit the rock opposite and there he stayed suspended, a sort of human arch over the abyss. He lacked the courage to open his eyes for fear of finding himself face to face with the void. He drummed on the wall with his fingers, anxiously seeking that familiar hold that somehow just eluded his questing hand. His nails scratched over the rock in vain; his feet slipped a little under the effort. Good God, the relief when his left hand found a sketchy hold! He clenched his fingers, let go his foothold, and swung his body across. He was now flat against the rock, hanging by one hand over space. Opening his eyes he saw an enormous hold for the right hand that spelled safety; he could not quite reach it, however; first of all he would have to find a hold for his feet – there must be plenty – just there. He realised this, and he also realised that if he were to look down, well, then, in a wild frenzy he would just let go. With all the strength he could muster he hugged the rock like a beginner, and scrabbled with his feet without finding any sort of lodgment. Then exhaustion overtook him, his left arm was strained to the breaking point, his joints gave; he screamed with terror, tried to fight off his invisible enemy, and felt that he was about to let go.

No! His right hand had found a hold hidden in a corner of the crack; with a last instinctive movement he relaxed, then drew himself together and in one muscular bound flung himself right into the crack. How good to feel the touch of the rock all around him! It took him back to the days when he would rush to his mother for safety. But was he safe? Not yet. For minutes that seemed like hours he remained in that position, jammed in the crack, eyes shut, head against the rock. But he was tiring quickly: so, still keeping his eyes shut, he fumbled for another hold. There they were, plenty of them, and he heaved himself up and into a little cave. At last he could relax. An edge of rock cut off the downward view; only a very steep grass slope lay between him and the top. He felt better now, in spite of that menacing cornice above that he would somehow have to get over. But the fatal spell had been broken, and he could breathe again more freely.

He left the safety of the cave with considerable regret, coiled up the rope that trailed behind him and continued his climb. Up here, on the slope above the precipice, grew primroses, gentians and moss.

But there was always that awful precipice! He could not stand it any more; his head spun round and round and so did the landscape. He crawled up on all fours, digging the head of his axe into the slippery grass to help him on. What a ridiculous and humiliating attitude it was – what on earth would his friends say if they were to see him crawling up like an insect! But deep inside him he cared not a rap, he had come to the end of his pride, he had said goodbye to self-respect and could only think of saving his skin. To escape from this precipice that obsessed him! Escape from the mountains which so clearly were no longer meant for him! Escape from this awful dizzy wall to the hard snow slopes on the northern side! He crouched there on all fours under the cornice, like a poodle trying to open a door. He could climb it directly if he could only make himself stand straight up above the precipice, drive in the head of his axe, and hoist himself upon it; but he could not bring himself to make this movement that would make victory certain. Instead he burrowed in the snow like a mole, scooping out a tunnel with quick little strokes of his axe, till it was big enough for him to crawl through. At last he came out on the further slope; at last his eyes could rest on something not so steep, not so vertical, not so desperate. Once more he felt that mountains were friendly beings; the snow-covered pastures of Carlaveyron revealed the gentlest of contours, delighting him. He stood up in the snow like a madman and started straight down in a standing glissade!

In a shadowed gully, the harder snow took him off his guard; he overbalanced, fell, and shot down the névé into a boulder-strewn corrie: his glissade ended at a big boulder which he struck with some force. The shock made him lose consciousness.

When he came to his senses the sun was very low on the horizon. Mist was rising from the plains of Sallanches, floating above the Désert de Platé, and filling the gorges of Diosaz. The sun was setting in splendour behind the Col des Aravis; the Chamonix valley was already deep in shadow, and the white glacier streams were lost in its steel-blue depths.

Painfully Pierre heaved himself up, as if awakening from a long stupor; he rubbed his face with snow that froze and reddened his hands. Then he noticed that he had bled copiously from a scalp wound. He set off slowly, trying to make out the mule track between the patches of snow, and made a long detour around the Brévent chimney and the tourists' way up it, protected by iron railings. He avoided everything steep and precipitous, and would have given his soul to be back among the flat and smiling fields below. He was glad of the approaching darkness that veiled the depths beneath.

When he reached Planpraz the shadows from the valley rose up to meet him. He picked his way down very carefully, refusing the shortcuts between the zigzags of the path, steering his course by the uncertain light that filtered through the forest trees. At long last he felt with delight the soft and springy turf of the meadows under his feet.

There was a glimmer of light at Moëntieu. Pierre made for it, with wavering steps: his mother would no doubt be waiting for him, and he must not show himself to her in this state, dirty and torn and bloodstained. He stopped at the trough, washed himself in the running water, put on his hat to conceal his scalp wound, and at last, satisfied that he was now fairly presentable, he pushed open the door of the chalet.

Marie Servettaz was indeed waiting for him, sitting motionless in the chimney corner, her knitting on her knee. She let out a sigh of relief when he appeared.

'Is that you, Pierre? Where have you come from at this time of night?'

But she got no answer. With a surly look Pierre crammed his hat further down on his head, hung his sack and ice-axe on the rack, and began to go upstairs to his room.

'The soup's on the fire, Pierre,' said Marie gently; then added, with a faint tinge of reproach, 'Why don't you tell me when you're going off? We've been anxious about you all day.'

He turned on her fiercely: 'D'you think I'm a baby?'

Marie did not attempt to answer. She ladled out the soup, and betook herself with a sigh to her own room.

Pierre sat down and ate his meal slowly, staring straight in front of him; he poured himself out a brimming glass of wine, then rose from the table and with heavy steps mounted the staircase to the upper storey.

Chapter XX

Uncle Paul was strolling down the Rue Joseph-Vallot, with his thumbs stuck into the armholes of his waistcoat, and on the back of his bald and glistening head perched a straw hat which had become a byword in Chamonix.

'Paul's changed his cap for his straw hat,' they would say. 'Summer can't be far off.'

But on this particular evening Paul, contrary to his usual habit, was saying very little. He smoked his pipe in short puffs and looked as if he had something on his mind. He passed the Café National without going in, proceeded down the road and eventually found himself on the outskirts of the town. It was the hour when work was ending in factory, field and office, and the street was fuller than usual. People were doing their shopping and exchanging local gossip. Everybody had a civil word of greeting for that important citizen, Paul Dechosalet.

'Good evening, Monsieur Paul. Here's the fine weather at last! Are the hotel bookings coming on nicely?'

'Not a thing! It looks like a bad season,' grumbled Uncle Paul.

This provoked discreet smiles, for everybody knew that Paul always liked to expect the worst – and yet every summer his hotel was invariably full. Like the cautious old peasant that he was, he preferred not to display his wealth. You never could tell!

Paul Dechosalet walked up and down the street, obviously expecting somebody. The country lasses were riding in on their bicycles from all directions with huge tin milk cans on their backs; they were bringing the milk, as they did every evening, to the municipal creamery. And there, in fact, was Aline getting off her bicycle; she stood holding the handlebars and hailed him cheerily. Uncle Paul took a few steps in her direction.

'I was waiting for you, Aline. Run along and empty your can, then come back and we'll have a talk.'

What on earth did he want to talk about, she wondered, as she rushed off to leave her milk. She was back in a flash and, wheeling her bicycle with one hand, caught up Uncle Paul, who had kept on down the street. They walked for a while in silence; then Paul, who had been maturing his words, came quickly to the point.

'It's about Pierre, Aline! I'm deeply concerned about him. You must have noticed, my dear, how terribly altered he's been lately. My sister's spoken to me about it. It appears that he doesn't open his mouth at home, he turns up just in time for dinner, bolts his food, and is off again, without saying a word. Three days out of six he comes in drunk, but there's worse than that – he never used to drink, but now he's in and out of all the bars in town, and the lowest ones at that! He seems to be avoiding his old friends, Fernand, Boule, all those fine young lads; they used to be like brothers together. And now he's gone all wild like this. I keep wondering what's on his mind. What's he like with you, Aline?'

Aline hung her head sadly and struggled to find words for her feelings.

'I can't understand his attitude, Monsieur Paul; he behaves to me just as he does to everybody else – he carries on in such a brutal, such a painful way. For no reason at all he'll order me roughly to go away, then a minute later he'll ask my pardon with eyes like a whipped dog's – and finally he'll go off to the fields by himself. We've seen him lying for hours at a time on his back watching the clouds. If only that were the worst … but you're right, he's taken to drinking. He goes from one café to another, almost always alone, he sits down and stays there for hours with his glass in front of him and his head full of horrible thoughts. It scares me just to think about it! And I keep wondering how I could help him out of it.

'Fernand, Boule and Paul have done the best they could to get him back, but he always finds some excuse for not going with them. The way I see it, it's his fall on the Dru that's done this to him … it must still be affecting him there … ' (and Aline pointed to her forehead).

'All the same,' argued Uncle Paul, 'he was perfectly normal for the first six months of his convalescence; his mother told me that all this dates from a certain day, about a month ago, when he disappeared for the whole day and came back without telling them where he'd been. Up in the mountains, no doubt, for his boots were caked as if he'd been walking for a long time in snow, and then when she was putting his clothes away my sister saw bloodstains at the neck. She wanted to ask him about it, but he flew into a rage, so she gave it up. His eyes were bloodshot and he swore at her. "Don't ever speak to me of today, Mother." She didn't want to make him worse so she didn't say any more.'

'I knew that, Monsieur Paul, and I've been trying to puzzle it out. All he would say, one evening when he was particularly low, were these words: "An old bundle of cast-off rags, Aline, that's what I am, good for nothing. You needn't worry any more about me – catch me setting foot on the mountains again!" And that struck me as so queer, coming from him; he used to be so desperately keen to start climbing again.'

'Aline, we simply must do something for him, and I believe that you're the only person who can make him see reason. If we can stop him from drinking, that's something. But Pierre never was one for the bottle; he's drinking because he's taken a bad beating about something. We must try to find out what it is ... I thought perhaps it might be something to do with you?'

'Oh, Monsieur Paul!' exclaimed Aline indignantly.

'I see I was all wrong, and I'm glad I was.'

What Uncle Paul did not add was that Pierre had often been seen in bad company in a dive outside the town. It was all so unlike him, it might have been an entirely different person they were discussing.

'We must stop this whole crazy business,' he went on, 'and there's only one thing to be done about it. You must do all you can – without preaching at him, for he's not a lad to take advice – but in loving him more than ever, in surrounding him with your affection, in trying to take his mind off his trouble. And the others must do their share. Tell Fernand and Boule to do all they can to make him come back to their gang. If necessary they can start by going to the café with him a few times, to get him accustomed to them again … then perhaps they could take him out a little with them – no real climbs, of course, but you know how it is, there's nothing like a meal up in a chalet with your pals to cheer you up. Now, are you going to help?'

'Of course I am, Monsieur Paul, I'm very grateful to you for taking such an interest in Pierre. He's such a good person, you know. He must be ill, or else there's something he won't tell us. Well, we'll try to find out! Thank you, Monsieur Paul.'

'You can call me Uncle Paul, Aline, for I'm sure that as soon as all this business is settled, you'll be getting married quickly – and I'll be one of the witnesses at your wedding! Now away with you, Niece – it'll be dark before you get home.' Aline sprang lightly into the saddle, one foot on the pedal, and the empty can on her back.

'Thank you, Uncle Paul! I do like you!'

Then away she went, with a smile on her lips; hope was springing up inside her once again, for there is nothing a girl likes better than a conspiracy on behalf of the man she loves.

Uncle Paul put his straw hat back on his head, wiped his moustache, took out a cigar, lit it with his lighter, and slowly walked back up the road to the square.

Chapter XXI

Early in the morning Paul Mouny came down on his motorbicycle from the village of La Tour, and immediately set out to find Boule and Fernand Lourtier. Fernand was sawing wood behind the house, and steadily stacking the logs under the gallery in neat symmetrical piles that smelled of pitch and resin. At the sight of Paul he left his bench and saw, and inquired cheerfully:

'Coming to give me a hand, Paul? I've still got quite a few to saw up.'

'Just chuck that and go and change,' ordered Paul. 'Georges gets back from Geneva today. We're going to meet him and celebrate his return!'

'Is Boule coming along?'

'Of course. You know – we ought to let Pierre know too.'

'D'you think he'd be likely to come? He's like a bear with a sore head these days.'

'Then all the more reason why he ought to come; he can't refuse to do that for Georges!'

'That's true; you ride up to Moëntieu, and I'll go across to Boule's.'

Paul headed his motorbike up the stony bumpy track to Moussoux; he took his machine as far as possible, up to the wooden cross that was erected during the last mission to the village, just behind the twisty path up to Moëntieu. Leaning his bike against the base of the cross, he climbed quickly up to Pierre's home. Marie Servettaz greeted him listlessly.

'He isn't here. He went off by the shortcut a quarter of an hour ago. You might find him somewhere near Ruskin's Stone, that's where he goes to daydream when he has one of his solitary fits.'

Paul followed the little path that cuts across the meadows and undergrowth from Moëntieu to Ruskin's Stone. Soon he spotted Pierre, lying on his side on the grass some distance away, head on elbow, looking across at the chain of Mont Blanc.

'Morning, Pierre!'

Pierre answered with a grunt which sounded barely civil.

'I've come to collect you,' continued Paul, in no way put out by this offhand reception. 'Georges is coming. So Boule and I thought that we should go and meet him and take him somewhere to celebrate – that's what I've come to tell you – to make him forget his condition a little.'

'Haven't got time to go down.'

'Haven't got time! Look here, you've got to come with us, you can't refuse to do that for Georges. He wouldn't be happy if you weren't there.'

'Well, I don't care.'

Paul, standing in front of his friend, began to get angry. He raised his voice:

'Pull yourself together, man. You haven't been yourself for some time now. Have we done anything to rile you without realising it? If we have, you should tell us: can't have misunderstandings among friends. We haven't? Then you haven't got any excuse.' And Paul became urgent: 'Hurry up, can't you. The bus will be up in an hour's time.'

'No!'

Pierre snapped out his refusal. His mind was made up.

'Look here, Pierre,' went on Paul, 'you're behaving very badly. Georges lost both feet in saving your poor father's client. He's got every right to expect your gratitude, and there you are not wanting to show him even a little by coming to meet him! I just can't understand you.'

Pierre raised himself up and hid his face in his hands.

'That's enough – shut up, you idiot! Can't you see that I'm absolutely miserable and don't want to see anybody at all? Haven't you ever wanted to shut yourself up and get away from people altogether? What do you think I've got to look forward to now? I only wish you and the others would leave me alone.'

'What in God's name are you talking about? You've got a wonderful life ahead of you. You're young, you're going to get married, and you've got a fine house of your own. What more d'you want?'

'I want – but what's the good, you wouldn't understand.'

'For God's sake, Pierre, please tell me. I don't know what's the matter with you, but I'm sure I could help and do something about it.'

Pierre gave a mirthless laugh; he was sitting down now and his hands played with the tufts of grass.

'Nobody can help me, Paul, nobody – not even Aline, though I'm very fond of her – not even yourself – and I'm fond of you too.'

'Oh, skip it! Stop thinking about your troubles, and come along with us. There's plenty of people with worse troubles than yours. Look at Georges, for one. There he is, a cripple for life, no more climbing for *him*. And it was all he had to live on; I know that American's given him some sort of a pension, and that the Provident Fund has made him a grant, but you can't get away from the fact that he's lost the toes on both his feet, and they can't be stuck on again.'

Pierre was in no mood to argue, and soon he gave in.

'Oh, all right, I'll come. It's for Georges's sake I'm going – I see the point of what you said a minute ago. It's quite true that my family ought to be grateful to him. Go ahead, and I'll catch up with you.'

'No, I'm waiting for you here,' insisted Paul, who didn't want to let him get away. 'I've got the bike at La Croix de Moussoux, and I'll give you a lift down.'

Pierre got up, spat out the grass stem he was chewing, and preceded Paul down the path towards Moussoux.

A few minutes later they were strolling along the road to the station with Boule and Fernand, and without knowing exactly why, Pierre suddenly felt very glad to be among his friends again.

The raucous note of an air horn warned them of the arrival of the mail bus from Geneva. Pierre tried to catch sight of Georges among the crowd of passengers.

Georges was the last to get down, very slowly and with the

help of a stick. His thin drawn face bore witness to all he had been through. Otherwise, he looked quite normal; but if you glanced at his feet, you saw that he had on two strange-looking shoes, shorter than you would expect, made of solid leather reinforced by thick rubber soles. In them he walked fairly easily, and he proudly demonstrated to his friends how, when he hit the reinforced piece hard with his stick, he didn't feel a thing.

The others said nothing, but looked at him with sad and troubled faces.

'Has it all healed up?' asked Boule for the sake of saying something.

'Nearly, but with these special boots I don't feel a thing.'

'Did they amputate your foot at the heel?' asked Fernand.

'Not quite as far back, but nearly; they evened it up, the surgeon told me. They took my bones out all right!'

'Can you walk then?'

'Just take a look at me,' and tossing down his stick, Georges cut a spirited caper.

'*Ça fait mé pi pas pi!* You're quite a boy, Georges,' smiled Boule.

'We'll go and celebrate my return with something. Coming along, you others?'

'Just what we were going to do, we decided to have some *fondue* together at Breton's.'

'That's a good idea. Lord, it's good to be back again in the country! Over there, in the hospital, there were days when I almost went mad.' (He looked up at the Aiguilles.) 'Well, well, it's an early season this year, we could do them all now. I've got to get into training again. My legs feel as if they were made out of flannel. Come on!'

They made for the top of the town.

Père Breton's café-restaurant was patronised almost exclusively by guides and other mountain folk. It was a long wooden room with two rows of polished oak tables: the walls were hung with the painted shields of various mountaineering clubs, and with a few magnificent mountain photographs. The café, which was over a hundred years old, used to be the starting point for the stagecoaches on the Martigny line; though it had been slightly modernised it had managed to preserve its old-fashioned character.

The room was full of customers, chatting over their drinks in a thick acrid fog of pipe smoke.

Georges and his friends made a round of the tables and hailed all their acquaintances. Everybody wanted to congratulate Georges on having escaped so comparatively lightly, and his remarkable recovery greatly impressed them all. Old Breton, who knew very well how to keep business booming, ceremoniously announced from his perch behind the bar:

'Ladies and gentlemen! Drinks on the house in honour of Clarisse's Georges!'

Cheers acclaimed this friendly gesture. There followed more drinks and toasts. To the Company of Guides! To the mountains! To the people of Chamonix! And they all tried to get Georges to sit at their own tables.

In the midst of all the hubbub, while Georges was relating his misfortunes down there in the plains, Boule had slipped away to the kitchen and called for Breton.

'Make up some *fondue*, Breton, and we'll have it in the kitchen.'

'Look here,' said the landlord, 'the place is full up tonight, and I've got enough on my hands already – but just go ahead down to the cellar. You'll find cheese and white wine there, so you can cook it yourself – I hear you've got quite a reputation for it!'

'All right, and don't mind if I put in a little extra! And by the way, put some bottles of *roussette* out to cool – we'll be needing them.'

Boule set to work in the old low-roofed, smoke-blackened kitchen, whose floor was paved rather unevenly with granite slabs. *Fondue* is almost a national dish at Chamonix: it is a speciality of Geneva, and the cantons of Vaud and Valais, and is also found in the Faucigny district of Savoy. It has to be prepared and eaten according to a solemn ritual, which must be scrupulously observed.

It was a revelation to see how carefully Boule prepared it. He was so impressed by the solemnity of the occasion that for once there was no smile on his lips. First he weighed a fair-sized piece of real Gruyère from the alp, and shredded it finely into an earthenware casserole rubbed with garlic; then he poured white wine over it, and cooked cheese and wine together over a brisk heat till it formed a bland and savoury cream that simmered gently. He added two glasses of Kirsch and went on stirring. Pierre, who had come along to give him a hand, lit a spirit stove on the kitchen table, and they all sat down around the bubbling *fondue* in the earthenware dish.

'Is it done, Boule?' they asked.

'Done to a turn!'

'Let's start then,' Georges murmured happily.

And every one of them cut a thick cube of bread, stuck it on his fork, dipped it into the *fondue* and drew it out dripping with cheese. Conversation died away, and they all worked away steadily till nothing was left but a golden crust at the foot of the dish. After drinking a glass of Kirsch as the ritual prescribes, they prepared to divide the 'crackling', this golden crust at the foot of the casserole that holds the quintessence of all the varied flavours of the *fondue*.

Breton, who was keeping an eye on their progress, did not wait to be asked for the long-necked bottles of *roussette*, and the white wine succeeded the *fondue*. Exhilarated by this dish that warmed the very cockles of their hearts, the young men began to talk in loud and confident voices.

Guides always come back to the inevitable topic. Sure enough, they were soon talking mountains. Only Pierre kept quiet; the wine had made him taciturn, and a sullen expression had come back to his face. But Georges was in great form, and full of plans.

'I'm going to start off on the Gaillands rocks, by way of training.'

'You're crazy, Georges – look at those feet of yours,' said Paul.

'But I've got my hands, haven't I, and with these special boots I can climb perfectly well. Anyhow, I'm going to take a crack at it. Who'll come with me?'

'I will, of course,' said Fernand, 'I want to see how you get along. But are you really thinking of doing regular climbs again? When you spoke to us about it at Geneva I thought you were joking.'

'Of course I'm not! What sort of man d'you think I'd be if I didn't climb! It'd be awful. There's no two ways about it. I'm hoping to do all the big climbs, and not just easy stuff.'

'All the same you should take it easy,' put in Boule.

'Why should I? It's all a question of determination. Remember Young, the crack English climber, who made the first ascent of the Grépon from the Mer de Glace? He lost a leg in the war. That didn't stop him – he started off again, and with a wooden leg at that! You should have seen him. He used to fix a sort of snowshoe affair on the end to keep it from sinking into the snow, and on rocks he made fine use of his iron tip.'

'That's right,' added Fernand, 'and it reminds me of the shock the Chief Guide got the day Knubel, Young's guide, came walking into the office and asked him in that German-French lingo of his:

'"My client's broken his leg: I want to get it fixed. Can you tell me where?"

'"Your client's had an accident? What, on one of the mountains?"

'"*Ja*, up on the Grépon," answered Knubel, "he's broken his leg."

'"But I never heard a word about it – do you mean to say you managed to get him down?"

'"*Ja*, it took us a long time, but we got back to the Montenvers."

'The Chief Guide was absolutely staggered. "You should see Dr Coutaz – he specialises in broken legs."

'"But I don't want any doctor," shouts Knubel in a fury, "I want a good carpenter – it's a wooden leg!"

'You should have seen old Cupelaz! We all stood by and roared.'

The guides burst into roars of laughter; Boule slapped his thighs and nearly choked with mirth. Only Pierre did not join in; he drank one glass after another, never uttered a word, and a hard look came into his face. Georges went on:

'Yes, it's all a matter of determination; if you allow circumstances to get the better of you, then you're all through. You don't want to see me guardian of a hut at twenty-six. That's an old man's job. But I'm determined to get back my place in the roster! Now here's a suggestion: what about taking you up the Dru for my first big climb – I'll lead it – eh, Pierre? We've both got a score to settle with it. What I say is that if you've been hurt somewhere, you should go back as soon as you can to wipe out the impression it made on you, otherwise you go on having a horror of the place and can't bring yourself to go back. We'll do it towards the end of June, as soon as it's clear of snow, for I can tell you I've had enough verglas to last a lifetime! Let's have another bottle, Breton!'

The others took it up enthusiastically.

'Let's drink to the Dru – it's done enough to the whole lot of us.'

'It certainly has. Boy, if you'd seen those pitches a few days after your accident – eh, Pierre?'

Pierre did not open his mouth. With his head in his hands, he stared fixedly at the wax tablecloth.

'What's up with him?' inquired Georges. 'He looks so strange all of a sudden.'

'He's been like this for a month,' explained Fernand; 'he's been an entirely different man.'

'Come on, Pierre,' urged Boule affectionately, 'cheer up, we're all so glad to be together again: you and Georges have come back a long way. See if you can't forget your troubles.'

Pierre still did not answer. Paul leaned across to look into his face and saw he was quietly sobbing.

'Good Lord,' he muttered, 'he's crying. What's the matter with him? Pierre, we hate seeing you in trouble like this – what *is* the matter?'

At last Pierre spoke, right from the heart.

He lifted his troubled face to Georges, and the words came in a dull monotone.

'Georges, you've just told us that you couldn't get used to the idea of never climbing again. And you talk of going off again with your stumps of feet, and I know you'll succeed in fighting your way back. But if *I* were to tell you that it's all over for me, and that I'll never again set foot on the mountains, that I'll be hanging around in the valley to see you start off – '

'*You*?' said Georges, absolutely flabbergasted. 'In heaven's name, why?'

'Is it because you think your family won't let you climb?' asked Fernand. 'You idiot – they never meant *that*. Your mother and

Uncle Paul and Aline all know that you'll climb again, but as an amateur on holidays – that's what they'd like. You'll make enough money out of your pension – and what could be pleasanter, I ask you, than going off with your own pals! No grousing or conceited clients – none of their heavy sacks to carry – believe me, if I could afford it, I'd take another guide and go off with him, just the two of us. Just remember how well everything goes when we're climbing by ourselves; the rope's always taut, the rappels properly placed, you know just what's happening without a word being spoken, you feel as if two separate bodies were thinking as one. I've never felt that with clients – at any rate, hardly ever, maybe with one or two top-notchers, but even so – they don't think as we do, and that puts a barrier between you. But the family will never stop you from doing that kind of climbing, I'm positive of that.'

Pierre shook his head sadly.

'Neither as guide nor as amateur – I won't be going back to the mountains.'

'Have you taken a vow?' joked Boule, and then could have bitten his tongue out for saying it.

'I've lost my head for heights,' Pierre burst out, and put his head on the table, overcome by such a shameful confession.

'Lost your head?' repeated Fernand. 'Don't make me laugh! We saw you up on the Dru – there was nothing wrong with your head then! I'd have said you had almost too much confidence.'

'But it's quite true. The doctor warned me – and I didn't want to believe him. So I went off by myself one night – and gave myself a sort of test.'

'Was that the night you were missing from home?' asked Fernand. 'Good Lord, I might have guessed it. And I suppose you fell? Aline told me there was blood on your jacket.'

'No, but I wish I had. If you'd seen me floundering for nearly an hour before taking that long stride across on the face of the Brévent – grovelling like a caterpillar, quaking like jelly, keeping my eyes shut so as not to see the drop below – and then, once I was across, the relief of finding myself on something slightly less vertical. The blood was nothing – just a scratch when I was glissading down the névé on the way back.'

'We're terribly sorry, Pierre.'

Pierre raised his head and went on:

'I've tried to hide it as something to be ashamed of; I didn't want to talk about it to anybody, that's why I kept away from you all – seeing you all in such good condition made me feel sick – it was awful! So I started drinking, and the more I drank the more I harked back to the whole miserable business. The only moments of peace I had were when I went off by myself to a clearing in the woods, and sat dreaming away and looking at the mountains. It did me good, just gazing at them – and I could live in memory there, and think out new routes that now I'll never be able to take!'

'But you will, Pierre, you will,' broke in Georges vehemently, 'and I'm going to help you. Take it from me, vertigo's a thing that can be cured, it's just a question of wanting to cure it. I'm telling you, my father had a client, a woman, who was a trifle deaf, and that gave her vertigo; he couldn't make her go up anything, not even the Aiguille de l'M. So Father set to work to make her believe she could get over it, and after three seasons with him, progressing by easy stages, she was jumping around like a goat on the slabs of the Grépon!'

'All very well, but I couldn't even walk along the ledge on the Brévent.'

'You should never have gone off by yourself … you should have told us,' Fernand reproached him. 'I'd have gone up with you without a second thought. But there's plenty of time yet.'

'No there isn't – I'll never start again. I'm not going to have you seeing me when I'm flopping around like a bundle of rags. No … I've given up climbing for good.'

'No such thing,' declared Georges. 'Look here, both of us have to learn our jobs again, so you come along with me. To begin with, we'll let the other boys help; then we'll take over ourselves.'

Fernand, Boule and Paul readily agreed. Georges got up, and taking Pierre by the arm, hoisted him up from his chair.

'We've had enough to drink for tonight; time to go home. Paul can give me a lift on his bike, the others will walk you up to Moussoux.'

And off they went.

It was a clear, cold night, and the stars shone and twinkled above the mountains. Walking down the road with his friends, Pierre felt like an invalid on the highroad to recovery. Simply unburdening himself of his troubles had done him a world of good; far down in his heart he felt a faint stirring of hope. It was still just a flicker, for the memory of that dreadful day on the Brévent haunted him like a nightmare. Once again he saw the yawning gulf under his feet, he shrank back with nausea at his heart, in absolute revulsion. He could not repress a shudder; the others all wondered what on earth was the matter. He shook his head sadly.

'It's no good, I'll never get over it.'

'We'll see,' said Boule gently. 'It's all a matter of practice.'

Before separating, they arranged a meeting.

'While we're waiting for the rocks to get into decent condition,' decided Fernand, 'we should take his cows up to the mountains next week. We're up at the Chamarillon alp; will you come up with us, Pierre? We'll meet here and all go up together.'

'All right, it'll give me something else to think about.' (Pierre gave a wry smile.) 'Perhaps on the pastures I won't be plagued by vertigo!'

'That'd be the last straw!'

'And the next day, we'll have a cow fight between the "queens",' added Fernand, to tempt him. 'You can put your money on my beauty; she's in fine fighting trim!'

'Oh, all right.'

'You can count on me.'

'Aline's coming up with us.'

'All right, you can tell her I'll be there.'

Chapter XXII

Fernand and Boule had foregathered like conspirators in the back room at Gros-Bibi's. Pierre's sad revelation of the other night had shocked them deeply, and they were trying to find a way to help him out of his dangerous frame of mind. With a nature as stubborn as Pierre's you had to take a roundabout way to gain your end. Suddenly Boule had an inspiration; his cheerful face looked broader than ever as he asked Fernand:

'Are you in solid with the doctor?'

'I think so, but why?'

'You go along to him and tell him what the situation really is: he'll be able to think of something, I'm sure. For instance, if he could persuade Pierre to do a little climbing – of course we'd be there too. You get over there now – it's his consulting hour – I'll wait for you here, I don't want to hang around his place.'

A few minutes later Fernand was ringing Dr Coutaz's bell.

'Hello. Is one of the family ill?' asked the doctor.

'No, Doctor, it's about Pierre. I expect you know all about it; ever since he's known what was the matter with him he's been a changed man.'

And Fernand told him everything that had happened at Breton's. Dr Coutaz listened gravely.

'It's just a question of time and patience, Fernand, you can't cure vertigo suddenly, just like that.'

'So it's really true, is it, Doctor, that Pierre's got vertigo? Poor chap – and do you really think that it can't always be cured? But you know, there *have* been cases. Georges's father cured one of his clients by starting her on easy climbs and working her up little by little to harder ones.'

'I'm sorry, but what you've just told me is sad enough, and

proves that I didn't make any mistake. It's just the opposite, in fact – he's made his condition worse. He should never have tried that climb by himself; the nervous shock he got will only intensify his horror of height and exposure.'

'But look here, Doctor, we can't let him go to pieces like that. We must give him some hope. We're all ready to look after him – Boule, Paul, Georges, and myself; with all of us around him, there won't be the slightest risk.'

He paused – and then burst out, 'Couldn't we persuade him that what you said was wrong?'

Dr Coutaz was taken aback by such a preposterous suggestion.

'It's pretty rough, Fernand, if you mean to repay me for my services by telling everyone that I don't know my job. Do you really mean it?'

'I do indeed, Doctor; as I see it, it's a matter of saving a man's life, and I think that's worth a lie. Don't worry, I'm not going to throw any doubt on your skill and your professional conscience. But there *is* a way. You like Pierre, don't you? You've shown you have, often enough – especially the other day when he had his accident. So I said to myself, we'll get together on this, the doctor and I.'

'Indeed, and when did you join the profession?' sarcastically inquired Coutaz.

'No, but I've got an idea.'

'Out with it, then.'

'If you'd only tell Pierre that all that story about vertigo was just an excuse to keep him away from the mountains; that you did it because of his mother – it wouldn't be hard for you to think up something. Anyway, you see the idea.'

'You can't ask me to do a thing like that, Fernand. To give Pierre a false sense of security would be the best way of killing him, for he might come off without any warning at all, and I'd have his death on my conscience. There's only one thing to be done, my boy. You must lead him back to it gently and look after him all the time. You can take him climbing with you, but you'll have to keep a very close eye on him, and you should never allow him to lead. In such conditions he may perhaps – and I say *perhaps*' (the doctor stressed the word) – 'get over his trouble. Take him on the Gaillands rocks, on short training climbs, then you can see how he gets on. Let me know how it goes; I'll willingly keep in touch and advise you; but I couldn't lull Pierre into a false sense of security. I realise it's put a great strain on his character and that he hasn't reacted quite the way he should; but he's a lad with plenty of resilience. If he goes around with you boys, that'll be half the battle. Rescue work of this kind is every bit as important as bringing a casualty off a mountain.'

Fernand left the doctor's only half satisfied. He could appreciate Dr Coutaz's scruples – but if it had been himself, he would certainly have found some way around them. He rejoined Boule at Gros-Bibi's.

'Well?'

'The doctor won't play ball with us. All the same, I'm convinced it's a question of persuading Pierre. If we succeed in making him believe that his head's all right, then it will be all right.'

'We can always have a shot at it... By the way, is it still OK about going up to the alp?'

'Yes, next Tuesday.'

'So long, then. See you Tuesday.'

They paid for their drinks, left the café, and went their separate ways.

Chapter XXIII

The great exodus had started around midnight: at irregular intervals the herds of cattle passed through Chamonix with a jingling of bells that woke everybody up. Merrily they sounded, joyful as bells that summon to a christening, responsive to the regular swaying of necks confined by leather collars, and keeping time with the cows' sober, steady gait. Now and then two of the animals would go for each other and knock their bells around, and the harmony would be lost. Shouts and yells from the herdsmen added to the general uproar. The spring migration would go on for a day and a night without stopping, but nobody in Chamonix would complain about it, for everybody in the district understood perfectly well that when the herds went up to the alps it meant that the good season had come back again.

It was a beautiful, clear, windless night, with only a tiny breeze stirring the alders down by the Arve. Lights sprang up in the windows; children had been wakened from sleep to see the cattle troop by; men and women, too, who took one look at the procession and then went back again to sleep and dream. The animals moved up from the valleys towards the heights as if driven by some irresistible impulse; they passed by in little droves of twenty or thirty head, usually grouped together by villages or hamlets, and herded by a number of wall-eyed curs who came and went all the time, tongues hanging out, and occasionally drawing attention to their vigilance by an outburst of barking. Behind them walked the animals' owners, each with his sack on his back and an iron-shod stick in his hand.

It was nearly midnight when Pierre Servettaz woke up. Alice, the elder of his sisters, had set coffee, bread and cream cheese out on the kitchen table; the two of them ate in silence, then went out to the barn. The cows were beautifully groomed in readiness for the occasion, their coats soft as silk, and they turned inquisitive muzzles towards the intruders, as if to inquire the meaning of a visit at this time of the night.

Pierre changed the light bells they wore in winter for heavier ones with a deeper note – most striking objects they were, of blue steel, hanging from wide leather collars with copper buckles and gilt fittings. He patted the beasts gently and carefully combed out the tufts of hair between the tawny horns.

'There you are, my beauties,' he said, 'all dressed up and ready for the mountains.'

Then, with a clanking of metal, he unhooked the chains that tethered them to their stalls and they ambled out one by one, ears pricked and lips drawn back, snuffling in the night air.

Alice went to the head of the little procession and gently summoned the leader of the herd.

'Come on, Parise, come along, that's a good girl, come along.'

Parise obediently followed her mistress and the others trooped after her. The jingling herd reached the highroad and made its way through Chamonix without joining any of the others, which were now converging from all quarters, from Les Houches, Servoz, Vaudagne.

Slow and steady, the nocturnal march began.

At Les Praz, after they had crossed the bridge over the Arve, wet with spray and loud with the roaring of waters, Pierre stopped to wait for Fernand, Aline and their cattle. From a long way off, Alice recognised the sound of one of the deep bells – it was Lionne's, Fernand Lourtier's fighting cow.

'He's bringing his queen up – listen! She's leading them, Pierre.'

In a minute or two vague shapes that were soon seen to be Fernand's beasts loomed up in the darkness. The two herds were allowed to intermingle, and the cows sniffed at each other with some suspicion, especially Lionne, who reared up, all ready to charge.

'Let 'em fight in the meadows before we start off again,' shouted Fernand from the rear, 'it won't take long, and it'll settle 'em down.'

The fight was a matter of shadows and of bells that came and went in the darkness. Lionne displayed herself arrogantly before each member of the two herds, but the others, recognising her as the rightful fighting queen, made off in alarm, or broke off the fight at the first clash of horns. Lionne retired in disgust and began to browse peacefully.

'We can go on now,' said Fernand, 'they know who's master; we'll have some real fun up at Chamarillon tomorrow.'

Pierre, who was watching the confusion of animals from a little way off, suddenly felt a gentle hand on his arm. He turned around. Aline was there, very trim in her blue gabardine skiing breeches and dazzling white stockings. She smiled in the dim light, such a radiant smile that Pierre drew her towards him and gathered her in his arms without saying a word.

Alice was busy getting the undisciplined mob of cattle on the move again, and before long they were on their way across the flat meadows of Les Praz. There was a glimmer of light on the Aiguille Verte, and the eye could just make out the crescent-shaped curve of the Col de Balme and its velvety pastures. The light strengthened in the east, and from the dew-drenched pastures rose the scent of honey and pollen.

At Les Tines, Georges joined them with his cows, and there was a few minutes' more fighting. Lionne, by now slobbering at the mouth, had found a rival worthy of her mettle, and would not let go; at last they had to be separated so that they should not fritter away all their energy before the big fight on the alp.

It was broad daylight when the procession reached Argentière. The cafés were open, and the drovers stopped to wet their whistles while the girls went on with the cattle. As the sun rose higher, the sound of shouting and ringing filled the valley. It was a terrific din, with literally hundreds of bells chiming together to produce a harmonious whole that drowned the savage roar of the torrent rumbling out of the Argentière glacier.

By the time the procession had left the highroad at the Montroc viaduct, there were several hundred cows lumbering along in unbroken sequence, and others could be seen trekking in single file up the zigzags leading to the alps of Chamarillon and Balme.

In contrast, the valley behind them seemed stripped of all its cattle, and the few animals that remained below (one for each family, to provide the daily milk) were tethered to their pickets in their corners of the orchards, and raised their voices in a melancholy mooing.

With horns held high, the others displayed new energy as soon as they felt the damp earth of the alp under their feet. The older beasts recognised the path and walked up unhesitatingly; as for the young heifers, the mountain air had gone straight to their heads, and they pranced and gambolled in the most skittish manner.

At La Tour, the last village in the valley, which squats under its heavy stone-tiled roofs among pastures bright with lilies, arnicas and gentians, Fernand, Pierre and Georges sorted out their cows from the mob and drove them into a dry stone fold. Wearied by their fifteen-kilometre walk, the animals peaceably settled down to graze without trying to pick any fights.

Paul Mouny waited for them at the door of his chalet. He was in high spirits and eagerly looking forward to the afternoon's sport. He could not help teasing Fernand.

'Well, Fernand, how's the queen? She'll have her work cut out for her; I've just seen Boucle go up, you know, Napoleon from Lavancher's cow. He's had her horns reinforced, the old devil! Yes, my boy, bound with steel so that they won't split – and I bet he's doped her too, because her eyes were red and she was slavering away; he was leading her on a rope.'

'My cow will square up to any of the others' – Fernand was emphatic; 'anyway, it's too early to dose her, I'll give her some feed and some wine at Chamarillon just before the fight.'

'You'd better come and dose yourself in the meantime,' and Paul invited them in.

He had a good meal laid out for them: sausage made of cabbage and dried meat, and a dry white wine from the shores of Lake Geneva. They sat down at the table, which, in fact, was a trough boarded over with a larch plank. Aline, as seemed natural, sat down next to Pierre, and pleading tiredness, leaned her head on his shoulder. The others paid little attention to these lovers' manoeuvres. Fernand made merry with Alice; it was her first outing with the young men and she blushed every time he told a raw joke. However, they soon had to be on the road again.

The climb up to Balme was long and uneventful; the cows greedily cropped tufts of grass and flowers by the wayside, and had to be constantly prodded on. The joyous peals that had accompanied their steady walk along the flat valley bottom had given way to a milder music, with the high clear notes of the lighter bells sounding above the muffled bass of the big bronze bells of the fighting queens.

The morning was well advanced when they reached Chamarillon. The head cheesemaker at Balme, and the partners in the syndicate that managed the alp, entered the animals as they arrived in a big clothbound register that lay on a rustic table out on the grass. Each owner declared the number of his cows, which were at once entered and marked. Then cowherds tethered them up in long barns that stood side by side in a fold of the hillside, away from avalanche tracks, and so rooted to the ground that they seemed to be part of the slope.

The animals had to be given time to recuperate after their ten hours' journey. Early in the afternoon they would be let out, and then all would be set for the great encounter, when out of those 200-odd cows would be chosen the queen of the herd.

The tradition of allowing the herd to choose its own queen is as old as the granite of the Aiguilles. People who only know the heavy, stupid cows of the plains, whose udders trail on the ground, should not assume that mountain cows are just the same. The alps that lie between Mont Blanc and Monte Leone above the Simplon have reared a special breed, sprung from the soil itself, that in all probability used to roam wild at the foot of the glaciers. It is a very powerful breed, black-coated, with tawny streaks on flanks and belly, and the horns are as wide apart as those of a fighting bull. The cows have something of the same bearing too, with their short necks, powerful withers, legs lean and lithe as a racehorse's, and small, firm hooves, admirably adapted for the loose screes, steep grass slopes and exposed ledges of the mountainside.

Each summer, when the animals foregather from all corners of the valley, their first meeting is marked by an epic combat, a fight to the death, in which the cows settle which of them is to be queen. Once chosen, she leads the herd up to the pastures, fights any newcomers among the neighbouring herds, summons her companions to the watering place by the stream that comes tumbling down through the slate quarry. And when autumn comes, and the first snow, it is she who leads the long tinkling procession down to the valley again. From such roots spring the Valaisian's passionate attachment to the sport. Owners of cows will make bets of heroic proportions with each other, and pay vast sums for the unique pleasure of having in their herd the alp's *reine à cornes*.

The rage had spread to the Chamonix valley, and the cow fights of the early summer brought a huge crowd of fans up to the alp. Leaving their beasts with the Valaisian cowherds, Pierre and his party went over to the Chamarillon refreshment hut. It was a plain little one-storey building, with all the rooms in a row, at the foot of a steep grass slope and commanding a fine view over the whole Chamonix valley. Near at hand the Aiguille Verte and the Dru glittered and dazzled above the larch woods of Lognan; further back, there was a glimpse of the Mer de Glace as it wound its icy way round the base of the Aiguilles, kneeling like suppliants under the majestic dome of Mont Blanc. Part of the frontier ridge too could be seen, with the Dent du Géant keeping baleful watch over the snowfields of the Col. To the north-west stretched the lower range of the Aiguilles Rouges, heaving their bare flanks above the Flégère woods, still flecked with snow right up to the reddish rocks of decomposing schist. Beyond the pleasant valley of Chamonix the flat and even outline of the Bellevue plateau formed a sort of backdrop to the scene; and beyond it stretched tier on tier of mountains, merging into each other in the blue distance.

The chalet stood on the edge of the rather featureless expanse of alp, a green carpet with here and there a crack in which slate workings could be seen, or the fan-shaped ravines gouged out by the sources of the Arve. The Swiss frontier was just over there; it followed the perfect crescent of the Col de Balme, and plumb in the middle, like a fortress, stood the Swiss inn.

Over to the north rose the long grassy ribs, with the Balme chalets nestling between them, which formed the alps of Balme. There too the herds were just now foregathering for the decisive encounter. The dark and dramatic Vallorcine peaks thrust their barren summits up from the grassy alps. Over towards the Col des Montets the forest seemed to be advancing against the pasture, and a few stunted larches had established outposts well above the tree line – a victory of nature over the barren inhospitable mountainside.

Inside, the dining room of the chalet was filled to bursting point, and louder and louder rose the hum of conversation. Through the thick fog of smoke that hung midway between floor and ceiling loomed the heads, bent well forward, berets askew, of the countrymen who crashed their fists down on the table to drive home the points of their strenuous arguments.

Visitors who hired guides during the summer would hardly have recognised, in these uncouth peasants with their heavy serge and corduroy, the expert climbers who led them up the mountains. They were no longer guides, they were barely even civilised; they had become once more, of their own free will, typical narrow-minded, heavy-featured mountain peasants. All their enthusiasm now was for the cow fights. Bets were being laid on all the known animals, especially on Boucle, the terror belonging to Napoleon from Lavancher. She was no heavier, no more spirited than many another, but she had been queen at Chamarillon for five seasons, thanks to the peculiar formation of her horns. Immense and powerful, they curved around till they practically met, thus forming a ring that protected her from all attack. Splendid fighters especially brought up from Martigny had so far failed to make an impression on her; at each encounter her adversary's forehead would come right up against her two steel-tipped points, which would gore the rival cow without letting her close in.

Napoleon was loud in his boasts. He was a sly, vindictive little man, who considered himself cock of the walk up there, and had no wish to give up his position.

'A thousand francs on my cow! Any takers?'

There were no offers; his queen had too unbeatable a reputation. They were all backing Boucle, who looked like a sure bet. Only the owners of the other cows backed their chances and laid bets for the second place; it seemed impossible that Boucle could be beaten.

Fernand stalked aggressively to the middle of the room. He was probably twenty years Napoleon's junior, but his enthusiasm and knowledge of cows were already well known, and his handsome queen had been much admired by other connoisseurs in his barn at home.

'I'll take you on, Napoleon,' he challenged, 'my cow's going to make mincemeat of that horned donkey of yours!'

Napoleon goggled at him, and the others hastened to restrain Fernand.

'Hold on, you're crazy to bet a lot of money like that,' Paul admonished him. But Napoleon motioned him back.

'Let it stand, he deserves a lesson' – then, turning to Fernand, 'by all means, if you want to lose your money.'

'That Boucle of yours doesn't scare me,' persisted Fernand, 'even if her horns are tipped with steel. If you've bound them, it must be because there was a risk of their breaking. That's right, isn't it? But there's one thing I want to warn you about: there's a bolt sticking out, and unless it's filed down I'll withdraw my bet.'

'I'm filing nothing,' growled Napoleon, 'and I'm taking no lessons from impertinent kids like you.'

Excitement was mounting, and Napoleon, who had already had a couple of drinks, began to lose his temper.

'I'm putting my 1,000 francs down on the table; we'll let the cheesemaker look after them for us – here you are, Hyacinthe.'

The stolid Swiss cheesemaker took the 1,000-franc note, and slipped it inside his waistcoat; but he felt obliged to warn Fernand, who was holding his note out too.

'You're making a big mistake! His animal can't be beaten. She's been champion for five years, and this is the first time yours has even been up. She'll be upset by the new place, and she'll have three times as many fights as Boucle. The other cows know her and don't challenge her any longer; they've accepted her as their queen. But your Lionne will have ten or twelve fights to take care of, and by the time she gets to Boucle she'll be played out.'

At this point Pierre broke in.

'Take my money too, Hyacinthe; just to show you that I'm not scared either by that old hack over there tied together by wire, I'll put 1,000 francs on Fernand's cow. Will you take it, Napoleon?'

Everybody was flabbergasted by the audacity of the two young men, and soon two camps were being formed. In their secret hearts they all wanted Fernand to win; Napoleon had bragged about his invincible queen just about long enough. All the same, they did not care to back Fernand openly; too damned risky. Napoleon was purple with rage.

'Done,' he shouted, and shoved another 1,000-franc note into the cheesemaker's hand.

Pierre slipped out by the back door; he had had enough argument and he wanted to find Aline. She was none too easy at the turn of events, and had come back to keep an eye on their herd in the stables.

'Hello, are you on sentry duty?' he asked with a laugh.

'I'd rather not leave the queen alone. Napoleon wouldn't stop at anything after what you said to him. You're crazy, the two of you; think of betting all that money! If Mother ever gets to hear of it ... '

'What's it got to do with her? It's our own money we're risking. Now, come out with me – Fernand and Paul are coming to take their turn at standing watch.'

Almost immediately the two appeared, flushed and excited by all the betting and talking. They brought Boule and Georges along with them. Paul was carrying a big carved bowl full of grain moistened with wine; they fed it to Lionne, who was chewing peacefully away in front of her manger, and she greedily set to work on the stimulating meal.

Then the four conspirators hoisted themselves up to the hayloft above the cowshed, where they could keep an eye on the animals without being seen themselves. You can never be too sure!

Chapter XXIV

Pierre and Aline went off, leaving the others to keep watch, and made their way to a little rhododendron-covered knoll that overlooked the valley. Aline lay down on the tangled branches that formed the springiest of couches, smiled in great contentment and stretched herself in the sun like a cat. Her loose brown hair straggled across the scarlet flowers. She drew Pierre down towards her; there they remained in a tender embrace, and Pierre at last knew peace and happiness. His black thoughts had scattered like clouds before the wind. He lived now for the moment, and could let his thoughts stray to the mountaintops without reopening old wounds: the mountains were part of his present bliss, and all he wanted was to clasp Aline even closer to his heart and put his lips on hers. The sun was high overhead. Now and then it passed behind a cottony cloud, and a shadow raced across the alp, chasing after the light; everything became a shade chillier. Instinctively the two lovers bowed their heads and held each other more tightly. Then the sun would reappear, and once more all was gaiety on the mountainside. Aline picked some sprigs of alpine rose, playfully covered herself with them, and her lips were as bright as the scarlet flowers. To Pierre she seemed more beautiful and more desirable than he had ever known her – perhaps this was because for the moment both love and mountains conspired together to intoxicate and overwhelm him. He and Aline shut their eyes the better to sniff up the powerful fragrance of the pastures, the better to feel the invisible caress of the breeze on thir sun-bronzed faces.

A tremendous clanging of bells brought them back to earth.

'Pierre!'

'Aline!'

'The cows are going out – let's go down before anyone comes

to look for us.'

'I wish we wouldn't, it's so lovely up here.' He helped himself to another kiss.

'Happy, Pierre?'

'Very happy.'

'No more horrible thoughts?'

Pierre was silent: Aline answered for both of them.

'We mustn't have any dark shadows in the future; as long as we're together, we'll always be happy, won't we, darling?'

Gently he stroked her lovely hair, now full of flower petals and dead grass.

'Let's go down.'

They jumped up. Aline shook the flowers off her jersey and they ran quickly down to the cattle.

The cows were trooping out of the barns; there was an ominous, apprehensive note in their mooing, and they picked up their heels and tossed their horns. Here and there a brawl developed; then the herdsmen separated the fighters and urged the whole troop up to the flowery plateau which had been cleared of stones in preparation for the fights that would determine who was to be queen.

Once up there, the men withdrew to a little knoll and left the beasts to choose the new one themselves. The greater part of the herd, in fact, were only too pleased just to browse to their hearts' content on the sweet grasses of the alp, and they shied away from any threat of violence; but some twenty queens roamed around restlessly, bellowing, sniffing at their rivals, spoiling for a fight, and soon a general scuffle broke out in the middle of the herd. One by one the fighters faced up to their adversaries. This encounter lasted barely a minute; there was a shock as the two groups hurtled against each other, then the losers broke off and turned to fly, each followed by her conqueror who belaboured the victim's side with shrewd digs of her horns. After an hour only six were left on the field of battle, coats stained with sweat and dirt, eyes bloodshot, foaming at the mouth. These quivering, high-strung creatures were the real mountain queens.

Those who had laid bets were all standing together, and voices rang high. It was getting near the end and for yet another time Boucle showed no signs of wanting to yield her position as queen. She stalked aggressively and ill-naturedly from one fighter to another, always using the same tactics. The other cow would make the first move while Boucle, standing squarely on her four hooves, awaited the shock, and allowed her adversary to wear herself out with each successive charge against her deadly horns. She stood rooted to the ground, awaiting her moment: then with a single twist of the head she outflanked the other cow and forced her neck down to the ground. While the loser fled away to seek oblivion in the herd, Boucle stayed there motionless, her head well down and her horns sticking out in front, while her great chest heaved in and out in time with her quick breathing. She pawed the ground with her small forefeet, scattering clods of earth all over the place; then in a fury of destruction, like a wild buffalo in the bush, she knelt down, gored the earth with her horns, and spattered herself with dirt while her blood trickled down into the trodden earth. Her bell, choked with mud, hung dumbly from her neck.

Then, with all her rivals out of the fight, the splendid creature swaggered through the herd, pausing here and there to administer a dig with her horns, or to order another animal off a particular juicy bit of pasture. Her reign was undisputed; the rest of them had clearly made their choice. Imagine her astonishment when, on reaching the edge of the plateau, she saw two cows still fighting in a sheltered nook on the edge of a deep gully down which a thin trickle of clear water ran over blackened schists.

The queen was absolutely amazed; she showed it by remaining rooted to the spot after letting out a heartfelt full-throated bellow. She pawed the ground with her forefeet to mark her rage and disapproval, and waited for the battle to end. The two cows, of whom Fernand's Lionne was one, were locked in a deadly struggle.

From his place among his friends, who all stood to win something on the fight, Fernand saw the dreaded champion approach. This was certainly going to be a great fight, the crowning one of them all! The spectators cheered; they watched Lionne win all her battles and greatly admired her real fighting spirit and her phenomenal stamina. She would certainly give Boucle a run for her money.

'Look out, Napoleon,' they chaffed him, 'you'll be losing your money.'

'I'm not worrying, I've got a sure thing with Boucle,' he answered, but his words carried more assurance than his voice.

Fernand was watching his queen; for the last ten minutes, in spite of being slightly lower down the slope than her opponent, she had been fighting head down with a powerful black cow, a fierce and lively animal. They were evenly matched, but with a final thrust Lionne overthrew her rival, who then knelt on the grass and bellowed her submission.

There was a cheer for Lionne's victory; then everybody turned to watch Boucle, who was now mincing towards them, bellowing and slobbering and shaking her head. Lionne lifted her horns, sniffed the veteran, steel-tipped warrior, still some distance away, and then, to the amazement of the spectators, she did not wait to provoke a fight but calmly walked down to the edge of the stream and drank deeply, lifting up her head at each mouthful, blowing out her nostrils, and thrashing her buttocks with her tail.

Napoleon was jubilant.

'She's running out, that precious queen of yours! She's running out! I told you it was crazy to put her up against Boucle.'

Fernand was horrified by Lionne's withdrawal, and wanted to lead her back to fight, but the others stopped him.

'You just leave her alone, Fernand; it's not for us to interfere. After all, it's the cows' business, not ours. No need to get worked up yet, it isn't all over; that cow of yours is pretty shrewd, she's just taking a break and a drink and pulling herself together.'

Placidly Lionne ambled up again from the gully and started to browse, just like any common-or-garden milker. That didn't suit the backers at all. And they yelled at her.

'Hey, Lionne, get a move on!' they yelled. 'Go after her, girl.'

It was with considerable astonishment that Boucle surveyed this newcomer, who browsed away on the Chamarillon alp, just a few feet off, without paying the slightest attention to her, Boucle, the queen of the alp! She determined to deal severely with this lack of respect, this affront to her own dignity.

So, going behind Lionne, she meanly gave her a sharp dig in the rump with her horns. Lionne spun around in a flash, startled by this unforeseen attack and, muzzle well down, pawed the ground and snorted.

'She's going to fight – hurrah!' yelled the *aficionados* of this strange mountain sport.

Boucle recognised an enemy worthy of her mettle and made herself ready. Head down, she looked around for the stance that best suited her tactics, on the slope above her opponent.

'It's not fair! It's too steep here,' shouted Boule, 'it'll make it more even if you move your cows over to the flat ground.'

'Leave 'em alone,' growled Fernand, 'the fight should take place wherever the cows happen to meet. Leave 'em alone, I don't care!'

In his excitement Pierre approached within a few feet of the fighters who stood there motionless, face to face, eyeing each other, their horns almost touching.

'Get back, Pierre,' bawled Napoleon, 'or you'll mess it up.'

'Don't get excited, I'm going back.'

The air was charged with electricity, and the spectators were as nervous as the cows.

Then the fight began. Boucle gave a short challenging roar and warily awaited the first assault. As a newcomer to the alp, Lionne was completely ignorant of the wiles and ruses of the old campaigner; she put all her weight behind her first charge and tried to hook her horns into Boucle's. There was a terrific shock as forehead met forehead with a hollow crack. Boucle received it with hindquarters drawn up, neck arched, and her back hooves dug well into the ground. Lionne had hurled herself on the steel-shod tips of her adversary's horns, and blood dripped from her gored forehead and trickled into her nostrils. She bellowed with pain, broke away, then came back to the fray. Boucle withstood the charge unflinching, disconcerting Lionne by her apparent impassivity. The latter tried a new tactic: she came forward gently, head on one side, trying to break through her rival's formidable defence. Without charging, Lionne put all her weight on Boucle's horns, but it was no use; with a quick jab sideways Boucle gashed her under the ear. But Lionne stoutly maintained her hold and, in spite of the blood streaming down her face, increased the pressure, trying to get her opponent off balance. Hooves firmly planted in the ground, Boucle withstood this terrific assault without giving an inch. For twenty minutes they remained locked together in this crushing embrace, never relaxing for a moment. It was clear they were tiring, though Boucle still seemed to be the fresher of the two. Lionne's black and tawny coat was marbled with sweat; there was froth on her fetlocks and breast; the skin was gathered up around her protruding eyeballs, and she restlessly switched her flanks with her tail.

Excitement mounted to fever pitch among the spectators. Napoleon was beside himself; he cheered his queen on, danced up and down gesticulating like a madman; then finding an old peasant from Servoz who doubted Boucle could win, he forced him into a fierce hand-to-hand struggle. Over and over they rolled on the grass, practically under the combatants' feet, and had to be forcibly separated.

Meanwhile the fight had taken a new turn. Boucle, while apparently standing still, was imperceptibly forcing Lionne back; she exploited the peculiarities of her horns by pressing the points against her rival's wounds, making unerringly for the exposed flesh that had to suffer still further. Pressing hard on the open wounds, with a quick movement of the head, she gouged her long horns deep into the mangled forehead. Clearly, it was becoming an unequal struggle and several of the spectators advised Fernand to put a finish to it.

'Call her off, Fernand, or she'll be maimed for life.'

But Fernand wouldn't think of it.

After trampling with all their weight on the spongy ground of the alp, the two creatures were now standing in thick mud up to their hocks. Each time a hoof went down, the mud splashed up over the combatants. Boucle, putting on extra pressure, was trying little by little to force her rival to the edge of the gully where she would be almost certain to lose her footing. The onlookers guessed what she had in mind, and sweated with apprehension as they followed every incident of this tremendous encounter.

All of a sudden, just when they had given her up for lost, Lionne reared up on her hindquarters and came down with all her weight on to Boucle's horns; then, with a lightning pass, she managed to force one of her horns under her rival's ear. With a slow sideways twist that sent a shiver running through the whole length of her body, she succeeded in screwing and twisting Boucle's neck. The outlook had completely changed. Caught in her own trap, betrayed by the peculiar formation of her horns, Boucle could no longer work free. At last, with a great snorting and bellowing, she yielded to this unexpected offensive. Her twisted vertebrae cracked and strained; she was compelled to give at the knees, while the glassy-eyed Lionne kept up the terrible pressure. Great veins swelled up almost to bursting point on her neck and chest; sweat poured down her coat in muddy trails. A sharp crack – and the onlookers saw a horn wrenched off and watched it fly through the air, while blood streamed down the gored forehead of the dethroned queen.

They cheered and cheered again, and Lionne answered them with a roar of triumph, a long quarrelsome bellow like a rutting bull's.

Boucle had broken away; and now, shaking her head all stained with dark blobs of congealed blood, she set off at a trot to bury her shame in the middle of the herd.

The new queen stood there utterly exhausted; she was bleeding, her flanks heaved convulsively, yet she took up her position proudly on a hillock and gave a few sharp roars to summon her companions and proclaim her sovereignty. Then she swung through the herd at a gallop, going from one beast to another, sniffing and snorting. They all made way for her; finally, shouldering aside four cows who were munching away in the juiciest corner of the alp, she settled down to browse in peace.

The head cheesemaker handed over the total stakes to Fernand and Pierre, and everyone came up to congratulate the lucky owner of the new queen. But it was getting late, so the company started down on the return journey to the valley; with umbrellas slung over their shoulders, sticks in their hands and rucksacks on their backs, they set off at a great pace down the mountain path. Napoleon had caught his cow, thrown a halter round her neck, and was now off to the slaughterhouse with her.

Pierre had collected his friends and was about to start down when Fernand stopped him.

'Easy there, Pierre, don't be in such a hurry. We must celebrate our victory, and we might as well do it now while we're all together. Let's have supper at the chalet here, and tomorrow we might all have a day out together – what d'you say?'

'Sounds good to me,' approved Georges.

Pierre would have liked to refuse, but the memory of the sweet moments of early afternoon came back to him. 'It would be wonderful,' he mused to himself, 'to be together like this for two whole days!'

'Are you staying up with us, Aline?' he inquired aloud.

'Of course she is,' answered Fernand, 'I told Mother we might stay up, and she said it was all right.'

'But *I* didn't say anything about it at home, and I don't want Mother to be worried, the way she was that day when I made such a fool of myself up on the rocks. And there's Alice too.'

'Look here, Pierre,' put in his sister gently, 'now that you're enjoying yourself for once, you'd be much better off to stay up here with the others. I'll go down and explain it all to them at home.'

'Will you really? And won't you be afraid to go down by yourself? Well, the days are getting longer, and you ought to be able to get a train at Montroc. All right, I'll stay! Tell Mother we're all going out somewhere tomorrow. By the way,' he added, a note of anxiety creeping into his voice, 'exactly what do you mean to do tomorrow?'

'What about walking from Posettes over to the Col des Montets?' suggested Georges. 'It's a beautiful walk with a marvellous view.'

'I'd love to do that.' Pierre was reassured.

'So long,' called Alice; and, hoisting on her light rucksack, she was off like a goat down through the dwarf rhododendrons, a true daughter of the mountains. The rest of them watched her as far as the edge of the grassy rib that plunges down towards the village of La Tour, concealing the head of the valley. Before finally disappearing she turned around, waved her scarf, and let out a carefree yodel.

Chapter XXV

Supper was a cheerful meal. The man who had rented the chalet had prepared a magnificent dish of smoked meat; appetites were excellent, and the young people ate to a continuous ripple of chatter and jokes. They had the living room to themselves, and the comparative silence outside contrasted with the unwonted liveliness of this first day on the mountains.

When they had finished eating they went out again to the now deserted pastures. The night was calm and silent, with only now and then a far-off tinkling of muffled bells from the cow barns to disturb the evening peace.

A strong breeze from the east blew across the hillside, bending the long grass and ruffling the pastures on the plateau into alternate strips of light and dark. Waves of every shade of green spread outwards in the breeze like ripples on a lake, endlessly renewing themselves. The alp had been transformed into a great swaying, shimmering carpet.

The young people climbed up the ridge just behind the chalet that overlooks the Combe de Varméne; there before them stretched the whole magnificent mountain chain. Georges and Fernand, once again caught up in their old enthusiasm, were chattering away about new routes and sensational achievements.

'D'you really think you'll be able to climb?' asked Fernand a trifle anxiously. 'Have you had a try yet?'

'Yes I have, down at Gaillands, and I got along fine. Of course I don't have the suppleness that my own toes would give me if I still had 'em, but I can tell you that when I got a nail on to a hold, it stayed there. I've been using my hands a lot, and I think that with a little more practice I could develop great strength in my fingertips; as long as I've got a good handhold, you can be sure I'm not coming off.'

Fernand turned to another subject. 'Tell me,' he asked Georges, 'why did we stay up here tonight?'

'Because of Pierre. I thought I was right about him. He seems a good deal steadier after even this one day. Love might very well prove a cure for vertigo! Hey, just look at the turtle doves!'

Pierre and Aline were enjoying another tête-à-tête. They had sat down a little way off from the rest, and were exchanging low whispers that must have been very sweet to hear, judging from the sparkle in Pierre's eyes and from Aline's bubbling happiness.

'Yes,' went on Fernand, 'he's more like himself, and I think that with my sister's help he'll get back his zest for life. They ought to get married in the autumn. If only in the meantime we could give him back his self-confidence! Look here, don't let on' (and Fernand put a finger to his lips), 'but I have a plan: tomorrow we'll be going right past the Aiguillette d'Argentière and you can pretend you want to try out your new form. The sight of you will make him want to try too, and I'll be surprised if it doesn't end up with him climbing too. And if he's well held, he'll get back his nerve – what do you think of it?'

'Hm – he's a pretty stubborn character when he wants to be.'

After spending most of the night before in driving up the cattle they were beginning to feel tired, so they turned back to the chalet. Before going down Boule drew himself up on his short legs and enlivened the night with a cheerful Tyrolean ditty.

Down in the valley lights were twinkling through the dusk; a fresh wind had sprung up, and it blew around the corners of the chalet.

'I'm going to put you in the loft,' said the warden, 'but be careful you don't set the place on fire.'

Candle in hand they climbed cheerfully up the narrow ladder to the hayloft, and proceeded to make their own burrows in the hay. No one commented on the fact that Pierre had burrowed in next to Aline. Once Boule had blown out the candle, all was quiet in the draughty garret except for the noise of breathing and the wind whistling under the slates in the roof.

Emboldened by the darkness, Pierre came closer to Aline; she laid her head trustingly on her lover's shoulder. He kissed her tenderly and as he felt her dropping off to sleep in the shelter of his arms, he could picture the smile on her parted lips. And, since it seemed to be making her happy, he joined her in her dreams.

Chapter XXVI

'Time to get up,' announced Georges, brushing the fine dust of the hayloft off his neck, his sleeves and his hair. 'Come on, down you go: it's light already.'

In a minute they were up and scrambling down the narrow ladder. They took a hurried bite and then were off across the alp like a pack of schoolboys on a holiday; there was no attempt at order, but Georges stumped on ahead, walking stiffly on his maimed feet; he was doing well and seemed to enjoy forcing the pace.

'What would it be like if they hadn't cut off your toes?' observed Boule. 'We wouldn't have a chance of keeping up with you. They must have fed you on rabbit at that hospital of yours!'

When they reached the cowsheds of Balme the cattle were emerging in a cloud of steam, and the gay jangling of bells rang out again over the mountain pastures.

Their path took them up over screes and boulders to the cairn on the Posettes. It was a view they all knew well, but they were compelled to stop and admire once again the incomparable mountain prospect. Aline did not often have a day out like this, and she was transported with wonder and delight. She hopped up and down beside Pierre and babbled away like a little girl who has been taken out for the first time to a longed-for treat.

'Oh, Pierre, I'm so happy, so terribly happy! I just love being up here in the mountains! When we're married, you won't leave me at home, will you, you'll take me climbing with you?'

'Of course I will, darling,' answered Pierre, trying to convince himself that he would.

Leaving the short grass of the alp behind them, they wandered into the larch wood, decked out with the tender green of the new shoots and melodious with the song of birds. Boule and Paul, that pair of inveterate sportsmen, tried to start up the blackcock nesting under the lower branches of the alder bushes. In front of them rose the ruddy, jagged line of the Aiguilles Rouges.

Emerging from the shade of the trees, the little party soon reached the Col des Montets, that spectacular couloir which resounds all winter to the roar of avalanches. It is a savage place, swept by a fierce wind that whistles down the couloir and blows itself out over on the Vallorcine side.

There was a short stop at the hotel on the Col, then Pierre and his companions started up again on the side of the Aiguilles Rouges. A little path, very difficult to trace, wound up through the bushes, skirted a huge erratic boulder on which perched a stunted larch tree, and slanted up the mountainside. Passing through a copse of larch, it then rose steeply towards some large slabs of polished rock that cut off their upward view. At first sight it looked as if there was no way around; yet these cliffs conceal the gullies and steep grassy couloirs that carry the path to the upper pastures of Chéserys.

It was hard work with the sun on them; sweat was dripping from every brow when at last the party stopped at the foot of the rock face. Just in front of them rose an enormous pillar of rock, detached from the main mass of the mountain. It was thirty metres high on its north side, and about a hundred on the valley side, and it pushed a squat head up into the sky. Stuck on to its flank, like a thorn in the stem of a rose tree, was an ugly little tooth barely fifteen metres above the gap between the two summits. It was a favourite practice ground for climbers: the younger and more daring guides had made many new routes up the rocks, where every degree of difficulty could be found, from the classic route up the ordinary way, to the frightful overhang on the miniature north face. And it was here, just as they were putting down their sacks at the foot of the Aiguillette, that Georges nonchalantly advanced a suggestion.

'Since we *are* here, suppose we limber up a bit? It looks like a good opportunity, doesn't it?'

'Good idea,' agreed the others – all except Pierre.

'How lovely,' said Aline, 'I'm longing to climb something.'

Pierre was not so keen on the idea; the prospect made him very uneasy.

'Go on if you like,' he said airily, 'I'll watch you from here. I've already told you that all this doesn't mean a thing to me.'

'Oh, come on, Pierre,' urged Georges, 'you know we agreed to start off again together.'

'Well, you start first.'

Fernand, Boule, Paul and Georges dived into their sacks and brought out ropes, karabiners, rings and pitons. The sight of all this carefully chosen tackle opened Pierre's eyes to the well-meant conspiracy.

'You've played a pretty cute trick on me,' he said. 'OK, I'll take a shot at it.' Then, as an afterthought, rather sadly, 'But if I do have an attack, don't make fun of me.'

'That's wonderful, Pierre, I knew you would. Everything will go beautifully. Here's your reward, I'll give it to you in advance.' And Aline bestowed a smacking kiss on his cheek. 'Are you glad?'

'Hm.'

'Where do we start?' she inquired.

'Up the easiest way,' announced Georges, 'and I'm going to lead. Pierre, you're going to see how well a cripple can manage as long as his fingers are all right.'

Paul was rather worried.

'Look here, Georges, don't you think one of us should lead on your first day out?'

'Don't be silly! If I saw someone up above me, and was certain of being held, I'd be overconfident. I want to see just what I can do. And anyway,' he added scornfully, 'the ordinary route's just kid stuff.'

Georges tied himself on, allowing thirty metres of rope between him and the next man, and began to climb. He gripped the rock firmly with his long, sensitive fingers, then hoisted his stumps on to the holds as best he could. He felt around but could not quite get them. Like many a man who has lost a leg and yet somehow always manages to feel cold in both feet, he too felt as if both his feet were perfectly normal. But as soon as he tried to place them on a ledge – lo, there was nothing but emptiness.

Yet somehow he gained height, and soon, with a long stride to the right, he was up on the ridge of the Aiguillette. Now his movements became more confident, he climbed with greater freedom, no longer sticking quite so closely to the rock. Confidence came back with a rush and there was pride as well as pleasure in his voice when he shouted down to them:

'I'm up: you can come on now.'

Fernand took Pierre's arm and showed him the route.

'You saw the way he went? What a man! Almost as good as he ever was. And you'll be just the same. Here, tie yourself on.'

Pierre did not at all enjoy putting on the rope. He was not feeling at all well and hesitated visibly, but Fernand, who had gone up ahead, was now pulling on the rope.

'Come on up, keep just behind me.'

And there, just at his heels, was Boule who, without waiting for a word from anyone, had made it his job to provide a safeguard in case of a sudden collapse. They might have been shepherding a child up the climb, or a very special client who had been entrusted to their charge. All went well for the first ten metres; Pierre stuck as close as possible to the rock, and as, strictly speaking, there was no sheer drop beneath him, he climbed up slowly enough, but confidently, testing the holds as he went; and Boule, whose head kept bobbing up below Pierre's heels, helped him on with encouraging remarks.

'There now, you're doing it all on your own.'

'Fat chance of that,' grumbled Pierre, 'with Fernand hauling me up like a sack of flour, so that I couldn't come off even one inch, and you guiding my feet on to their holds. Of course, it's easy like this. But suppose I were leading?'

'It'll all come back gradually if you listen to us. But you shouldn't try to do everything the first time.'

They were up to the traverse now. With one spring, Fernand was astride the ridge, and moved a few metres up it to belay his rope round a spike of rock; then holding it taut, he called to Pierre to come on. Pierre, in his turn, took the long stride across to the airy little ridge and straddled it woodenly. His hands gripped the rock, and he laid his head on them, prey once more to doubt. Only a few metres separated him from the summit, a few airy metres, for the Aiguillette tapers off here and Pierre was looking over on to the steep drop of the south face. It took a terrific effort of will to go on. Fernand, watching from his stance above, saw Pierre turn pale and shut his eyes. He said nothing, but signalled to Boule to come up quickly in support. Boule, hanging by his hands in a most unconvincing attitude, managed to put himself between his friend and the alarming drop beneath. But Pierre still made no move, and remained stuck there like a lizard on a sun-baked stone.

'Taking a nap, Pierre?' Boule shouted.

'It's coming on again – the dizziness.'

'Don't worry. Aline's still down there, she can't see you.'

Down from the summit floated Georges's cheerful voice –

Là-haut sur la montagne
L'était un vieux chalet …
Murs blancs, toits de bardeau,
Devant la porte un vieux bouleau –

'You'll be perfectly all right,' Boule assured him, 'no need to hurry; the rope's taut, I'm right here beside you – just open your eyes and look up, we're practically there.'

Pierre opened his eyes and despairingly clutched the rocks. He felt like a shipwrecked mariner in a gale clinging to a fragment of wreckage. The whole landscape was in motion, spinning round that damned spike up there – glaciers, woods, pastures wheeled and circled in a frenzied dance, even the Aiguillette was rocking on its base. It was an appalling sensation that made him turn pale and cling to the rock with all his might. Then with a sudden access of courage he decided to follow the experiment through to the very end. The presence of his friends gave him some confidence.

'I'm going up,' he announced briefly.

Fernand had shinnied up to the tiny summit platform in order to thread the rope through the ring fixed in up there. Boule kept close behind Pierre's heels. Poor Pierre. He staggered like a drunken man, he kicked out wildly in his attempts to find the holds, his feet kept on going into the wrong places, but Boule guided them back into the right ones. These few metres seemed absolutely endless. At last his head appeared over the top and with a final effort he heaved himself on to the platform. Boule let out a cheerful yell.

'He's up, Aline! It all came off without a hitch.'

But Fernand said nothing. He was thinking that vertigo must indeed be a frightful thing if it could transform an exceptionally brave man into a puppet like this. He had never realised till now the depths of his companion's distress.

With Paul to lead her, Aline now climbed up to join them. She came up like a cat, and her face shone with pleasure.

'Can you see her? She's a real guide's daughter!' Fernand remarked to Pierre. 'Later on, if you like, you can take her with you as porter!'

Pierre's only answer was a melancholy smile.

Georges wanted to make an experiment before starting down.

'Stand up on the top here, Pierre – yes, stand right up.'

Pierre summoned up all his resolution, got to his knees, and tried hard to stand up on the minute pedestal. No good: everything began to spin round him again, the landscape started up its infernal dance. He gave it up.

'No, I can't manage that yet; it's too much for the first time.'

'He's right,' put in Paul, 'we should take it very easy.'

They prepared to rope down on the north side, a descent of over twenty-five metres. There is an overhang in the lower part, and when you reach it you spin around and around like a spider at the end of a thread.

Boule slid down first, agile as a monkey on the rope. Then Fernand motioned Pierre to follow. Pierre mechanically passed the rappel line around him and started over the edge.

'OK?'

'OK, I'm off.'

He shut his eyes almost as soon as he began to feel the drop under his feet, and he continued to descend without seeing a thing, letting the line run out through force of habit, knocking against the bulges, scraping his fingers against the rock. He preferred to endure these minor miseries than that infernal whirligig of peaks. He landed with a bump in a tuft of rhododendrons and sank into them as into an eiderdown. At the touch of solid earth life surged through him once again. He opened his eyes like a man coming out of a bad dream, unroped, and sighed with happiness and relief.

'I'm down!'

Now it was Aline's turn. She had never roped down before, and Paul and Georges were giving her instructions. She did not like the idea of letting herself down into space at all; however, she managed to overcome her repugnance, but made such a clumsy start that she rebounded off the wall and swung to and fro against the rock, clutching the line that was cutting into her thigh.

'I don't like this one bit,' she shouted in disgust.

Pierre watched her from below; he had recovered his sangfroid, and it was the guide in him that now shouted up instructions.

'Hey, Aline, don't hold on so tight! Let the line run through your fingers!' Now he was angry. 'For God's sake let it run' – and now encouraging, 'very nice – now lean back a little – legs at right angles to your body – feet against the rock, and *dance* your way down.' Impatiently he stamped his feet. 'Look down, damn it – kick off from the rocks to keep your body well clear. That's better – you'll do your next rappel fine.'

Aline, still panting with excitement, rolled in the grass beside him and flung herself into his arms, entangled as she was in the rope.

'I thought it would never come to an end!' Then, coming back to the thought that was never far from her mind: 'There, dear, now you see how well you can climb. What d'you think?'

'With two men nursing me like that, of course it was all right, but we haven't done the hardest thing here.'

Georges came down last from the Aiguillette with the ease and assurance of a veteran climber.

'Pierre,' he said solemnly, 'if you and I can't climb the way we used to, it's because we haven't got enough guts. We shouldn't throw in the towel at the first trifling setback.'

'You're dead right, Georges, but you know if it hadn't been for the others I couldn't have done it. As it was, I had one bad moment.'

'It'll all come back to you, Pierre; if you like we'll do a few more things like this till you feel sure of yourself again. That's the best cure, you know.'

They sat down in a ring on the slabs at the foot of the climb, unpacked their provisions, took out their wine bottles, and ate and drank and laughed a great deal. The sun had described its arc round the chain of Mont Blanc, and shadows were creeping over the mountain. The breeze from the Col des Montets played on the rock face above them. Far away on the further slope could be heard the sound of bells, strangely muted, and overlaid by the deeper voice of waters. It was the dominant note of the pastoral scene, punctuated at times by the creaking and cracking of the glaciers against the furrowed flanks of the high mountains.

Exhilarated by the mountain air and by their own high spirits, the young people began to sing. Boule started it off and then the rest joined in, each singing his own part. Against the deep male chorus, Aline's voice rose crystal clear; and when it came to the refrain, Boule's jubiliant yodels out-soared them all, like a song heard above the mountain wind.

But this enchanting interlude had to come to an end. Georges, with one idea firmly planted in his head, interrupted the concert, coiled up the ropes, and stirred up his lazy friends.

'The Petite Aiguillette – that'll be a decisive test.'

'Are you out of your head, Georges?' asked Paul. 'That's not a climb for your first day. It's too hard – we'll come back some other time.'

'No, let's go now, while we're still well warmed up by the other climb.'

The Petite Aiguillette is nothing more than a splinter stuck on to the sides of the bigger one. Just a single spike, fifteen metres high on one side, sixty on the other. From the gap between the two Aiguillettes there is barely fifteen metres' climbing; but so steep and so exposed that few guides dare to take it on. Climbers who have led it can be counted on your fingers, and it was rated at 150 francs in the tariff of expeditions.

'Good pay for fifteen metres,' acknowledged Boule.

'It isn't enough,' objected Fernand; '150 francs for the risk of breaking your neck – that's much too little. To my mind they should have left this little rock alone – open to anyone who thinks he's capable of climbing it; but why on earth tempt young men to have a shot at it by the promise of quick profit?'

'You're dead right, Fernand,' said Pierre.

'You know,' put in Georges, 'I've already climbed it three times; so you just let me carry on.'

'I've done it several times – but never led it,' said Fernand.

They crawled into an underground crack, a curious well-like chimney that emerged just at the foot of the Petite Aiguillette. Seen from this angle, the face looked terribly exposed. There was a smooth slab that ended at an overhang; the overhang then had to be turned by a very delicate step, then an ill-defined little arête led up to the summit.

It is only a matter of seconds for a competent climber; people can either do it, or they can't. Under the overhang there is a fixed iron piton; it is the only safeguard for the leader, and even that would not prevent him, if he fell, from swinging like a pendulum over space in a position from which it would be extremely difficult to rescue him. Less daring climbers have adopted another solution; from a projection of the Grande Aiguillette they throw a rope over the summit of the Petite and climb up in perfect safety, held from above. But this inelegant method did not appeal to our young sportsmen.

Georges was standing in front of the slab like a boxer squaring up to his opponent. He gave the end of his rope to Fernand, who would safeguard him as best he could from here, which would not be very much. Before launching out he kicked his absurd boots against the rock – they were rounded like clogs, and gave him feet like an elephant's. With his knife he scraped off the grass and dirt stuck between his bootnails, took a deep breath, and started up. The rest of the party followed his progress with considerable anxiety, but they relaxed a little as they saw how beautifully this master of his craft moved up, making the utmost use of each of the infrequent handholds, gripping the slight irregularities in the rock surface with his great fingers, coming back a bit, in perfect balance, the better to place his maimed feet on some tiny ledge or wrinkle. He climbed very quickly up to the overhang. He had to turn it by an extremely delicate movement that would bring him on to the ridge. They could see him hesitate a moment; then, having calculated every movement, he embarked on the delicate traverse. Half his body disappeared from their sight, hidden by the bulging rock wall; his left hand, the only one now visible, was well placed on a good hold.

From this stance against the wall, Fernand watched the rope, which had suddenly stopped running through his fingers. What was happening? He could not see a thing from where he stood, but Aline, who had stepped back a little to follow the leader's progress better, suddenly gave the alarm.

'Pierre! Pierre!' she shouted. 'He's in trouble! His foot isn't holding – the boot's slipping as if he couldn't find a good hold.'

Faint gasps from above underlined the desperate effort Georges was making; they could only guess at it. Anxiously they stared at the hand clutching the rock; suddenly it began to tremble.

'Oh my God!' broke from Pierre, and before anyone could guess what he was up to he had flung himself at the slab, without a rope, without any kind of safeguard. Aline managed to stifle the anguished cry that rose from her constricted throat. Fernand, all too aware of his powerlessness, stood with great drops of sweat on his brow, bracing himself to take the strain on the rope. The rest, rendered speechless by surprise, waited for the inevitable climax.

With a few controlled movements Pierre was up to the overhang. He caught hold of Georges's rope, tied it to the piton, then he in turn launched out on to the delicate traverse till he was able to put all his weight on to Georges's hand and prevent him from letting go.

'Hold on, Georges, I'm here, it's OK, you're held now.'

He could feel that great knotted hand tightly clenched under his own fingers, and guided it around the corner out of sight. Those below heard a deep sigh and then Georges's voice, queer and strained.

'Got it! Lord – I couldn't get a grip with my nails on that little hold just the other side of the arête. I was spreadeagled all over the face, and I was getting pretty tired; if you hadn't come up, I would have let go.'

'Go on up, for God's sake,' said Pierre feverishly, 'get a move on, I'm not roped.'

And Georges suddenly realised that without a rope his friend was none too well placed, and might easily have another attack of vertigo. He swarmed quickly up the last few metres and without wasting a minute flung his rope down to Pierre.

'Here, catch!'

Pierre caught it with tremendous relief, tied himself on, and continued the climb. Now it was his turn for the bad step. Nothing beneath him – and now, for the first time, he looked his enemy squarely in the face. He even laughed. In the heat of action, something seemed to have suddenly cleared in his brain – as if someone had drawn back a veil. And, oh, blessed miracle, the larches had stopped spinning around, the whirligig had ceased, the landscape was motionless and the Aiguillette that he embraced was firmly planted, and no longer oscillated slowly from side to side as it had done that morning.

He shouted with joy and let out a triumphant yodel that reverberated in the still air. The others, who had not heard him sing for such a long time, were dumbfounded. Up in her rocky perch, looking like a little Italian with her kerchief knotted under her chin, Aline shed a few happy tears and didn't even bother to wipe them away.

Fernand winked at Boule.

'We won't need to bother that doctor of ours again!'

But Paul Mouny, the most level-headed of them all, was not at all pleased.

'What a pair of idiots! Break your necks, eh – you came mighty close to it. What's the idea of trying rocks like these when you've only got stumps for feet? And Pierre running up the slabs like that without roping, without any kind of safeguard. And he'll be telling us in a minute that he's afraid of vertigo. I've never heard of anything so crazy.'

'Come on, Paul,' urged Fernand, 'we're taking a bottle up to them on top, they deserve it.'

'Ask them to let you down a rope.'

'Catch me!' cried Fernand. 'Boule, take the sack; I'm off – so long!'

And he was off with a song on his lips, unerringly finding the right holds; then he disappeared behind the overhang. He was still singing when, five minutes later, he climbed on to the summit and clapped Pierre on the back.

'We're one up on the doctor, eh?'

Now that the moment of action was over, Pierre fell victim to a new unease. Once again the world had begun to spin around. He shut his eyes, but there was a sick feeling in his mouth; he crouched in a little hollow in the rock and leaned his head against the sun-warmed stone. The others eyed his pale face anxiously. With his hand, he motioned them to keep quiet.

'It's nothing – just a final attack – it'll pass off.'

Boule uncorked the bottle, poured the sparkling wine into the mugs, and feeling called on to propose a toast, declared: 'Well, boys, here's to our next big climbs.'

There came a shout from Aline below.

'What about me? Have you forgotten all about me?'

'Just you stay there, Aline, it's too hard for you; we'll be down in a minute.'

They came down on the doubled rope and were soon back on the platform. It was very cool in the shade; Pierre felt his anguish miraculously cured, and in its place he experienced a blessed peace, a matchless serenity.

'You know, Georges, if it hadn't been for you I could never have done it. But when I saw you being so brave, I drove myself to it;

I don't think I'm quite cured yet, but I'm certain now that I'll be able to climb again. So if you're in favour of it – what about going on with it?'

Georges gave him a friendly poke in the ribs.

'Whenever you want … It's the least I can do for you, after all, you saved my life.'

'Don't worry about that – plenty of time for you to pay me back. It's all in the day's work for a guide.'

They trudged down the path towards the valley. The sun was gradually withdrawing itself from the earth; a few light clouds floated midway up the high peaks. Above, everything was gilt and burnished by the setting sun; below, rock and pasture, forest and glacier were indistinguishable in the blue half-light, and only the torrent stood out clear, a silver thread between the pinewoods.

Chapter XXVII

All this side of the mountain lay deep in shadow. The sun had gone behind the tree-covered ridge; now it crudely lit up Aiguilles and glaciers, and only a few scattered rays filtered through to the damp and mossy hollow that holds the stagnant waters of the Lac des Gaillands. The aspen branches gleamed silver, outlined against the setting sun. Occasionally a trout jumped, breaking the calm surface of the lake, snapped at a fly and dived again with a swirl of ripples that spread out across the pond and spent themselves in tiny waves against the steep reed-covered banks. A frog let out its breath and flattened itself down in the rippling grass.

The cliff towering over the lake was covered with luxuriant vegetation, and streaked and seamed with cracks and gullies. It stretched right up to the peaceful forest above, and was overhung by a fringe of pine branches.

Pierre Servettaz slowly coiled up the ropes and examined them carefully before passing them to Georges, who stowed them neatly away in his sack. They had been doing some practice climbs on the hardest routes of the Gaillands rocks. Pierre's rope-soled shoes were slashed and muddy; he himself was still covered with earth and dead leaves, which he had collected during his tussles with the briary overhangs. Georges had been trying out a new pair of boots, specially made for him, with a solid edge of rubber in place of nails: 'Tyres, that's what they are,' had been Pierre's comment. They were exhausted and content, for they had successfully negotiated some exceptionally difficult routes; the big overhang, the Steiger Chimney, the Red Slab. Pierre had come through with flying colours. He was no longer the helpless puppet of two months back. He had regained control of his nerves, and though he occasionally felt vague qualms, each new climb had given him back a little more self-confidence. Yet up till now the pair of them had not ventured on a full-scale high-level expedition.

This evening they felt in the pink of condition. Seated on the damp grass at the water's edge, in the romantic setting of the little tarn beneath the great cliff, and invisible from the road, they chatted away quietly.

'Just look at those Aiguilles, Pierre! They're drying up fast; the snow couloirs have never been in such good condition. We'll have to make up our minds … The weather's fair, the days are long now, I feel on top of my form, and as for you – you could go anywhere you wanted!'

'I'm not so sure, Georges! I wonder how I'd get along in a real ice couloir, with a slope plunging down 1,000 metres beneath me? Even before this business I used to be pretty scared; what'd it be like now?'

'If you want to know, just go and find out,' was Georges's answer. 'What do you say to a real first-class expedition? For instance, the north face of the Aiguille Verte? The Argentière couloir must be in splendid condition; it's only been climbed once or twice. If we could get up, then we'd be ready to take up the mountains seriously again.'

'Don't you think that's a pretty big thing to take on? And it's not as if it were difficult rock – it's a snow climb.'

'All the more reason. It's a first-class climb, with ice and snow; a prolonged effort, a very steep slope more than 1,500 metres high, with ice on the rocks, steps to cut, and a difficult descent by the ordinary route. A really magnificent climb. Doesn't it tempt you?'

'Of course it does. But I get a sinking feeling when I think of trying it.'

'You'll just have to get over that. No use looking for more rock climbs. You've shown what you can do, I know you could go anywhere now, and you'll climb better and better as the season goes on. But a real mountain – a four-thousander! We'll have to take a shot at it!'

'All right. If you want, we can ask Fernand and Boule.'

'That's just what we shouldn't do. If they came we'd be relying too much on them: me with these fancy hooves of mine, and you with your buzzing ears. But if we do this climb on our own, with no outside help, then we'll show what we're really capable of.'

'You're absolutely right, we have to know once and for all. Shall we sleep up at the Jardin d'Argentière?'

'Yes.'

'When?'

'Tomorrow night. Mind, not a word to the others.'

They set off down the road to Chamonix, and Pierre's lithe catlike stride in his rope-soled shoes contrasted strangely with Georges's jerky gait in his special boots. They separated like conspirators at the entrance to the town.

'So long, Georges, till tomorrow!'

'So long!'

Chapter XXVIII

Next morning came. To avoid arousing suspicion, they had set out separately: Pierre on his bicycle, Georges by the little electric train that chugs along the valley at regular intervals.

They had arranged to meet on the moraine of the Argentière glacier, by the big rock that marks the start of the Lognan footpath. Pierre arrived first, in the heat of the afternoon. His sack was heavy: he slipped it off his shoulder with relief, and leaned against the big boulder, keeping an eye on the zigzags of the path, while he mopped his streaming brow. Soon he spotted Georges, several turns of the path below him, bent under an immense load. They met without a word. Georges sat down beside Pierre, breathed deeply, rolled up his shirtsleeves on his sinewy arms, and then, anxious to break the silence, let out a yell that dropped into space.

'Lord, what a sirocco, Pierre! But it'll hold up, it's an easterly wind.'

Pierre did not think it worthwhile answering yet: he emptied his sack and checked over the contents.

'I've got sixty metres of line,' he announced, 'in case the bergschrund's tricky coming down. Have you got enough rope?'

'Yes – forty metres of the eleven-millimetre rope.'

'That should do. And the ice pitons?'

'I've got twelve, though they weigh a hell of a lot, not to speak of four snap-links, helmet, crampons, gloves, glasses. God, what a lot of junk!'

'Yes, I've got all these too. We can bivouac if we have to.'

'Better not have to. A night out would be damn cold at 4,000 metres.'

'Well, we've got all these clothes.'

They started off again very slowly and made their way along the left bank of the glacier. The path climbed up through a straggling larch wood, between two narrow gorges whose roaring torrents were full with the melting of the snow.

Once again, they were passing beyond the tree line; only a few stunted larches tried to go any higher. Twisted, rickety, and battered by the snows and frosts of winter, they looked like suppliants praying to the gods of the mountaintops. The alp of Lognan displayed its carpet of juniper and dwarf rhododendron on the high mountainside – a veritable flower bed that stretched right up to the crumbly moraines and the glaciers. Milky torrents flowed out from the glaciers and tumbled in foam down to the narrow gorges and waterfalls; and, towards the east, the Argentière glacier streamed down to a great icefall of séracs, whose pillars, columns and cornices gleamed as if fashioned of the most delicate ivory shot through with sapphire blue.

The Lognan chalet-hotel, a solid two-storey building, overlooks this waste of glacier; it is the hut nearest to the climbs in the Argentière basin, but Pierre and Georges would have to pass it by. A pity – a rest would have been very welcome; it would have been very tempting to spend this night in warmth and shelter. Pierre, especially, hesitated.

'Suppose we slept here, Georges?' he suggested. 'After all, it would only put us back an hour and a half in the morning, and it would be a lot more comfortable than that awful shack at the Jardin. It's half broken down, anyway, and I imagine it'll be full of snow.'

'No – you know it's a serious business to be set back an hour and a half, Pierre. If we want to find the snow in good condition in the couloir, we shouldn't spend the night here. We can rest here now, if you like; but then we've got to get moving.'

Pierre said no more, for he knew that Georges was right and spoke from experience. What he could not admit was that he was now very frightened of going up there at all. Here, there was still life and civilisation. There was an excellent guardian at the hut; there were rooms and beds, and looking straight down from here to the valley you could even see the pastures and fields and little clusters of chalets by the Arve.

All this was very reassuring to a beginner, for Pierre felt this day that he was a beginner again. He might have been climbing the High Alps for the first time. Already he was shivering at the idea of the steep slopes they would have to climb tomorrow; he shuddered as he thought of the lonely vigil ahead of them, away up on the glacier that was silent as an undiscovered territory. His nervous apprehension betrayed itself in a physical uneasiness that made him more heavy, more clumsy. Georges noticed this, and knew this condition well enough to realise that in one minute the desire for security might triumph over the love of adventure. So he cut short the tempting rest at the Lognan hut.

'Come on! Let's get going! If we hang around here, it'll foul up the whole night.'

Unlike Pierre, he was bursting with energy, and full of a wild joy at the prospect of once more battling on the heights.

Taking the path that starts above the hut, they reached the left-hand moraine of the glacier. The track follows the actual crest of the moraine; on one side lies a savage waste of ice which cracks and disintegrates into indescribable chaos; on the other, the charm and gentleness of pastures starred with gentians, arnicas and primroses. What a contrast! On one side, the smiling prospect of the alp, bounded by the elaborate candelabra of the larches, where the streams weave iridescent threads, where hazelcocks call under the sundrenched alders; on the other, a polar region of ice and granite, over which now blew an icy wind. And these two such different worlds lie side by side for nearly an hour's walking, till the crest of the moraine narrows down and becomes no more than a wrinkle of grey pebbles which suddenly disappears in the huge rock face.

Stepping on to the glacier, the two walked quickly over the ice, strewn with fallen stones, then presently came in sight of last winter's yellow snow, all honeycombed by running water. Georges went on ahead, followed by a silent and apprehensive Pierre. He was beginning to wish they had never started: only his desperate pride kept him from turning around, from leaving everything and bolting for the valley. He calculated that by hurrying down he could just reach Argentière before nightfall; but he was ashamed of his weakness, and in adjusting his step to Georges's short stride, he noticed the maimed feet that were marking out his path for him, as if showing a faintheart his duty. How could he think of running away while Georges there, in front, was showing such an example?

Gradually the angle of the glacier eased off. It looked as if the slope came to an end a little higher up; a reef of ice stood up on the skyline, sharply outlined, white on blue, like the threshold of a new world. The two climbers kept on past the shattered rocks, made a detour around some wide crevasses, and climbed up a snow incline to the upper plateau.

Possibly somewhere in the world there are glaciers longer, higher, and more broken than the Argentière glacier. Yet you cannot help being impressed when you reach this high and icy valley, practically level, seven kilometres long, and bounded by a wall of rock and ice which has no equal in Europe. There is such a sharp contrast between the deceptive mildness of the plateau, riddled with crevasses invisible under the dazzling white blanket, and the kilometre-high precipices that stretch like an impassable barrier along the left bank of the glacier! At its head, an equally redoubtable barrier separates France from Italy and from Switzerland. No three other countries have such a superb meeting-point. Mont Dolent, which marks the boundary, raises its icy mitre more than 1,000 metres above the glacier.

On the right bank, the outlook is a little less grim: that is to say, the slopes are slightly less steep, slightly less forbidding; but there too is a barrier of red rock, twisted and shattered, gouged into deep clefts down which wind little tributaries of ice. But the eye is always drawn back to the north-facing walls, each more baffling than the last. Some daring climbers have forced new routes up them; one by one, the rocky ledges, the ice slopes, the hanging glaciers, have had to surrender to man and yield their secrets to climbers whom nothing could daunt.

Yet there is still some untrodden ground, which with a thousand glances of its icy armour mocks those who venture on that plain of ice. As you survey it, you think of far-off places – Greenland,

Spitsbergen, or even the mysterious glaciers of the Himalaya, or the desolate valleys of the Caucasus. It is as beautiful and as impressive, and when you step on to it, after the wearisome plod up from Lognan, you feel as if you were going into some secret chamber of the earth; the glacier is only a canyon with no way out of it, barred on three sides by rock and ice, while on the fourth, the valley side, it appears to open on to an abyss. You can see nothing of the landscape beyond. You guess vaguely that beyond the shelf that drops over into space there is an enormous hole, at the foot of which live men. You can see a few modest peaks far off on the hazy horizon, but every part of you that thinks and dreams is here monopolised by the perpendicular walls that dominate, crush, submerge, and are apparently just about to topple over on the explorer who dares to violate their mysterious solitude.

The two guides had halted on the edge of the glacier and were sitting on their sacks in the snow. Georges scrutinised the lofty walls with an experienced eye and let out a whistle of admiration.

'Look at this couloir, Pierre! Did you ever see such a straight line! Seen face on, it looks unbelievably steep. Looks like we'll have a little step-cutting tomorrow, especially towards that bulge in the middle where the ice is gleaming. The bergschrund looks pretty bad. All right, we'll take it on. What d'you say to it?'

'Hm.'

Pierre could find nothing to say. He hardly dared to lift his eyes to examine the hazardous route they would take tomorrow, the sight of which so delighted Georges. He wished that they had arrived there after dark, so that they would have seen nothing, and could have attacked the mountain without having time to think of what lay in front of them. Now he would be haunted all night by the dizzy vision of this thin streak of snow dividing the mountain, plunging in one swoop from the summit of the Aiguille Verte, 4,121 metres high, to the glacier plateau – 1,200 metres without a break, without a resting place, without any easing of the angle of the slope, without any sun-warmed rocks for the hands to grasp! For hours – maybe for days – they would have to stand on slippery little steps and risk losing their balance at the slightest movement.

In that case, he knew it would be useless to count on the support of the rope; it would be almost nonexistent. If one man were to fall here, then the whole party would fall – in such places the rope can only be a moral link between the climbers.

Obsessed by his fears, Pierre determined to drive out thought by action; he rose to his feet and quickly buckled up the straps of his sack. 'Come on, Georges, let's not stay here, it's beginning to get cold.' But his words were only a flimsy cover for his uneasiness. Taking the lead, he made a beeline across the great glacier: the snow was deep, and heavy, for the sun had been on it all afternoon. Pierre was very tired, but he refused to change places with his companion, for this healthy exhaustion acted like a drug on his uneasy spirit. He hoped to arrive at the refuge completely played out; then he might stand a better chance of sleeping. The two men were wading up to their thighs in slush; their boots were soaked through. What a damned nuisance it was; it would mean spending the night like this – well, they'd have to be on their guard against frostbite.

After two exhausting hours on the interminable glacier, they reached the little moraine of the Glacier des Améthystes; somewhere among its huge grey rocks lurked the hut, half submerged in the arête. What a miserable, neglected hovel it was! It was certainly in deplorable condition. The movements of the glacier and the moraine had cracked and split it; the little windows were jammed. A huge mass of snow blocked the entrance, and the climbers had to clear it away with their axes before they could get at the door. After many attempts, they managed to open it just wide enough to let them in. It was dark and freezing inside. The wind had blown through all the cracks and crannies, the blankets were covered with snow, and the damp mattresses smelled of decay. The hut had been condemned, and practically abandoned. There had been talk of building a new one, higher up on the rocks, but they had been discussing the site now for several years. It had to be sheltered from avalanches, and every autumn specialists would come and build little cairns which they would then return to inspect next spring. Usually, all their work had been swept away by some unpredictable fall; and they had to begin all over again on another site. The work needed patience, experience and perseverance. In the meantime, the old hut was in the throes of dissolution, wrenched out of place by the moving soil of the moraine. The wind howled through it, and all around it the jackdaws, attracted by the sight of the climbers, croaked mournfully in the evening breeze.

The two men set to work, cleaned out the hut, put the blankets outside to get more or less dry. Then Pierre melted snow on the little spirit stove for their evening soup. It took a long time, but at last they were eating an indeterminate hot soup that sent warmth flowing through bodies chilled by the cold and dampness of the hut. They were so busy preparing for their great expedition that night was on them before they knew it. They made tea and poured it into their water bottles; they took off their wet boots and stuffed them with straw, wrung out their woollen stockings and delicately hung them up to dry in front of the spirit stove. It was getting late, and the cold penetrated everywhere; the melted water from the roof dripped from a gutter on to a corner of the table, with a monotonous drip-drop sound that would shortly cease, when the frost came to arrest the translucent stalactites glittering like silver-spangled candles under the broken roof.

Deeply moved by the unbelievable silence and calm of evening, and by the mountains standing over them on all sides, the two climbers hardly spoke, exchanging only the few necessary words, and a short abrupt phrase or two. 'Pass me the kettle ... Make sure of those crampon tapes ... Need some more snow for tomorrow morning ... We ought to lie down and take forty winks ... D'you think we'll bivouac tomorrow night?' The questions usually received no reply. Each of the two was full of his own thoughts. Pierre was the victim of a new unease. It was too late now to go back. He would have to start, against his will, on this expedition out of all proportion to his present powers. In his mind's eye he could see again that sinister couloir embossed with black ice, and it appeared even steeper and more interminable, as if it were reaching far above the earth, right up to the stars.

Very different was Georges's state of mind. He felt brisk, light-hearted and happy, and dying with impatience to be off. If it weren't that he realised the importance to their enterprise of two hours' sleep and rest, he would have started off straightaway into the night by lantern light. But that would be crazy. He must be sensible, and rest, and keep calm. The struggle that waited for him tomorrow would be severe, yes, very severe, it was their lives they were staking; and they didn't have the right to stake them unless they were sure that they had all the trumps in their hand.

Reason triumphed at last. 'Let's lie down, Pierre. Got to keep up our strength!'

They had chosen the least damp part of the shelf, and lay there rolled up in blankets. They had put on all the clothes they had brought with them, helmets and sweaters, but still they could not get warm. They hugged each other tight to pool the heat of their bodies. They had blown out the candle, but they could not get to sleep; they knew they would not have been able to sleep for thinking of this melancholy vigil in the derelict and ruined hut. So they forced themselves not to think of it, and now and then, overcome by tiredness, they dropped off. A few minutes later they woke up with a start, certain that they had slept for hours. Then they turned over again, trying to find more comfortable positions, till finally, worn out by exhaustion, they suddenly fell fast asleep, as if losing consciousness altogether.

Chapter XXIX

Promptly at midnight Georges threw off the blankets, lit the candle and shook Pierre, who got up mechanically. Silence reigned in the hut – silence and cold. Dazedly they eyed their half-frozen boots, which they had to rub with their hands for a few minutes before they could get them on their feet. Even so, they had to force their feet in, for their damp socks stuck against the stiff leather. It was like putting on clogs a couple of sizes too small. Steam began to rise from the little pannikin of tea warming on the spirit stove. They tried to eat, but their stomachs rejected the idea of food at such an unusual hour. Well, it couldn't be helped – but they could certainly have used it, for once well away on that ice slope, there would be no halt till they got to the top – and that was some distance away!

The hut had been tidied, the door carefully shut, sacks fastened, and at one o'clock they were ready to start. The lamp lit up a little circle of snow-covered stones, and nothing at all beyond. It was inky dark, with only a few paler streaks showing over against the great rock walls. These were the ice couloirs. A terrific roar broke the baleful silence of the night; somewhere opposite a sérac had heeled over and crashed on to the glacier in a cloud of dust.

Picking their way over the wobbly stones, they reached the lowest slopes of the mountain, and the snow became steeper. They climbed slowly on for an unconscionably long time, heads well down, examining the crevasses that suddenly confronted them, like skylights opening on to unseen depths below. They contoured around a clump of séracs; it was now just light enough for them to make out the landscape, and an icy dawn came up to meet them as they reached the edge of the bergschrund. They had been going for three hours; this would be the last stop.

Above them, the couloir went up so steeply that they had to crane their necks to see the top. An insignificant little cornice barred the way out; the foreshortening made it look quite close. But Georges and Pierre were not to be deceived by this trick of perspective. It was a tremendous undertaking they were now embarking on, for there were 1,200 metres of that vertical-looking slope to be climbed; from here it looked so steep in parts as to be almost overhanging. Pierre could not keep his eyes off the summit high above. That little cornice up there fascinated and intrigued him. He was frightened now, but he would not give up; he realised the difficulties ahead, but far from wanting to shirk the ordeal, he had only one thought in his head: to fling himself into the struggle. Does not real courage consist of victory over fear?

Georges was calmer, and full of common sense.

'Better have a bite here. We've got to nurse our strength. We won't be able to count on another stop after this. The slope's too steep; we'll have to cut steps all the way up to the bulge, without any chance of a breather.'

They forced themselves to swallow something: biscuits, chocolate, an apple. They filled their pockets with prunes and lumps of sugar, and fixed on their crampons, threading the tapes with meticulous care.

Georges had not even raised the question of who was to lead. He took it for granted he would go first, and assumed command of the party with no objection from Pierre. He tied himself on at one end of a fifty-metre rope, fastened a few ice pitons and snap-links on to his belt, made sure that his axe sling was firmly around his wrist, and finally turned his attention to the next stage of the climb. The bergschrund was very high and wide, and the upper lip overhung the lower by several metres. There were no rocks visible except on the extreme right, but if they tried that spur, they would be forced out well beyond the couloir. And they had pledged themselves to follow the most elegant route, a straight line from base to summit.

They scouted along the edge of the crevasse, looking for the easiest point of attack: a fragile snow-bridge allowed them to reach a little chimney in the ice of the upper lip. To climb up it would be the only possible way of surmounting the overhang.

'It'll need a lot of steps,' grunted Georges, 'but it should go all right, it's just a matter of patience. Ready, Pierre?'

'Yes, I'm ready. Let's get going.'

Georges tested the snow-bridge with his ice-axe. It was a thin yet solid arch of snow spanning an apparently fathomless gulf. Pierre stepped back a pace or two, planted his ice-axe firmly in the deep snow, and made ready to safeguard his companion on the next stage.

The snow-bridge abutted on to the ice wall of the upper lip. Georges set to work scooping out holds in the bare ice, buckets for feet, pigeonholes for hands, and mounted very slowly.

He had to do all his cutting with one hand, a tiring job, with the cold freezing his fingers through their woollen gloves. He got up five or six metres; then, on reaching the overhang at the foot of the ice chimney, he hammered in a long piton and passed his rope through the ring; it ran through beautifully.

'Well, that's that,' he announced.

He came down again quickly on the rope and recrossed the snow-bridge to snatch a minute's rest beside Pierre. He took his gloves off, blew on his fingers and rubbed them vigorously to restore circulation; then advanced once more to the attack, climbed quickly up to the piton, using the steps he had already made, and gingerly inserted the upper part of his body into the crack in the ice. It was too narrow for him to cut steps in the usual way, so he stuck his ice-axe in his belt, took his knife and cut out some little handholds, then shuffled up by the pressure of his crampon points on the sides, just as if he were climbing a crack in a rock face. His progress was exceedingly slow, and he was getting tired, but he managed to get up about ten metres in this fashion. Now he was overhanging the yawning gash of the bergschrund that plunged down into the blue depths below. Finding a little knob of ice, he used it to stand on for a moment and rest. A second piton, thin as a knife blade, was driven into the ice. Lifting his head he could see the top of the little chimney a few metres above him, and beyond it the sky, which he seemed to be looking at from the bottom of a well.

'Just one more heave and I'm up,' he shouted cheerily down to Pierre.

Without a moment's respite he continued to battle his way up hugging the ice, or moving up by the pressure of hands and legs on opposite walls. The crack widened, and he continued to climb with his body arched over space, his hands firmly gripping tiny holds that quickly filled with icy water. To get out of the crack involved a last delicate manoeuvre. He braced himself up on the points of his crampons that scratched and scored the blue ice and, taking out his axe again, managed to drive it into the upper lip; then very gently he hoisted himself on to it and with a final effort crawled on to the snow slope above. The sun touched him just as he straightened up, and he let out a triumphant yodel. He could feel the warmth all around him now, his muscles played more freely, his blood ran more warmly. After struggling in the shadow and chill of the ice chimney, it was like coming back to life.

Down below Pierre was absolutely frozen and his teeth were chattering. But the fears he had been so ashamed of had miraculously vanished in the face of real difficulties. It was a new man who heard Georges's happy cry, a man eager for action. The rope ran out easily down the ice chimney. Pierre tucked his ice-axe into his belt, checked his crampon fastenings yet again, and started up in great spirits. As he went he used his hammer to knock the precious pitons out, and clipped them on to his belt; it was his turn now to hug the ice and worm his way up towards the sun. An intensely blue patch of sky overhead showed him the way; at last, quite breathless with his rapid ascent, he sat down beside Georges. Beneath them yawned the bergschrund, beyond it lay the glacier, whose surface curled, writhed and cracked like boiling porridge.

They turned and looked up.

It had taken them three hours to get across the bergschrund, without gaining any height worth speaking of. When they stood up, their bodies almost touched the slope that mounted skywards so dizzily; there was nothing to break the uncannily monotonous line of the couloir except a trough scooped out by avalanches on its even surface. From this point, everything was foreshortened; there was nothing to indicate the scale or emphasise the verticality of the whole scene. There was nothing but this white wall scored and grooved by the stones that chipped away its surface; dirty at the edges, under the rock ridges now encased in verglas, with a black trail marking where stones had fallen in the rare intervals of thaw.

To begin with, the couloir was hard snow; it was possible to get some sort of foothold in it, to make a step with one hearty kick. Pierre was now leading, for Georges's injury handicapped him here; he made steady progress up the slope, keeping well to the side of the avalanche groove and its polished marble-like sides. It felt like climbing up a colossal ladder that would take him into a strange new world. He used his hands as well as his feet, driving the point of his axe into the snow, and pressing the other hand flat against the slope to keep himself in balance. His crampons bit into the hard snow; in this way he got up a rope's length. And when he looked down between his legs, it was like nothing on earth – a gigantic slide, narrowing into the distance, and coming to an end in the bottleneck of the bergschrund. As soon as Pierre had climbed his fifty metres, at top speed and without a halt, he drove his axe deep into the snow, belayed the rope around it, and took it in evenly as Georges climbed up. The slightest movement, the slightest loss of balance, would be fatal. But he could snap his fingers at the very idea. Never had he felt so absolutely confident, and last night's misgivings had vanished like a bad dream; all that concerned him at this present moment was how best to safeguard his friend's advance. Their two lives were firmly linked by the rope that made them equal sharers in risk and danger. As he leaned against the slope he could see, framed between his legs, Georges climbing upwards, nose touching the snow, rigorously observing that inflexible rule of mountaineering, that you must always have three points of contact; two legs and a hand must be well placed before the other hand moves, or two hands and a leg before you move the other leg. Georges indulged in none of those daring manoeuvres by which people steady themselves in a tight corner with cold sweat breaking out all over their bodies.

Georges was close to him now. It was his turn to drive in his axe and pay the rope out to his friend. And still they climbed; the sun was shining full on the ice slope and they put on their aluminium-rimmed goggles; but even through the smoked glasses they were dazzled, so bright it shone. The ultraviolet rays burned their cheeks, and they scooped out huge handfuls of snow to rub on their faces. Tiredness was forgotten; there always comes a moment when it vanishes, when the human machine seems to be so beautifully tuned up that men can keep going for hours, days, nights, and days again without feeling the least exhaustion.

The angle became even steeper, and because of an imperceptible change in the orientation of the slope, the good hard snow up which they could safely walk in crampons had given way to treacherous powder overlying black ice. They were barely halfway up the couloir, and yet, in that limited perspective, the summit looked near enough to touch by hand. They took their bearings by the rock ridges beside them, and glanced quickly over the great face on which they were stuck like a couple of flies on a windowpane. Poor little manikins caught in the clutches of this most inhuman mountain!

Up here, every gesture had its value, every movement counted for something, every response could kill or save; this was no question of gaily overcoming a difficult short pitch, a situation so common on a rock climb. Here the climber must concentrate all his attention and determination, force himself tirelessly to repeat the same movements. Up to this point all had gone well, and if the good snow had continued, Pierre would have had every hope of reaching the summit dome in another hour or two; and now, under the harmless-looking top layer, this ice appeared to menace them.

'This is no joke,' he muttered.

His axe no longer bit into the slope; he felt it bounce back from the black ice that lay under ten centimetres of powder snow. Carefully he examined the slope above; his eyes scanned it slowly, trying to see the best line to follow.

There was one possible solution: to traverse sideways to the rocky spur by the left bank of the couloir – that tempted him strongly. An hour's step-cutting, at most, and he would be able to rest on sound rock, and then make his way up pretty easily to the top. But there was nothing particularly creditable in simply trying to sidestep any difficulty. Before starting, they had made up their minds to go up by the couloir; they would have to go through with it, and the man who had quaked in advance at the idea of cutting steps on a slope of seventy degrees now found considerable satisfaction in examining the difficulty. With a few energetic strokes of the axe he carved himself out a comfortable platform for his feet; it was not so much a step as a bucket, to use the jargon of climbers; then, taking out an ice piton, he hammered it in. Now he could allow himself a little latitude, and he beckoned to Georges to come up. When he had joined him, Pierre indicated the next stage.

'D'you see it?'

'Hm – looks tricky,' admitted Georges. 'Just look at that slab of ice gleaming in the sun; we'll have to keep to the right edge of the couloir.'

'No use – it'd be even worse. It's covered with powder snow, and I suspect it's lying on ice. I'd just as soon tackle the obstacle direct.'

It was Georges's turn to watch the couloir plunging down between his legs.

'Lord, what an angle! And what a fall, if you slipped!'

'If you fell, you'd slide down and shoot over the bergschrund the way you do when you're ski-jumping,' said Pierre optimistically. 'Maybe you'd survive.'

'Bourrisson did after rolling down 600 metres on the Col de la Tour des Courtes!'

'And there was that Englishman on the Col de Miage.'

'And Fernand from Praz-Conduits on the Thendia glacier!'

And they recalled all the miraculous escapes of the last few years in which by some extraordinary stroke of luck climbers had survived a sensational fall.

'But for the moment,' declared Georges, 'our business is to go on, and not to fall off. Let me go ahead now; you must be pretty well fagged out.'

'No, there's too much hard ice up there – you'd be handicapped by those big hooves of yours!'

'Well, what about your head?'

Pierre turned face outwards and spat disdainfully. 'Listen, boy, I don't know if we're going to pull this climb off or not, but I do know that vertigo's a fraud. I'm in good form today; let me carry on.'

'Certainly, if you want to.'

Pierre fingered the ice pitons bristling at his belt to verify their exact position, made sure that his axe was well slung on to his wrist, and set to work again on the tedious business of cutting steps. Chips of ice broke off under the axe; he took a slightly slanting line up the slope, moving with the utmost assurance, nicking out small holds for the hands and cutting beautiful, narrow, long steps for the feet. He was cutting his way up the high mountainside, and it was slow work. Down below Georges watched him; then all of a sudden, tired of this forced inactivity, he leant his whole body against the slope and bathed his burning face in the snow.

Pierre had now come to grips with the stretch of blue ice that had gleamed so brightly in the sunlight; it was so hard that it flaked off and he had to hack out each step with short, precise axe-strokes. His crampons barely bit into the ice on the steps, and the slope was by now so steep that, when it was a matter of changing feet, he had to cut an extra nick.

So absorbed was he in his step-cutting that he never noticed some stones, loosened by the sun's heat, come bounding down the couloir. Georges gave a warning cry –

'Stones – look out!'

He just managed to press himself flat against the slope, and as there had been no time to finish the step, he was balancing on the points of his crampons. An object as big as his fist whizzed past his ears, then another, and a third, which by all reasoning should have fractured his skull, merely whipped off his beret, barely grazing his scalp.

It had been a near thing. Very slowly Pierre recovered his pos-tion. It took some doing, and he started off again on his interminable step-cutting.

'Rope's nearly out,' warned Georges.

Phlegmatically, Pierre hacked out another platform, drove in another piton, and brought his friend up beside him. His arm was heavy and felt half-paralysed; he could barely grip the handle of his axe.

'You're tired, Pierre; let me go first.'

'No, you won't; I'll see us through on the ice. I swore I'd do it. You can lead the rest of the way.'

If only they could drink something! But they could not even think of it. Taking off a sack would have been far too dangerous a manoeuvre – no false moves in a place like this!

Pierre put his lips to the ice slope and sucked the melted water greedily. He started up again as lightly as a ballet dancer, and as soon as he was a few steps up, Georges took his place on the platform. So the ascent continued; a desperately monotonous business. The sun was by now high in the sky; they reckoned it might well be noon, possibly two in the afternoon; they were not going to avoid a bivouac this time! Their sacks were heavy and their stomachs empty; hastily they took a few prunes out of their pockets and munched them to deaden the pangs of hunger.

Pierre managed to get up a hundred metres further at the cost of unprecedented efforts. He noticed a patch of snow not far off that looked more inviting; he slanted across to it, and found to his delight that the snow was half-thawed and easy to manipulate. He got his hands and feet well dug into it; in his impatience he would have climbed up the whole way like this, but he had forgotten Georges away behind, still grappling with the bad stretch.

A pull on the rope, followed by a shout, brought him back to his responsibilities.

'Easy, up there, or you'll bring me off.'

Pierre turned around to watch his friend, and quite suddenly, as he observed Georges clinging to this incredible ice slope by the tips of his fingers and crampons, he was overcome by vertigo! Everything spun around; the couloir corkscrewed down below him, as if it were trying to bore its way into the glacier. With a great effort of will he managed to exorcise the awful scene, and leaned his whole length up against the snow slope. Georges, now near at hand, yelled at him to get going; he started, went up a rope's length by the simple expedient of digging his hands and feet into the snow, and then, when he seemed to have reached some sort of a stance, he squatted down. It was the merest projection, but the angle was now no more than forty to forty-five degrees, and compared with the dizzy precipice they had just come up, this particular slope looked both level and inviting.

They extracted the flask of tea from the sack and took a long pull at it. Oh, the beautiful freshness of the tea in their parched mouths! They could have gone on drinking for ever, but had to ration themselves strictly, for they still had a night out ahead of them. And what a night!

With a few strokes of the axe Georges had scooped out a sort of seat in the snow slope; at last they could rest. The heat was now stifling; the red handkerchiefs which they knotted around their heads made them look like a pair of Italian bandits, a bizarre enough sight in this deserted spot. Beneath their feet the slope plunged down as if it were constantly being renewed from above. All the time the heavy avalanches roared down; before long they saw one break off just a hundred metres below them and wipe out their upward tracks like an eraser.

'We'd better not hang around here,' growled Georges, 'we're right smack in the line of fire. Better ease off a little towards the right-hand edge!'

So off they set again and Georges, now in the lead, stamped his way up a sort of steep rib of snow; at last the heavy snow came to an end, and gave way just underneath the summit to a slope that ran steeply up to the enormous cornice that barred the final approach.

On their right, over to the north, the ridge of the Grands Montets, with its rocky towers and battlements, jagged as the teeth of a saw, projected above the ice slopes.

Still the ascent continued, and now that victory was near it seemed boring and monotonous; the enemy that had kept them going in the heat of action now flagged, and they were beginning to feel extremely tired; but they were determined to reach the top at all costs, and would not allow themselves even the briefest respite.

Pierre tasted the sweets of victory – a double victory, over the mountain and over himself. At long last he was at peace, and he climbed with the serenity of a man who knows beyond all doubt that he will attain the goal he has set himself. He was already planning great things; he would be a porter this year, but next year he would pass the test, and he could see himself with the guides' round badge on his jacket. 'You're going to be a guide,' he repeated to himself, 'you're going to be a guide' – and he turned a proprietary eye on the tangle of mountaintops. This was his kingdom by right of conquest! He had paid dearly for the winning of it, yet not so much as his poor old friend stumping up the snow in front on maimed feet. Pierre could not restrain his happiness.

'Georges,' he yelled, 'Georges, we've done it, we're all right! There's no doubt about it, I'll be a guide!'

'Me too!' bawled Georges, without turning round. 'And no later than tomorrow, when we're back and we've shown them what kind of men we are.'

Far below, the level glacier gleamed like a mass of molten metal; heavy trails of smoke floated towards the Col Dolent. Suddenly the climbers noticed that they had overtopped the nearer peaks.

Over to the east the Swiss Alps stretched line upon line towards the horizon, links of a chain separated by seas of cloud. There was the Grand Combin, so near and so enormous, mounting guard over the Val d'Aosta, and further back the white and magnificent Weisshorn, the pointed tooth of the Dent Blanche, and the Dent d'Hérens whose black rocks were streaked with ice. Beyond soared the challenging spike of the Matterhorn, its symmetry deformed by the nose on the Zmutt ridge that looked so blue in the shadow of the mountains, and the polar wastes of Monte Rosa, floating far above the earth. Further to the north lay the heaped-up mess of the Oberland peaks, a tangle of summits and glaciers. Lower down were the ridiculous little blue hillocks of Faucigny and Chablais which, seen from here, appeared to be no more than wrinkles on the face of the earth. And near, so near that it looked as if one could have tossed a stone into it, was the deep hollow of the Chamonix valley, with tracks and forests, villages and roads, standing out like an enormous relief map. But the splendours of the distant landscape took away nothing from the beauty of the foreground, with all those peaks so close to them, yet separated by impassable avalanche-swept couloirs. But their gaze always came around again to the smooth and shining slope that curved down to the glacier. And as he gazed, Pierre could not help murmuring:

'And we actually came up there!'

Certainly they had won their victory, certainly they had come up there; and now they could afford to laugh at their fears. It was as conquerors that they reached the summit cornice. It overhung most dangerously; if it were to break away, it would sweep them like straws down the slope to the gaping bergschrund. It was the last obstacle, and not the least.

Pierre took the lead again.

'Let me tackle this, Georges, I've had an account to settle with a cornice ever since that one on the Brévent.'

While Georges watched him, alert to check any slip, he attacked the obstacle with his axe, broke off the stalactites of ice that hung menacingly down and snapped like glass at his touch; then scooping away with the blade of his axe he began to tunnel through the cornice, wriggled himself in, poked the shaft of his axe right up, then pulled it out again. Through the tiny oval hole he could just see the opposite slope.

'That's done it, we're there!' With a few blows of the pick he finished knocking off the cornice, then hoisted himself on to the summit, to be sent staggering immediately by a great gust of wind; but he recovered in a minute and began yelling like a madman with delight.

Then the two of them, standing on a ridge as narrow as the gable of an Alsatian house, hugged each other and shook hands – for two cents they would have embraced! They did not give a moment's thought to the descent. There is no easy route on the Aiguille Verte, and to get down they would have to face the steep and dangerous Whymper couloir, a funnel for stones and avalanches. No matter. They could make light of it now. Let darkness come, and with it the inevitable bivouac; they had conquered, and they were certainly not going to give the mountain any further chance to defeat them.

Chapter XXX

They considered what to do next.

'It's too late to go down, and the snow would be too soft in the couloir,' said Pierre. 'Let's stay up here till sunset; then we can bivouac lower down the ridge, on the rocks. What do you say to that?'

'What about going on all night?' suggested Georges.

'No good – we're tired, and anyway there's only a stump of candle left, and there aren't any steps. Sooner or later we'd be forced to bivouac – so we might as well pick a good place now.'

'What if bad weather catches us here?'

'Just look around – we're not taking much of a risk.'

There was clearly nothing more to fear; the elements were on their side. Sunset lingered on the high peaks. It was already dark in the plains, but up here on this summit, over 4,000 metres high, they towered above the shadows and were still touched by the tender gleams of the dying day.

Twilight set the west afire with violent, livid streaks, like a display of Northern Lights above the shadowy valleys. They felt like castaways stranded on a polar ice floe, at the edge of a sea of shadows that was already lapping their snowy reef. Now only a few points held the light: the 4,000-metre summits, five or six glowing centres that kept watch, like so many lighthouses, over the sleep of men below. One after another they went out; and at last there were only two left: Monte Rosa to the east, Mont Blanc to the west. Monte Rosa dimmed its light, then vanished into darkness, and finally the invisible watchman, decreeing it was now time for all to rest, extinguished the last gleams illuminating the dome of Mont Blanc.

But down in the valleys at once appeared the lights of men.

The larger places could be recognised by the luminous halo around them; the sparkling row down there must surely be Geneva, and over to the north, that delicate pattern of lights would be Lausanne. Beyond these larger clusters, flickering little lights appeared and disappeared all over the range, even in the remotest parts. That faint light nearly 2,000 metres below them, keeping solitary vigil in the heart of the Mont Blanc massif – surely it must be the Couvercle? Snug between its walls, men would be nearing the end of an evening spent around the common table; no doubt they would be busy getting their sacks ready for their departure in the small hours. Tomorrow, perhaps, some of them would climb up as far as this magnificent summit where Pierre and Georges were about to bivouac.

The cold brought them back to the realities of the present moment. They went a rope's length down on the Talèfre side and sheltered from the north wind down on the arête. A precarious shelter it was, for the wind blew across the Col de la Grande Rocheuse, that sickle fashioned in ice that makes an impossible and neglected col between Argentière and Talèfre.

The first rocks loomed above the ghostly Whymper couloir. That was where they would go down tomorrow, before the sun could loosen the stones from their icy bed. In the meantime they contrived to hack out a little platform, and shovelled out enough snow to make a pretty comfortable hole. They lined it with their ropes, to provide some sort of insulation against the cold. Inside this little grotto there was just room to move, but their labours had induced a gentle glow and they were anxious to keep the warmth in. Pierre took out the spirit stove and melted snow in his pannikin. It was slow in melting; the water then came quickly to the boil. They put in some tea and sugar – their last remaining provisions. The brew tasted wonderful. They huddled together, struggling against their increasing drowsiness, for they knew very well how dangerous sleep would be at such a temperature. So they made themselves very busy; they carefully unlaced their crampons (the straps were beginning to freeze), put their feet in their sacks, muffled their faces in their helmets, all but their eyes, and then, with nothing left to do, they began to sing. Under the brilliant night sky of the high peaks, they bawled away at the tops of their voices.

Pierre went through his whole repertoire: mountain songs, drinking songs, and even an occasional aria from an opera. Georges, who could not sing a note in time, provided the bass. When they had sung everything they knew, they stopped, quite exhausted, and dozed off for a while; but not for long. The cold woke them up and the singing began again; it was better than just sitting with chattering teeth.

Nights are short at the end of June when you are 4,000 metres up. As light slowly filtered back they began to suffer in earnest from the cold. They lit the spirit stove and warmed up a fresh brew. They were still numb from the night's exposure, and prayed for the sun, which would surely not be long now. Mont Blanc was already aglow – and a warm puff reached them, encircled them, and brought them back to life. Snow that had been grey and livid now sparkled from every crystal. They left their foxhole, took great breaths in the sunlight and slapped each other vigorously on the back until they were ready to face the descent.

The first step was extremely difficult: the top of the couloir was bare ice; they could not think of going down that way, for endless time would be lost in cutting steps under such unfavourable conditions. They decided to keep close beside the rocks to the right of it, to begin with. Pierre went down first, cutting splendid steps in hard snow that was easy to deal with. Georges followed more slowly, placing his stumps very carefully in the steps. After their long confinement they were giving him considerable pain. Both climbers handled the rope with scrupulous care. To begin with, the slope was extremely steep, almost as steep as the north face, but they could progress from rock to rock and safeguard themselves satisfactorily at every stage. All the same, they foresaw the moment when they would have to cross the couloir and reach its left bank under the precipice of the Grande Rocheuse. This passage of a bare 100 metres had unfortunately been the scene of several accidents.

'After all we've been through on the way up,' argued Georges, 'we don't want to come off here. Drive a piton in here, and another one in the middle of the couloir, and then we won't have to worry.'

Pierre launched out on to the delicate traverse. The ice, polished and hardened by everlasting falls of stone and snow, was black here, and hard as the granite that it covered. Occasionally the axe would rebound from it with a hollow sound, without having made a single dent; the angle of the slope forced the climbers to cut with one hand only, and it was becoming an extremely dangerous process for the leader. After an hour's hard labour, Pierre reached the middle of the couloir, drove in a long ice piton, and continued on with this extra assurance. Very carefully he negotiated several smooth grooves, and then discovered to his immense relief that the ice was becoming less hard to his feet, and was gradually giving way to snow. He climbed up the farther side, made himself a nice little platform, and got ready to bring his friend across.

Poor old Georges! With his stumpy boots it was not easy for him to walk in the long shallow steps that Pierre had made. He cursed his clumsiness, yet somehow managed to do it; he wanted to pull out the piton in the centre, but his position was too precarious and Pierre shouted to him to leave it.

'Don't bother – it's not worth falling off for!'

He undid the ring that clipped his rope to the piton and went on – only ten metres more! But the steps cut by Pierre, now at the top of his form, were too widely spaced for Georges, who had to hack out some new ones for himself. He went about it calmly, with an occasional look at the couloir that twisted and plunged into space.

'Talk of falling!' he said. 'It's even more sensational than the other side with all those rocks sticking up.'

Far away below their eyes came to rest on the gentle contours of the upper basin of the Talèfre glacier, the great bowl of snow that lies just under the pinnacles of the Verte; when they reached it, their troubles would be over.

Georges resumed his step-cutting with increased energy, but his axe, striking on a hidden rock, suddenly flew out of his hand. Fortunately his instinctive reaction was to stay where he was in his steps, and not try to clutch at the axe that went bouncing and tinkling down the slope until it disappeared from sight.

He cursed roundly.

Pierre brought him safely across the rest of the way, pulling very gently on the rope. They took stock of the situation.

'No use pretending it isn't a damned nuisance,' said Pierre. 'The first man has to cut the steps, and the second has to safeguard him. And you just can't do that with only one axe. Oh well, never mind – better the axe than you, don't you think?'

'We'll just have to take it easy, that's all. The sun's getting hotter.'

The snow was certainly in splendid condition now. But for the angle of the slope, they could have run down it, digging their heels well in. But there was always that gulf below – and those rocks – and the furrows down which stones were beginning to swish silently.

'All the same, we'd better get a move on,' urged Pierre, 'otherwise when it comes to crossing the bergschrund we'll catch all the avalanches that converge down there.'

The Whymper couloir is not, strictly speaking, a genuine couloir, clearly defined like the one on the north face. It is rather a fan-shaped corrie, a collection of several couloirs, each steeper and sheerer than the last, that converge towards the glacier and unite to leap over an enormous bergschrund. They come down from the Moine arête, from the Grande Rocheuse, from the Col Armand Charlet, from the Aiguille du Jardin, and the route up the Verte proceeds across this intricate network, passing from one branch to another, and varying according to the year, the day, the month, the state of the snow, and so on. Early in the summer the couloir is simply an enormous snow slope, but by autumn it has been transformed into a colossal stoneshoot, tilted at an angle of forty-five degrees, and covered with a fine network of ice. At that season the couloir is under continual bombardment and there is no use attempting it. At such times the Verte can only be climbed by its arêtes which, thanks to nature's ingenious arrangements, are then free of snow, and frequently offer an easy climb.

Our two climbers, with all their experience to help them, made their way down through this vertical maze, calculating in advance exactly where they ought to leave a strip of snow between two furrows in order to reach an easier one.

They were keeping up a good pace. Pierre, having transferred his axe to Georges, went down first, face inwards, as if he were climbing down a ladder. He kicked his toes in hard to break the firm snow and make steps for his companion, and dug his hands well in, since the surface was beginning to thaw slightly. Gradually the slope eased off and they did not slacken pace. They no longer bothered to safeguard each other, but moved down together, face to the slope, seeing nothing of the landscape in general, nor of the drop beneath them; but their trained ears caught the swish of the little early-morning avalanches in the furrows. In a few hours, they realised, the snow might easily peel off in a major avalanche that would sweep down the whole couloir as far as the ice – and if so, it would be certain death for anyone who happened to be in its path. So they continued down at full speed.

In this manner they reached the rocky rib that overlooked the bergschrund, which could usually be crossed only at its eastern extremity, where a little secondary couloir came down from the Aiguille du Jardin. The climbers made quickly for this miniature couloir that broadened out into a great snow slope, and suddenly found themselves on the upper edge of a fault over twenty metres high. There was no possible way down. It looked as if they would have to make a tremendous detour by the rock. But could they bear to be baulked at this eleventh hour? Down below lay the even surface of the snowfield, seamed and cracked by great yawning crevasses.

They did not waste a minute.

'We'd better make a bollard,' suggested Pierre.

Their technical skill was once more being put to the test. They scooped out the snow till they reached the hard ice beneath. Then they hacked out what looked like an outsize mushroom, or a bollard on board ship. When it was completed they wound the spare rope around it – a thin line, six millimetres in diameter – and prepared to go down.

Georges went first, safeguarded by Pierre. In a minute he was spinning around and around and could not see a thing below him but the velvety darkness of the great crevasse; snow and water poured down the rope and through his clothes. After many attempts, balancing himself on the end of the line, he managed at last to set foot on a narrow snow-bridge, then to climb up the farther side.

Pierre followed quickly, assisted in his descent by Georges who, as soon as he was down to his level, gave a direct pull on the rope that brought Pierre over beside him.

Then they flopped down in the snow.

Their tremendous ordeal was over, and now they were very tired. Their eyes, insufficiently protected by goggles, were red and watery; this positively tropical sun whose rays were reflected from the snow made them dazed and dreamlike. They could have drunk the ocean – but there was not a single drop left in the bottle!

They coiled up the line, shortened the rope between them to fifteen metres, and set off again down the glacier.

Chapter XXXI

The rest of the descent seemed endless. They skirted round the foot of the huge Moine arête, bristling with secondary summits, made their way over hummocks of ice, or through a wild chaos of enormous séracs carved in the shape of cubes, towers and arcades. It was a relief to emerge from that labyrinth where they walked thigh-deep in snow, and to find a steeper slope just by the Aiguille du Moine. They began to run madly down in some old tracks that were still frozen; having forgotten to take off their crampons, they had to splay their feet out, and so looked somewhat like ducks waddling down to a pond. They were desperately thirsty. Before long they reached the first patch of grass, and the Clapier du Couvercle. There was the old hut, peaceful under the shelter of a great boulder, like a casket of precious wood abandoned in the open jaws of a strange monster.

An old man with a long moustache was smoking his pipe on the little wooden balcony, standing with his back to them and gazing at the mountains and at the path from the Montenvers up which the first parties of the day would soon arrive. Hearing a noise behind him, he turned around quickly, so startled that he removed his pipe from his mouth and just gaped at them without a word to say.

'Morning, Uncle!' Pierre hailed him jubilantly.

'Morning, Red Joseph,' was Georges's greeting.

'*You* – and *you!*'

Red Joseph, quite flabbergasted, at last brought himself to ask some questions.

'Where on earth have you come from at this time of day, and looking like that?'

'The Verte, north face,' answered Pierre briefly, 'but for God's sake before you do anything else, give us a bite and something to drink. Drink first, we're dying of thirst.'

They passed into the little hut, hanging their solitary ice-axe on the rack, then, seated astride a bench, took off their crampons.

While Red Joseph heated up the coffee they told him a little more about it, and his astonishment grew with every word of their story.

'But look here, Pierre, there's one thing I don't quite understand. They told me you suffered from vertigo – and even' – Joseph was a trifle embarrassed – 'and even that you'd changed a lot. As for you, Georges, if anyone had told me that you'd ever do such a climb again – well, I think I'd have bet my moustache that the thing was impossible! But what an extraordinary idea it was! What was the point of doing such a first-class expedition just by yourselves, without clients?'

'To show what we *could* do, Uncle; because we've made up our minds we're both going to be guides … and by the way, if you've got any clients you'd like to pass along to me … '

'Well, I can't say I'm surprised, really. I was pretty sure you'd end up like this.'

'The way I see it, Uncle, vertigo and frostbitten feet, all the risks that go with climbing, they were just invented to sharpen our appetite for life. It's only when you've been injured, or weakened in some way, that you can really appreciate being alive.'

'What you're saying amounts to this, that life's only worth living when you're willing to risk losing it?'

'That's just about it. Life's got to be a struggle. It's no good standing aside, or always looking for the easy way. I nearly did that, Uncle, and when I remember the mess I got myself into, I'm thoroughly ashamed of myself. It was Georges and the others who showed me what I ought to be doing: Georges especially, and *he's* never given up struggling to get back his old form!'

'He's right about you, Georges; it's been a fine bit of work; you've got guts! But look here, lads, taking life the hard way doesn't mean running unnecessary risks. If you're not to be afraid of risking your life, then you must see that you never do risk it except when you've got all the cards on your side. When I was just a boy, I remember once starting off on a big climb – can't quite recollect which it was now – with a pal of my own age. Just the two of us, like that, with no experience, and no proper preparations! We climbed up and up, and when we got to the top, we realised we'd forgotten to bring the rappel line that we needed for the descent. We spent a terrible night in a hole in the rocks, we hadn't any spare clothes, and our teeth chattered all night – there was hardly any food either. We just dashed off like a couple of scatterbrains. As you can very well imagine, Father began to get anxious, and it was he who found us after a day of searching and calling. I must have been sixteen then, but I swear I got the best hiding of my life. "Take this," said Papa between strokes, "take this, you rascal, to teach you to use your head! You don't just have to climb up, you've got to know how to get down. If you do anything, you must do it properly – you must prepare for it!" And down rained the blows, all over me. Ever since that day I assure you that I've thought twice before undertaking anything; I've taken such care over my preparations that when I did come up against some difficulty, I was ready to tackle it.'

'All the same, Joseph,' demurred Georges, 'there are times when you can't possibly guess what's coming next, and if you never took a crack at it for fear of falling, you'd never get anywhere.'

'I agree with you there, you've got to know when to take risks open-eyed, and for some useful end; even so, you may fall, but then you're in the hands of Providence. Do you remember when you were bent on climbing the Dru last year in spite of the verglas and everything else? If it had been simply for the sake of finishing the climb, I'd have said you were wrong, but you had a sacred duty to perform – bringing down poor Jean's body. Under those conditions, you were right to risk your lives; but that was an exception. Our lives don't just belong to ourselves alone, we haven't the right to dispose of them as we like. It amounts to the same thing as saying that just as we have no right to commit suicide, so we've no more right to risk our lives as long as Providence has marked out some duty for us.

'A death should always serve some purpose. The great scientists, explorers, soldiers, sailors, the pioneers who have fallen in some just cause or for the sake of some work that's valuable to others – they have a claim on our respect and our memory. It's for that that we shouldn't fear death, and should try to get the most out of life, the most that it's right for us to get.

'You understand what I'm trying to tell you, Pierre,' went on Joseph, as the young men listened gravely. 'You must never spare yourself till you're dead; and you must look upon rest as a foretaste of death. Work, struggle, and act – and lead a hard life. You'll find more happiness that way than if you spent your life loafing around.

'You're both of you going to be guides. It's a grand job – and it's a hard and dangerous job too. I wouldn't have exchanged it for anything else. But you must be careful – it isn't child's play. You won't be doing any more climbs just by yourselves, like this one you've just finished. You'll have the care and responsibility for other people's lives: the people you take on your rope will put their trust in you, and will ask you to help them out in their inexperience. The actual work will be twice as hard; instead of having a pal who can help you and safeguard you, nine times out of ten you'll have a creature who's liable to pull you off at every step. Lord, once I had a client who came clean off on the rope ten times during our descent of the Whymper couloir. And I can tell you that each time it became less amusing. I've never been able to figure out how I managed to keep him in his steps.

'Remember that a client is sacred – and that when you take your turn at the Bureau, you're entering into the most solemn engagement with him to help him accomplish dangerous things, and bring him back alive.

'But that's enough. Here I am jabbering away, and all the time you're dying for a drink.

'We're going to drink to your recovery, the three of us. There's no one in the hut, it's still too early in the season – all the better, nobody will interrupt us.'

Joseph brought out a bottle; he was moved, but didn't want to show it, and as he poured the sparkling wine into the mugs he wiped his long moustache with his horny fingers.

After a drink or two Pierre and Georges, who were pretty exhausted by this time, decided that they had better go down to the valley without further delay. They set off down the crystal-gatherers' path, clattered down the steps at Les Egralets and crossed the Mer de Glace without stopping. Once more they looked like men whose job it is to climb these heights.

The last train from Montenvers brought them down to Chamonix in the evening. Their faces were burned by the sun and the snow and drawn with exhaustion after two practically sleepless nights. Down in the valley the air seemed stifling.

They walked through the town without stopping anywhere and marched resolutely into the Guides' Office, where Jean-Baptiste Cupelaz was bringing his records up to date. The Chief Guide raised his head and, like Joseph, looked startled and confused to see them.

'Well, this *is* a surprise! You look as if you'd come a very long way!'

'We've done the Verte by the north face, as a training climb.'

'Whew – that *is* a climb.' The old guide whistled his admiration.

'Put me down for the Guides' test, Jean-Baptiste!' demanded Georges.

'Are you going to start guiding again? With those feet of yours? Are you crazy?'

'I've just shown you I'm not! I wanted to make sure I could do everything.'

'All right, all right, I'll start getting your record ready,' answered Jean-Baptiste slowly; then he grinned maliciously into his beard and added: 'The boys on the Committee won't like it at all! And how about you, Pierre – do you want to be put down also?'

'Me? I'll start as a porter this year – I'm not old enough yet to be a guide, but you can begin to get my record ready for next year.'

'Splendid, my lads – *ça fait mé pi pas pi!* – but they can't say anything about it, it's all in order. The rules don't say anything about a guide having to have two legs; they only require you to be able to do your job. All the same, the Committee won't like it!'

Jean-Baptiste Cupelaz opened a bulky minute book with detachable numbered pages. In his large and clumsy handwriting he wrote: 'Licence for the guide Georges à la Clarisse'; and in another, 'Licence for the porter Pierre Servettaz.' He tore out the leaves and handed them over.

'There you are, ten francs each. Now you can take your turn.'

Carefully folding the precious slips of paper away in their pocketbooks, the two young men left the office.

'Shall we go to Gros-Bibi's?' asked Georges.

'Not now, old chap,' replied Pierre soberly, 'I've still got another job to do. So long, we'll be seeing a lot of each other now!'

'So long.'

Pierre cut across the skating rink, a derelict place in summer, skirted the woods of Bouchet and came out on the road up to Mouilles. The valley was now deep in shadow, but the sun, hidden by the woody hillocks of the Prarion, still lit up the mountains above the trees. The Blaitière torrent rumbled and grumbled in its rocky gorge; the long stalks of the oats and green barley swayed in the evening breeze.

From a long way off Aline saw him coming up the cart track, happiness glowing in his face. She had no need to ask for any explanation.

Gently he took her hand and asked:

'Is your mother in?'

'Yes, she's in the living room.'

'Come along, we've got a lot to tell her.'

They stepped over the worn threshold of the old chalet, leaving the door wide open behind them.

There was no sound in the village but the murmur of running water dropping from the wooden conduit into the trough.

Slowly night came on, and one by one the lights appeared, all up and down the valley.

About the author

Roger Frison-Roche was born in Paris in 1906 of Savoyard parents. Moving to Chamonix and away from the city as soon as possible, he got a job in the tourist office and began in earnest the training for a *guide de haute montagne*, which he passed in 1930. He founded his own rock climbing and mountaineering school, and was active and successful in mountain races. He wrote articles on these events, becoming so popular that he was made editor in chief in 1935 and sent to Algiers, working on *La Dépêche d'Alger*. He also began to write a serial about the life of a young Alpine guide for weekly instalments in the paper. These were put together to form *Premier de Cordée* (*First on the Rope*) – the book that took him to fame. Frison-Roche travelled widely during the war as a correspondent and joined the Resistance in the Savoyard region. He later became obsessed with the landscapes of the desert and the Arctic after many trips to the Sahara and to stay with the Inuit, which became the subject matter of many of his subsequent books, as well as his beloved mountains. After having lived around the world and in various parts of France, in 1960 he moved back to his home town of Chamonix, soon after to be elected president of the Union Internationale des Guides de Montagne. Roger Frison-Roche died on 17 December 1999 in Chamonix.

CPSIA information can be obtained
at www.ICGtesting.com
Printed in the USA
LVHW041345030221
678263LV00039B/983